HOW TO DATE A DOUCHEBAG

THE STUDYING HOURS

SARA NEY

First Edition: September 2016
Library of Congress Cataloging-in-Publication Data
How to Date a Douchebag: The Studying Hours – 1st ed
ISBN-13: 978-1537432625 | ISBN-10: 1537432621

Thank you Internet for providing the inspiration for the dating quotes at the beginning of each chapter. They're all based on *real* conversations, pick-up lines, come-ons, and texts between actual people.

For more information about Sara Ney and her books, visit:
https://www.facebook.com/saraneyauthor/

"When I first saw her sitting
across the library, head down,
I thought it was going to be easy.
I thought maybe if I worked
her long enough, she'd drop her
panties and drop to her knees
for five minutes with me.
Well guess what? I was wrong."
– Sebastian Osborne

Foreshadowing

Jameson

Some days I stay home to study, but not very often.
The library is my solace.
My refuge.

Where I come to listen to the sound of pages being turned, the faint sound of laptop keys clicking, the light treading of footsteps padding across the worn hardwood floor. The building is one hundred and three years old, one of the oldest landmarks on campus, and full of history. Full of carved wood and dark corners. Full of knowledge and the secrets of scientists, philosophers, and students.

Really. It's the only place within a five-mile radius where I can be alone with my thoughts.

The only place without roommates, their music, their phones, and the constant flurry of activity at our off-campus rental. I never know when there's going to be a strange guy chilling on our couch, strangers in and out, or flirtatious giggling before bedroom doors get slammed shut.

The uncomfortable echoes of your roommate's bed squeaking, followed shortly thereafter by frenzied moaning in an otherwise silent house is…

Awkward.

And that's putting it mildly, because honestly, how do you get that sound out of your head?

You don't.

Instead, you escape to the library.

1

I don't worry about the distracting sounds of shouting or teasing or interruptions. Or the smell of overcooked Ramen noodles. I don't usually have to worry about being distracted, either.

Except for today.

Today I'm focused on a table full of disturbances near the entry in the form of four very large, very *athletic*-looking guys. Loud guys. Arrogant guys.

Relatively attractive guys.

Today, I can't concentrate.

I spot them long before they spot me, allowing myself a brief study respite to watch the largest one with a critical eye. With shocking dark hair and darker eyebrows, he hasn't looked down at the open book in front of him once. Rather, he's been glancing around the library's reading room.

Just as I'm doing.

Arms folded across a broad chest, his legs are spread, his expression impatient—almost as if he can't be bothered with homework.

As I conclude he must be waiting for the sky to open up and the universe to do the work for him, our gazes clash; those severe, ruthless slashes over his eyes shoot into his hairline while the lips surrounded by five o'clock shadow curl. Discriminating eyes so pale I can't discern their color from here begin their gradual descent down the column of buttons on my sweater before settling on my chest.

I shiver.

He smiles.

The sadistic creep *knows* his stare is making my skin crawl.

He relishes the fact.

Guys like him? Surely college will be a short blip on the roadmap of his life, a pit stop on the way to bullying co-workers, business partners, and probably women.

This guy? He's a douchebag—one with a capital D.

Blinking myself out of our stare-down, my blue eyes travel

around the table, mooring on the hulky blond guy tapping away on his keyboard, head bobbing to whatever music is bumping through those shiny black Beats. Then they land on the Latino slouched deep in his chair, staring at the ceiling and chewing on a yellow number two pencil.

Last but not least? The guy with the thick neck and thicker tattooed arms.

Fascinated, I lower my head to peer coyly from beneath my long lashes; he's clearly trying to focus on his work, aggravation with his rambunctious tablemates marring his handsome face and causing his shoulders to strain. Every so often, he shifts restlessly in his seat before giving his head a shake.

Blows out a puff of frustrated air.

Shifts in his seat. Shakes his head. Puffs out air.

Shampoo. Rinse. Repeat.

Until…

The entire table is interrupted by a pretty co-ed with light brown hair. It's tossed akimbo on her head in a casual, messy bun, but even from here I see the heavily lined eyes and bright red lips. The smoky-eyed look doesn't necessarily go with her black leggings and Iowa sweatshirt, but who am I to judge?

She slithers up to them brazenly, hip resting on the edge of the table, dragging one fingertip across the smooth surface, up and over that tattooed arm. Skims her nail across the bare skin of his forearm.

His head flies up, startled. Focuses on her.

I suck in the breath I didn't know I was holding at the sight of the grin he gives her.

Leans back, crosses his solid arms.

Spreads his legs.

She's cute.

And obviously his type.

I watch the show, riveted as he rises, muscled arm sliding around her slim waist…remove an earbud in time to hear a forced, enthusiastic giggle erupt from her throat...catch the the low timbre of his voice as he leads them deeper into the library, toward the last row of backlogged magazine and newspaper periodicals...suck in another breath when he smacks the girls' rear end with a sexually charged palm...sigh, disappointed when they turn the corner, disappearing from view.

Well then.

Removing my black-rimmed glasses, I rub the sight from my tired eyes, wondering for a brief moment what it would be like to be *that kind of girl*—the carefree kind who lets boys lead her into dark rows of books.

For funsies. Because it feels good.

Not the kind of girl who spends all her waking time studying because her grades suck and she can't afford not to.

I replace my glasses, the hairs on the back of my neck prickling with awareness as I pat a dainty yawn away, shifting my gaze.

Meet cold, intimidating gray eyes.

They crinkle knowingly at the corners as if to say, *I see you watching, but sweetheart, don't hold your breath —he'd never date someone like you.*

And he'd be right—the figure that just disappeared into the library stacks? He *wouldn't* want to date me. Wouldn't look at me twice given the chance.

Have sex with me? Maybe.

Date me? No.

But guess what? I wouldn't want him either. Because I can tell just by looking at him that he's probably a douchebag, just like his creepy friend.

And I'd want *nothing* to do with a guy like that.

4

"You're not trophy wife material.
You're more of a
participation ribbon kind of girl."

Sebastian

"**D**ude. Do me a solid and see if that's her."

I ignore his entreaty, determined to start this essay for a class I have first thing tomorrow morning, a class I need for graduation. I thought coming to the quiet library would give me the solace I need to get the assignment done, but apparently I was wrong.

So wrong.

"Are you listening to me? I need you to walk over there and see if that chick staring over here is my tutor. Please, I'm shy."

I pause. "Zeke, I'm not walking all the way over there just to see if she's your tutor. Do it yourself."

My head lowers and I go back to my paper.

"I'm the captain of the wrestling team, asshole."

My pen stops for the second time. "No, *I'm* the captain, asshole—or have you already forgotten? Doing your dirty work isn't part of my job description."

Whining but undeterred, my friend tries again. "What if I ask you nice?"

"Nope. You've already been a dick too many times today."

This perks him up considerably. "Speaking of dicks, what if I give you a blowjob?" he purrs. "Then would you do it?"

"*I'll* do it for a blowjob," our friend Dylan interrupts from across the table—the table that appeared large enough to accommodate all of us when we sat down but now feels like the size of a maxi pad.

"Shut the fuck up, Landers. No one asked you." Zeke sneers. "Osborne, go see if that's my tutor."

Jesus Christ he's relentless. "She's not your tutor."

He twists his torso to glance at her, dubious. "How do you know?"

We all crane our necks to get a good look at the girl in question, sitting across the dimly lit library commons. My dark eyes settle on the unassuming girl hunched over a stack of books and wielding a pencil, furiously writing away.

Intense and serious, this girl means business.

She's not here to fuck around.

I've noticed her in passing a few times myself, but have never spared her a second thought until now, chalking her up as just another warm body taking up an entire table my friends and I could have used.

Academic. Unadventurous. Probably a fucking prude if the pearl necklace circling her neck is any indication.

She barely batted an eye when I passed her with Cindy—or Mindy or whatever her name is that rhymes with 'Indy'—and hauled her to the storage room to get my dick wet.

"How do I know she's not your tutor?" I repeat. "First off, her face is buried in those books—she hasn't looked around once the entire time we've been here."

Zeke's dark eyebrows raise. "Bullshit. She's been watching us this entire time."

I ignore his expression and power on. "Secondly, she doesn't look like she needs a job. I mean, did you not see the fucking pearls around her neck? No way she needs the money."

"Maybe she likes helping those in need," Dylan jokes.

"I'll give her a need: I *need* a good grade in biology." Zeke ridicules us, studying her intently. "Virgin Mary over there looks like the fucking librarian. A girl like that is going to be single forever."

"Yeah but look at her: she's undeniably not waiting for anyone," Dylan observes.

Zeke shoots him an irritated scowl. "Did you just use the word *undeniably?*"

Our friend ignores him. "Or maybe she took one look at your pissed-off face and decided the job wasn't worth the forty bucks

7

you're going to pay her. And what's up with her sweater set? I bet she could use a good, stiff dicking." Dylan's booming voice cuts through the din, the rasp of it slicing through the peaceful university library in the most unquiet way. "She does look like a total bitch."

Zeke's laugh is crude. "Maybe that's the problem—she's had a dicking and it's still stuck up her ass." He checks his phone for the fifth time. "If she's not my tutor, then mine is a no-show. Would you please just go over there for me? I'm too lazy to haul my ass out of this chair."

I stare him down, shaking my head at his presumption before bracing my hands against the wooden table and rising to stand. "Fine. What's your tutor's name?"

He unfolds the scrap of paper resting on his pile of books and reads out loud. "Violet."

"Aww, how pretty." I shuffle leisurely across the library, weaving through the intricate labyrinth of tables, crosshairs on the black cardigan sweater set. *Violet.*

Her smooth, classic ponytail is pulled high, not a hair out of place, and black glasses are propped on her head. Wearing a simple white tee shirt and a black cardigan, a single strand of gleaming ivory pearls circle her neck.

That's right, I said it —fucking *pearls*.

Hot pink earbud cords dangle down her neck.

I saunter closer, approaching her cautiously, much like you'd approach a stray dog, or a girl you know is on her period—warily, guardedly.

Relaxing my fingertips on the edge of the solid wood table, I wait for her to glance up. Notice me. Say something. Blush.

But she doesn't. In fact, if this chick senses my presence, she's Level: *Expert* at hiding it.

Clearing my throat, I throw out a casual greeting and try to look bored. "Hey."

Her hand continues to move across her notebook, finger trailing the middle handwritten paragraph. Head still bent, her quiet voice murmurs, "I'm not a tutor, so don't bother."

I guess that answers my question. I turn toward my friends, both of them giving me a thumbs up, and shake my head. Negative Ghost Rider. Zeke furrows his brows, pissed off as usual, and glances down at the folded paper in his hand with a frown. He wads it up and tosses it to the floor.

Well.

I guess that settles it. Except…

"Your name's not Violet?" I press for more information, willing her to look up at me.

She doesn't so much as flinch.

"Sorry to disappoint you, but no."

I force out a chuckle, leaning on the table with my hip and crossing my arms. "Just checking. My friend over there got stood up by his study buddy and now he's moping."

"Why didn't he come over here himself?"

"Too lazy to get up." My tone is matter-of-fact.

"Not to be rude, but if he needs a tutor, maybe laziness is part of his problem."

Good point. "Good point."

"All right, now that we've established I'm not this mysterious missing Violet, I really do need to get back to studying. You're killing my mojo."

"Right. Sorry to bother you." The apology slips out and manages to sound sincere.

The girl hums out a dismissive, "Mmm hmm," and resumes pushing her fingertip along the lined notebook paper, all without glancing up at me.

It's really fucking annoying.

I mean, my pride is taking a real beating here. It's not everyday that I'm dismissed, and certainly not by some *nobody* in the damn library, a dull classmate with a long stick shoved up her entitled ass.

Do I just turn and walk away? Or do I try to get the last word in? I stand here, not really knowing what to do, and shove my hands in the pockets of my jeans.

This chick has managed to annoy the crap out of me in less than a minute *and* has the balls to reject me—and I'm not quite sure how to handle it.

"You can walk away now." She reads my mind, a slight edge to her voice.

The fuck is wrong with this chick?

"Chill," I grind out. "I'm going."

Sauntering back to my table is a quick journey, and both my friends have amused expressions plastered across their idiotic faces. I drag out my chair, rejoining them with a glower.

"That didn't look like it went so well," Dylan ventures.

"Fuck. Off."

"That's not Violet?" Zeke asks.

"Nope." I flip a topography textbook open. "Not Violet."

"Hey OzMan," Dylan muses thoughtfully. "I bet if you went back over there and put the moves on her, it would give her something to brag about for weeks. Give nerd girl a reason to live."

Somehow, I doubt that. "She'd have to take her face out of her book long enough to acknowledge me first."

"Bet you could get her to cream her white granny panties."

"No shit I could. Like it would be hard?"

Zeke laughs. "Let's be honest, she's not wearing granny panties—it's probably a chastity belt."

Not that I mind white granny panties; they all slip down a woman's thighs the same way: slowly and with a sweet satisfying sound when they hit the floor.

I smirk knowingly. "Yeah, probably."

"Do you suppose she's a virgin?" Dylan wonders out loud.

Zeke snickers, glancing over his wide shoulders toward the librarian, who's walking the perimeter of the room. He lowers his voice. "Fuck yeah she is; look at her. She'll be a post-gasm crier for sure when she finally takes it up th—"

"All right, enough." I cut him off sharply; even *I* have my standards when it comes to degrading woman. Granted, they're not high, but I have a few—and condescending them sexually is one of them. "You're being a douche."

I give the girl another glance over my shoulder, my tone softening. She really is kind of cute. "Besides, why do you even care?"

"I don't. I'm just saying, for all the fucking bragging you do, you couldn't get *that* chick to bang you, I guarantee it." He tips his head in her direction. "I saw the way she blew you off, and it's not the *blowing* you're used to receiving."

True. Take last night for example: it took me almost no effort at all to get laid on the back porch of the hockey house. Some small talk, a few flirtatious smiles, and I'm against an outside wall screwing some girl who didn't even give me her name.

"…and I bet you couldn't get her to put her *mouth* anywhere on you. I'll even pay you a hundred bucks."

Wait. Rewind.

One hundred bucks?

That gets my attention and my head snaps up. Why?

Because I'm broke.

The truth is, I didn't grow up going to the best schools. I was a talented wrestler from the beginning, but wasn't able to afford extra training; our family didn't have the money. When I was in middle school, my sister landed her first real job out of grad school but soon ended up embroiled in a legal battle—the details of which I won't get into—that depleted much of my parents' retirement.

Money for wrestling clubs and college went right along with it.

So yeah, unlike most of my friends, I'm not blessed to be here at the expense of my parent's deep pockets. I have no limitless credit cards or monthly allowance.

Nope.

I might have been blessed with a God-given talent for pinning opponents to the wrestling mat, but financially I'm only armed with an athletic scholarship (one I can't afford to fuck up) and a job. That's right. A *job*.

As in J-O-B.

As in, when I'm not in class, at practice, or studying, I'm busting my ass working up to *twenty* hours a week, driving the fork lift during the night shift at some rinky-dink lumber yard fifteen minutes from campus. It pays the rent on the shithole I share with my teammate Zeke, a football player named Parker, and his cousin Elliot.

The job helps pay what expenses the scholarship and my parents can't cover—utilities, gas, and groceries—with little left for much else.

And if anyone finds out, I'm screwed.

Technically, I'm not supposed to be working; my contract with Iowa prohibits it. But there's nothing I can do—I *have* to work, usually at night, when I should be sleeping, studying, and resting my body.

The body that takes a regular beating and is my only ticket to a Big Ten education.

An additional few thousand grand per year in scholastic scholarships help—those are sponsored by the insurance company my dad works for—but I could really use the money Zeke just threw down, even if it's only a hundred bucks.

So.

I find myself studying the girl again, scrutinizing her with renewed interest. Buttoned-up cardigan. Serious face. Sleek, dark hair. Mouth pulled into a straight line, pink tip of her tongue peeking out of the corner, indisputably from concentration.

I *guess* I could stand to have her mouth on mine for a few seconds.

I give Zeke a stiff nod, and because I know he'll pay, I say, "Make it five hundred and you have a deal."

He snorts. "Done."

Leaning back in his chair, my teammate crosses his bulky arms, urging me on with a flick of his fingers. "Best hop to it, Casanova, before she catches you staring and runs off with her tail between her sewn up legs."

"The girl I hooked-up with
last night woke up this morning,
rolled over, took one look at me
and said, "Oh thank god
you're hot," then went back
to sleep."

Sebastian

"**I** thought we already established I'm not a tutor."
        The girl is hunched, boxed out over her textbook, highlighter poised above the right margin. She still hasn't looked up, but at least she acknowledged me before I had to take drastic measures like clearing my throat and beating on the table.

I call that progress.

"Right. I got that the first time I came over."

Her neon highlighter stills, hovering above the book fanned out in front of her. She clicks it closed once, removes an earbud, and holds it suspended in the air as she waits for me to say something. "Is there something I can help you with?"

She tips her head to the side, waiting, listening for me to speak but continuing to study.

I decide to go for broke. "I need you to kiss me."

Nothing.

No reaction.

No balking, no blushing, no comment.

Like this sort of thing happens to her on the regular.

"Would you look at me, dammit?"

That does the trick; *that* gets her attention.

Her head lifts, her long brown ponytail cascading over her right shoulder, classy and sophisticated.

Her eyes are brilliant blue, lashes long.

Our eyes meet.

Gazes connect.

Heartbeats pound.

Whatever the fuck cliché you want to throw out there— they're all annoying, but there you have it. She's watching me warily, those blue eyes narrowing in a surly way.

Agitation flares her nostrils.

Very unpromising.

Dismissing me after a long stretch of silence, she pushes the earbud back in place, head lowering, highlighter resuming its even, effortless strokes across the paper laid out in front of her.

"You're ridiculous," she mutters with a cool flick of her wrist. "Go back to your friends."

"I can't." Might as well be brutally honest; maybe she'll appreciate that. It actually seems like something we have in common: zero tolerance for bullshit.

I can work with that.

She lifts her head and rolls her eyes. "You *can't* go back? What does that even mean?"

I smirk, anticipating the bomb I'm about to drop. "Sorry, sweetheart, that's impossible. I'm here on a mission and I can't go back until it's accomplished."

I hold my hands up helplessly, beseeching.

"First of all, don't ever call me sweetheart again. I'm a stranger to you. Secondly, I'm not interested in whatever *games* you little boys are playing. I have serious work to do here, so…"

The girl puts down the yellow highlighter, rifles through the writing utensils on the table, and chooses a blue felt-tip pen. Whatever she's working on has her full attention, and she goes back at it like I'm *not* still standing here bearing down on her—all six foot two of me.

Despite the fact that I'm not attracted to her the way I'd be attracted to, say, someone willing to bang me, the competitive D1 athlete in me refuses to budge from this spot; rather, I re-strategize.

I move closer to her chair, large hand resting on the corner of the wood table. Inches from her laptop, encroaching on her personal space, my coarse fingers tap the corner of the desk, slowly stroke the wood. A few more caresses and I'm pulling out the chair beside her, conscious of my teammates watching from across the room.

Nosy assholes.

The legs of the desk chair scrape against the old hardwood floor, causing more than a few heads to snap in our direction.

I straddle it, crossing my arms over the back, and face her head on.

Head tilted to the side as she copies notes from a laptop, she's handwriting them onto paper. The first thing I notice when she brushes the errant ponytail back over her shoulder is the smooth skin at the curve of her neck, then the small diamond studs in her lobes.

I observe the soft fabric of her cardigan—and I know it's soft because I'm pretty sure the last sorority girl I fucked had the same sweater; it's the uniform of snotty collegiate women everywhere.

This girl is all class.

She's also blatantly ignoring me.

I watch her a few minutes more as she continues copying classroom notes from her laptop into a spiral notebook, snubbing me. "Why are you copying notes you've already taken?"

Long, loud sigh. "Repetition. So I can memorize them."

Hmmm. Not a bad idea.

Perhaps I'll try it sometime.

"My name's Oz, by the way." I give her a megawatt smile, mouth filled with pearly, perfectly straight teeth that have dropped thongs, bikini briefs, and boy shorts all over this campus—and, truth be told, at several other universities.

Who am I to discriminate?

Still, the girl says nothing.

"Oz Osborne," I repeat, just in case she's hard of hearing, because she's still not answering me. Holy. Shit. What if she's *deaf* and can only reads lips?

I wait for the name recognition to set in. Wait for her eyebrows to shoot up or cheeks to flush. Wait for any sign she's heard of me; they all have.

But my salutation is met with an uncomfortable, deafening silence; so she's truly never heard of me, she's playing it cool, she

17

can't *hear* me—or she just plain ol' doesn't give a crap.

Scratch, scratch, scratch goes the pen across her paper.

Awkwardly, I'm stuck sitting at her fucking study table while my friends gawk from nearby, Zeke's smug gloating visible from across the room. Arms crossed, he leans back in his chair, pencil shoved behind his ear, watching instead of studying like I'm a sideshow.

His arrogant, angry brows rise.

Whatever; I've got this. *No* snotty chick is going to give me the cold shoulder; I'm Sebastian *fuckin* Osborne.

Undeterred, I clear my throat and try again.

"Anyway, as I was saying, my name is *Oz*. Nice to meet you." I lean my elbow on the edge of the table, my chest hovering perilously close to her personal space. I raise my voice and over-enunciate—just in case she *is* deaf and can't hear me.

"See that group of guys over there?" I tip my head toward the table my teammates occupy; they're egging me on with lewd gestures. Classy. "On second thought, don't look. They're assholes."

The girl sniffs.

"They also don't think you'll kiss me." Each word rings out clear as a bell, loud enough to get her attention.

"First of all, lower your voice." She rolls her eyes but keeps her head down, writing. "And secondly, your friends are right. I'm *not* kissing you."

"Ah! Good—so you're *not* deaf. I was getting kind of worried."

Her head shoots up. "Oh my god, what did you just say?"

"I thought for a second you were deaf and that's why you were ignoring me."

"You are an insensitive *idiot*." The appalled look on her face speaks volumes, her tone horrified when she parts her lips to say, "I can hear you, *smell* you—gosh! Even *see* you! I am one hundred percent ignoring you."

"I introduced myself to you four times."

Eye roll. "Haven't you heard of stranger danger?"

"I left my white kidnapping van back at the crack house, so you're safe—for now."

The witty comeback interests her, and she raises her head in disbelief. Sparkling eyes meet mine for the second time since I commandeered her table, assessing me the same way I studied her: with awareness, curiosity, and...

Humor.

She's amused by me, I can tell.

"You're kind of absurd, but...funny." She pauses. "*Oz.*"

"Thanks? I think."

"*Sooo...*" The girl taps her pen on the corner of the desk, squints at the corner of her computer monitor, and eyes me expectantly. "We're done here, right? It's getting late and I don't have a lot of time left to study."

I clear my throat. "Just one kiss and I'll leave you alone."

"What part of *no* didn't you get? Did your jock brain not learn that word?" Her voice is measured, slow, like maybe I don't understand English.

"Technically you never told me *no.*"

She stares back at me, expressionless.

I persist. "What about a small one? Just a quick peck on the lips. No tongue."

My joke goes without even the barest trace of a smile.

"Fine." I laugh. "*Some* tongue."

She slaps down her pen and threads her fingers together, blue eyes blazing. "Stop."

One word.

Stop.

Even I'm not dumb enough to push.

Fine, I'm going to push, but just a little. "C'mon babe. Don't make me walk back over there with this long tail between my legs."

At my innuendo, her keen eyes dart quickly between my legs,

land on the crotch of my jeans, and widen before she catches herself doing it. If I hadn't caught it myself, I'd think I'd imagined it.

Her lips purse.

The girl reaches up and pulls the black glasses down off her head, propping them on the bridge of her pert nose, and shoots a scornful glance across the room at my table full of teammates.

"I know how this whole thing must look, but I promise you, my intentions are honorable. We're just trying to have a little fun, yeah? No harm in—"

"Honorable?" The pink wires are still dangling from her ears when she reaches up and removes them, dropping the earbuds onto her laptop. "A little fun? At whose expense?"

Speaking of expenses, I'm about to lose five hundred big ones to the motion of her hand rising to cut off my reply.

"Tell me this: you come over here, try to get a kiss for *god-only-knows-what-reason,* and I'm supposed to be flattered by your attention? Please. Who do you think you are?"

I open my mouth to tell her, but she cuts me off.

Again.

"Do you win some special status—a plaque with your name on it, perhaps? The prime parking spot at your fraternity house for the month of September?"

She wants me to be direct? Fine. "I'm not in a fraternity, but yeah, actually, I do win something. I get five hundred bucks if you kiss me, and honestly, I could *really* use the money."

Now she's leaning back in her chair, balancing herself on the legs like a dude. "Ah, so you interrupted my research to act like an asshole on some lark. For *money.*"

"Yeah, basically." I shrug. "Five hundred bucks *is* five hundred bucks."

We have a reckoning then, regarding each other with unconcealed interest. She does little to disguise her inspection of my body, masked expression unreadable as she starts at my boots and works her way up.

I *know* when her eyes hit the flat of my sculpted abs. *Feel* when they run idly over my shoulders and hesitate when they flicker to my spread legs, to the crotch of my jeans.

Long dark lashes coated with black mascara flutter. Flawless pale skin flushes. Her lips, I can't help but notice, are pursed but pleasantly full.

Pretty damn cute, except I am completely unable to tell what she's thinking.

"You have one hell of a poker face you know that?"

"Thank you."

I lean in. "What's your name?"

She rolls her blue eyes.

Nonchalantly, I shrug. "If you won't tell me, I'll have to insist on calling you Sexy Librarian."

Her eyes take a joy ride up and down my thick arms folded over the chair, the full sleeve of tattoos. "See that woman over there with the gray bun and cardigan cataloging the dictionaries? *That's* the librarian."

Now I roll *my* eyes. "No shit, she looks like one—but if we're comparing, all you're missing is the gray hair, bitter expression, and nerdy glasses." Her hands touch the frames surrounding her blue eyes. "Never mind, you hit two of the three. A *tri*fecta of sexual repression."

"I'm not sexually repressed."

At the base of my thick neck, I pretend to have a necklace around my throat and finger an imaginary pearl. "Could have fooled me."

Her eyes narrow. "If this is your way of trying to be charming, you're failing miserably. I thought you were trying to *kiss* me."

"Does this mean you're thinking about it?"

She pauses for a heartbeat, picking up her pen and drawing little circles in her notebook. "It would surprise you if I said yes, wouldn't it?"

I chuckle. "Yes."

"Hold on—I want to remember this moment when I say the words." She squints at me like she's taking a picture in her mind, then slowly says, "*Yes.* I'm thinking about it."

Not. What. I. Was. Expecting.

Is this chick for real?

"Seriously?" I blurt out, brows planted in my hairline. "You're not just fucking with me?"

Her shoulders rise into a shrug. "Sure, why not? I could use three hundred dollars.

People don't surprise me very often, but Sexy Librarian…she just shocked the shit out of me. "*Three* hundred dollars?"

What the fuck!

"No offense, but I'm not giving you more than half the money; that's not part of the deal."

She lifts her earbuds, placing one back in her ear, then the other with a smug, satisfied smile. "See you around then, Oz."

I catch her eyes rolling again before her neck bends, pen flying into motion as she goes back to studying.

I sigh. "Fine. Fifty bucks."

"Two fifty."

She never lifts her head.

What the hell? "This is bullshit. You seriously won't kiss me for *free?*"

"Absolutely not." She looks up and down my chiseled torso, eyes taking in my dense biceps and tattoos with only mild interest. An eyebrow cocks. "You're not exactly my *type.*"

Liar.

"Kitten, you couldn't be less my type even if you were sitting in that chair wearing nothing but that goddamn necklace."

Liar.

"Please don't ever call *anyone* kitten. It's worse than sweetheart. I think I just threw up in my mouth a little." Then she boxes out, adjusting her entire body, rearranging herself away from me.

Head bowing over her notebook, her shoulders slump a fraction before she raises her head to look me directly in the eye. "Know what else? That was a shitty thing to say to someone."

"What! You just said the same freaking thing to me!"

Even so, when her mask of uncertainty gazes back at me,

I'm not gonna to lie—I feel like a total dickwad for having said it back.

Kind of.

Sort of.

Fine. *Not really.*

Nonetheless, I let out a long, drawn-out sigh, like I'm about to do her a huge favor to make up for it. "Okay. I'll give you half the money."

Her nose wrinkles in distaste. "That's your apology? Pity money?"

I refuse to say I'm sorry. "Take it or leave it."

"Fine. I'll kiss you, but only because you wore me down."

"You just fleeced me out of two hundred dollars!"

"Two hundred and *fifty.*"

We size each other up under the dim lights of the library, the table lamps casting a warm glow over her smooth skin and heart-shaped face. Shadows dance when she cocks her head in my direction, waiting for me to say something.

I try to look her up and down to mentally catalog her tits, hips, and ass, but it's impossible with her sitting down.

"Can you do me *one* favor?" I grumble. "I think this would be less awkward for me if you stood up."

She sniffs indignantly. "Less awkward for *you?* I'm about to put my lips on a complete stranger, and now you're getting picky. Keep piling up those favors."

"Instead of bitching you should be thanking me for the opportunity."

A huff. "That's right—you're paying me because you are the *epitome* of morality and trustworthiness. It practically oozes out of your pores."

"*Jesus* lady. I *said* I was going to give you half and I will."

"I'll believe that when I see it." She huffs again but stands, rises to her full height, and shocks me again. A petite little thing, she barely reaches my clavicle, and I'm tempted to see if I could rest my chin on her head.

"If you don't trust me and I'm pissing you off, why would you agree to this stupid stunt?"

This gives her pause and she seems to consider my question. "Curiosity. Besides, isn't it okay to make poor choices every once in a while?"

I glance down between our bodies, noting the full breasts straining against the buttons of her black cardigan, and grin. Sorry, can't help it; Sexy Librarian's got a great rack beneath her *proper* sweater, with its row of *proper* buttons, and now they're pressing im*proper*ly against my chest in the most improper way.

"What did you say your name was?" My question comes out huskier than intended.

Her pouty mouth slips into another satisfied smirk. "Sexy Librarian."

"No, seriously."

She pauses, inhaling a breath of air before exhaling it.

"Fine. If you must know, my name is James. James Clark."

I know it's fucking *rude*—and probably really obnoxious— but I let my eyes bug out of my head and my mouth fall open. "Your name is James? Like as in *James*, James?"

Patiently, she waits me out.

I just stare at her, reconciling the masculine name with the feminine figure in front of me. Then, I say the first thing that comes to mind: "Don't guys get confused when you're fucking them? Doesn't your dude name get confusing for them?"

James's blue eyes flare, but she otherwise doesn't react. She's obviously used to this response to her name.

"James is short for Jameson." The implied '*asshole*' tacked to the end of her sentence lingers in the air, squeezed between our bodies.

My dark eyebrow shoots sardonically into my hairline and my lips twist into a smirk. "What—the two extra letters on the end made it so long you had to shorten it?"

"Something like that." Bemused, she bites down on her lower lip. "Are you going to kiss me or what? I have a thirty-page paper to finish by midnight, and I'm only on page twenty-two."

"*You* have to kiss *me*."

"Oh sheesh." A loud sigh and she fiddles nervously with the top button of her cardigan. My eyes settle on the sliver of creamy skin there before she says, "Lucky me, this just gets better and better, doesn't it? All right then Oz, hold still. You ready?"

So fucking ready.

"I'm ready Jim." I chuckle. "Lay one on me."

As she presses her body closer, I catch a whiff of what smells like baby powder and something floral. I inhale, staring down at her chest. I mean, since her boobs are squished against me, I might as well take advantage—and shockingly, she lets me.

Rises to her toes. Flutters her lashes.

Purses her pouty lips.

I expect a chaste kiss to settle on my cheek, just a brush of her lips, or a quick peck on my jawline.

I've never been so wrong in my entire fucking life.

And truthfully, I've never been this turned on either. Trying to get James to kiss me has been fun, an actual, honest to God, *chase*—one I've enjoyed every second of.

So I watch her lips and revel in the feel of her—

Stop it fucker.

Focus.

Jameson's warm hands cup my face, cradling my jaw. Her thumbs begin a slow, steady stroke along my cheeks, gliding back and forth until my neck tilts involuntarily, eyelids getting heavy as I watch her in wonder. I'm truly enthralled as this weird, unassuming stranger searches my eyes.

Instinctually, my lips seek the contact of her palm, wanting to place a kiss there. As if sensing my intention, her head gives a shake. *"Don't."*

A whisper.

A sigh.

Her buttons dig deeper still into my chest when she arches higher on her tiptoes to rest her lips against the outside corner of my mouth.

Rests them there, inhaling. Presses those lips to one side, then the other.

My bottom lip.

Gives my cupid's bow a quick flick of the tongue.

My nostrils flare as I stand, ramrod straight and stiff, waiting…waiting until Jameson pulls back, her smooth hands lingering, never leaving my person, blue eyes memorizing every detail of my face.

Debating.

My dark, hawk-like gaze follows the teeth that drag over her lower lip and pull, follow the tongue darting out to moisten her mouth.

I don't move a single muscle in my body, but can't help goading her. "I don't have all day here."

"Shhhh," she admonishes. "Quiet please. When you talk, it makes me want to slap some sense into you."

Her pink mouth hovers just a breath away, teasing, the air between us growing oddly combustible. The energy between our lips emits a slight electric sizzle that I'll lie in bed questioning later— but for now, my dick twitches inside my dark jeans and my fists clench and unclench at my sides, fighting to gain some control of the situation.

It proves impossible.

My legs get restless, and suddenly adrenaline is coursing through my entire body. I could do a hundred laps around campus—which is so fucking ridiculous.

She's not even my usual type—blonde, stupid, and easy.

She's a *nobody*, and I don't screw nobodies.

Not usually.

Lips pursed, she finally presses them over mine.

Sighs.

My lips part and like a good girl, she slides her tongue unhurriedly inside.

I'm hard. So fucking hard.

Jameson tastes fresh—like peppermint gum and strawberries—and suddenly I find my hands circling her slim waist, pulling her flush to my body so I can grind my erection into her thigh as our lips part. Farther. My tongue seeks its way inside...all the way inside.

As deep as a lifeline.

Within seconds we're making out like unsupervised high school students in their parents' basement, right in the middle of the damn library, surrounded by our peers.

I groan when she bites my bottom lip then sucks on it.

From behind, I hear my asshole teammates at the table across the room catcalling—not loudly enough that the librarian will come over, but loud enough that Jameson breaks the kiss, pushing back on my solid rock of a heaving chest with a moan, distancing herself, hand poised at her lips.

After a few steadying breaths, she breathily asks, "Was that good enough for a payday? Satisfied now?"

Fuck no. "I won't be satisfied until I'm fucking you on a table in a study room." I grapple for her hand. "Come on."

Her eyes widen in surprise when I reach forward to grab her arms. Intention: pull her back in for another kiss. Reality: she evades me, sidestepping away, her ass hitting the table, jostling the lamp, and knocking her pens off the edge with a clatter. An unsteady hand flies to her swollen lips, gently caressing them with the pads of her fingertips.

"I'm *not* that kind of girl."

My blazing eyes take her in, head to toe: jeans, white tee, black cardigan, gleaming pearls.

Pearls. Jesus H. Christ.

"Then what kind of girl are you? One that's not into having a good time? Or are you just a tease?"

I visualize the scene with her in my mind. Haphazardly shoving our books off the table to the floor. Clearing it off so I can set her on the edge. Slide off her jeans. Caress her in places…all over. *Inside* places with my dick. Her clit while I watch her come, spread out on the study room table.

"You won your bet," James begins slowly, smoothing a hand down her ponytail. "You've won your money, and I've mollified my curiosity." Her big blue eyes, guarded now, roam to the table where Zeke and Dylan sit, watching. "You should go. Your friends are waiting."

I give a jerky nod, my hand reaching down to dramatically adjust the hard-on in my pants. "Thanks for the blue balls."

Her lip twitches. "You're welcome."

I give her another onceover, taking her in from head to toe, seeing her differently than I did ten minutes ago. In the blink of an eye, she's gone from straitlaced and unadventurous to sassy and weirdly erotic.

Damn shame she's not giving it up.

Finally, I turn, presenting her with my back before striding away, one heavy footfall after the other, toward my friends. I get halfway across the library when her bubbly little voice rings out, a soft beckoning.

"Hey *Oz?*"

I stop.

Instead of facing her, I turn my head only a fraction, presenting her with just my profile. "*What.*"

She's quiet for a few seconds—so quiet my morbid curiosity *forces* me to turn. Jameson stands in the soft lamp light in the dim corner, her eyes sparkling with wit and humor.

Captivated, my brows raise impatiently. "Well?"

"A little friendly advice?" Her pouty lips part and I'm drawn to them as they mutter, "*Never* judge a girl by her cardigan," just loud enough for me to hear.

That gives me pause. "Thanks for the suggestion, but I don't need it."

━━━━━━━━━━━━━━━

Two hours and twenty minutes later, that quietly uttered advice is all I can think about: never judge a girl by her cardigan.

Never judge a girl by her cardigan.

What the hell does that even mean?

Irritated, I punch my pillow, wadding it up under my head and staring at the ceiling, wide awake, trying to shove the visual of a certain set of pearls out of my mind and focus on something else— like Rachel Ididntcatchherlastname's perky tits, that little dick-tease. Or Carmen Whatsherface's tight little ass. Or that kinky brunette I let blow me in the library before...

I spit into the center of my palm before it disappears down into my mesh gym shorts. For better access, I push the waistband down my hips, past my raging hard-on. Gripping the base of my rigid shaft, I give it a few pulls to take the edge off before committing to the task, pumping it in a steady rhythm until my breathing becomes harsh.

My brow furrows in concentration and the tip of my tongue licks my bottom lip, my teeth biting down with every stroke. Shit it feels so fucking great, even though it's my own damn hand.

Unfortunately.

It takes me a few minutes to get off, and with a few more jerks I blow my load, groaning when my palm is filled with warm, sticky cum.

And like every romantic cliché in the existence of time, it's not the gorgeous, flawless face of a hot blonde I'm whacking off to, but the fresh face of Jameson Clark. Her immaculate hair. Her clear eyes. Those black glasses perched on her nose.

The universe is a bitchy, relentless mistress indeed.

Rising from bed, I snap the elastic waistband of my shorts around my lean hips, run a hand over my six-pack, and pad barefoot to the communal bathroom I share with three other guys to rinse my hands—and my cock.

#DOUCHEBAG

"Every time I have sex with him,
I have to say 'wrong hole.'
It's starting to give
both of us a complex."

Jameson

My heart is still beating a mile a minute when I climb into bed, flick the light off, and flop down on my back to stare at the ceiling.

Oz.

Oz the asshole.

Cocksure. Ridiculous. Aggravating.

Lewd.

Sexy.

Oh god he was sexy. The *things* his tongue did to my mouth in the short amount of time we were kissing are still taking my breath away, if my labored breathing is any indication.

Hair fanned out across my pillow, my hand slowly traces the exposed skin of my hipbone. My boxers are threadbare and folded down at the waistband, my fingers brushing...*brushing* along the elastic seam.

Closing my eyes, I let them trail inside my shorts, teasing myself with a light caress. Back and forth...closer and closer to the apex of my thighs until my legs, of their own accord, spread just a bit wider.

Oz...

Huge.

Firm.

Tattooed.

Tall Oz loomed over my table like some kind of modern day gladiator, broad and imposing.

Bored.

His penetrating eyes had looked down at me warily, if not fully jaded...but that can't be right; guys like him have the world by the ass and don't appreciate it. And yet...as he stood there, mocking me, there was no mistaking the lack of enthusiasm for his quest.

Until I'd lain my mouth on his.

I squeeze my eyes shut, remembering his lips. Full, soft, and gentle—if one ignored the sardonic smirk. His tongue—

Oh god.

Not my type, not my type, not my type, I chant.

Not my type at all.

Yet here I am, moaning in the dark, my fingers finally finding that one wet, aching sweet spot I've neglected far too long. Stroking myself, my eyelids flutter shut and I drown in the vivid image of Oz Osborne. Imposing. Potent.

Serious.

There's more behind that boastful smirk than he's presenting to people for show, of that I'm sure.

Not someone I've ever seen around campus, he came out of nowhere tonight with his hulky body and arrogant countenance— like he owned the place. What kind of guy demands control of a *library* for heaven's sake? God, I can't stand guys like that, conceited and full of themselves.

And yet...

The fingers from my free hand find my mouth in the dark, resting on my lips while I stroke myself with the other. Chaffed from the scruff on his face, my mouth feels branded, despite the mercenary intent of our kiss.

Oz.

I roll over and face the wall, groaning at the memory of his powerful arms; I'm a sucker for tattoos, and he had an armful beneath the sleeves of that worn navy blue tee shirt. His strong, dense arms. Solid chest. Toned back.

He's not my type. I have to keep reminding myself of that as I stroke between my legs, seeking that release.

He's not my type. He's...

A long, blissful sigh on a cold spring night. An incredible moment I won't soon forget. A vain, stubborn ass with deplorable taste in company.

He's everything I don't want.

And yet…

Somehow he is.

"Don't send me any boob shots.
Send pictures of your bathroom
and the inside of your cabinets.
I need to see what kind of clinger
I'm dealing with here."

Sebastian

"**D**ude, isn't that the chick from the library?" Zeke nudges me with a meaty elbow, though I can barely hear him over the throng and the music. I lean in closer. "What the fuck is she doing out in public? Shouldn't she be cataloging books or some shit?" he complains unnecessarily.

"Looks like she came back for another piece of the big D." Dylan laughs next to him, smacking me in the bicep. "That kiss she gave you the other night was hot."

Yeah. It was.

"I went home and jerked off to it," Zeke admits, taking a pull off his beer bottle. "I had the worst stiffy walking home."

Yeah. Me too.

My gaze searches the room, finally landing on Jameson huddled near the door wearing a heavy winter jacket—full-length goose down—along with mittens and a scarf. I cringe inwardly, wondering what the hell she's doing here, and why the fuck she's dressed like a goddamn Eskimo princess.

None of the other chicks here are wearing clothes—well, they are, but barely—and here comes Jameson Clark, bundled up for a trip to the Arctic Circle.

It's thirty degrees outside, not thirty *below*.

Still, I watch her enter the living room with a small group of friends; one I recognize as a regular on the fraternity row party circuit, another is my roommate Parker's regular fuck buddy. All of them are very nice girls, I'm sure, but with groupie mentalities—though not a single one of them is as conservative and buttoned up as James.

Jameson. Jim.

I try to listen as Zeke criticizes beside me, but instead find myself glued to James as she slowly lowers the zipper on her puffy

36

coat. Drags the zipper slowly down her body. Pulls the lapels apart, arching her spine to pull her arms free.

Tossing her head back, she laughs at something Fuck Buddy says and does an odd little dance on her heels as her friends grab the end of her scarf and unwind. Then, all together, they remove Jameson's thick mittens and stuff them in the pockets of her puffy coat.

She shakes out her long, dark brown hair.

That goddamn hair.

It's mussed and damp from the snow flurries outside, and kind of sexy as shit, even if a bit unkempt.

I look away, but not before catching sight of an emerald green cardigan that's probably some pretentious fabric like *cashmere*, pulled over a V-neck tee shirt, jeans, and—my eyes skim her body from tits to toe—black heeled boots.

Yup. *Way* too many clothes.

"What's she doing here?" Zeke nudges me again, a bored inflection to his deep voice. "I didn't think they let geeks out of the library on the weekends."

"Let's be honest, she's their DUFF," someone else says.

I cringe. Designated Ugly Fat Friend? Hardly.

Everyone stands around laughing, and our friend Jared sputters, "She's not their DUFF, morons. She's not fat."

Or ugly.

Not even close.

Calmly, I shrug, not wanting to call any more attention to Jameson, but not coming to her defense, either. "Who cares? It looks like she came here with Parker's booty call."

I might sound blasé, but inside I'm fuming.

Now that I've kissed those lips, I know she's not as prissy as she looks. I know her tits are real, her lips are demanding yet pliant, and her tongue does this magical swirly thing that makes my dick stiff. I know she likes sweaters, studying, and the library.

And let's not forget her sarcastic, shrewd little mouth.

So it's kind of pissing me off that these assholes are making fun of her.

"Let it go guys."

Zeke shrugs his wide, NCAA wrestling championship-bound shoulders. "Whatever man, just letting you know she's here. I'd keep my eye on that one if I were you; you know how the nerdy ones are. *Clingy*," he pronounces knowingly, like he's some god-damn Yoda for nerdy chicks.

"Stage five clingers," Dylan adds, trying to be helpful—until I jab him in the ribcage with my elbow. It's one thing for me to de-grade Jameson behind her back; it's another completely for my friends to do it, and I've had enough.

"Okay, okay, I get it." Dylan coughs from the contact, sputtering on his beer. "Big fucking deal—she showed up at a house party."

"I'm running to grab another beer. Anyone want anything?" I ask, not waiting for their answers and already heading toward the kitchen. The solo keg on the yellow linoleum floor summons and I answer its call.

Beside it? Jameson Clark.

What a coincidence.

"Here, let me get that for you." I reach down for the keg nozzle, grab the red cup out of her hand, and give the handle on the barrel a few hard pumps.

Despite the blaring music filtering through the house, I still manage to catch the sound of her foot tapping on the kitchen floor.

"You owe me more than one measly foamy beer, *Oswald*," she teases.

Did she just call me—

"Oswald?" I search the throng around us. "Who the hell are you talking to?"

Jameson scrunches up her nose, causing the freckles across the bridge of her nose to wink at me. It's kind of really fucking cute, actually—or is that just the three beers I've already chugged down talking?

"Uh, you? Oz. *Oswald*."

I laugh then, a loud, booming laugh that echoes in the small, shitty kitchen.

"You seriously don't know who I am?"

Lips purse, and she takes a dainty sip of the red plastic cup, tapping on the rim with her index finger as she drinks. A thin line of white foam coats her top lip. "I don't know—should I?"

I guess that answers that question.

"Sweetheart, Oz is a nickname. Haven't you googled me yet?"

Amused blue eyes roll. "I'm sure you google yourself enough for the both of us."

Shit, she's right. I do google myself a lot.

Nevertheless, I persist. "There is *no* fucking way you don't know who I am."

She gives me a sidelong glance, thinking. Taps her cheek with the tip of her index finger. "Are you an actor? Have I seen you on TV?" Snaps her fingers together. "I know—your father is an important politician. The president of something or other? No? Hmmm…"

My grin widens. "You're a sarcastic little asshole, did you know that?"

"I take that as a compliment coming from you. Luckily, my sarcasm is usually a sign of affection when I'm warming up to someone."

"Wow, this is you being *nice*?" Over her shoulder, I watch Fuck Buddy and the other girl nudging their way through the crowd toward us. They stop when they reach Jameson's side, both of them primping their long blonde hair with flirty, well-practiced flips.

Even with both of them at her side, Jameson resumes her teasing.

"Of course I'm being nice; you owe me two hundred and fifty

dollars. Or have you already forgotten?"

"How could I possibly forget when you're hell bent on reminding me? Instead of cash, why don't we get creative?"

She lifts a well-manicured brow. "Creative?"

"Yeah. There are other ways I can pay you, starting on my knees with my tongue. Or if you're not a fan of orgasms, I'll let you—"

"Stop!" Jameson shouts in a rush, hands going up in the universal sign for *time out*. "Stop talking! *Jesus*. Okay, fine. How about you just pay me when they pay you?"

"You didn't let me finish what I was going to say."

"Trust me, I know where that was headed."

Fuck Buddy's mouth drops open.

"Uh, James—not to interrupt, but...why is Oz Osborne trying to pay you in sexual favors?" Her chest sticks out, tits on full display in a bright pink top with a scoop neck, her bleached blonde hair artfully curled and spilling down her back. She flips it over her shoulder again and smiles wide.

Nice. Very nice.

Very friendly, I'll bet.

She's so smoking hot it's no wonder Parker fucks her on the regular.

If Jameson notices me noticing her friend, she doesn't comment on it. Instead, she takes a healthy swig of beer, leaving another coating of foam on her top lip. I avert my eyes, removing them from her friend's breasts, then watch as Jameson's pale pink tongue slips out. Licks the foam. Laps more foam from the top of her red cup like it's whipped cream.

Jameson collects herself, fanning her face before introducing her friends. "Uh, Oz, these are my friends, Allison and Hayley. Allison and Hay—well, you obviously already know who this is, and I'm assuming *you* didn't have to google him."

The girls glance between us, rusty wheels turning inside their beautiful blonde heads.

"Um…" the blonde in pink drags out. "What's going on between the two of you?"

"Nothing," Jameson deadpans, recovering her quick wit. "If you don't count the fact that he owes me money for services rendered."

Her *duh* inflection has me sputtering in surprise, the beer in my mouth dripping down my chin in the un-sexiest dribble when a delighted chuckle leaves my throat. I can't remember the last time I choked because something was funny, let alone on alcohol.

Or maybe I'm just getting drunk.

Grabbing the hem of my shirt, I lift it to wipe the drool, noting with arrogance that both Allison and Hayley are hungrily gawking at the solid, tight, six-pack abs on display. I take my sweet time lowering my shirt.

Let the ladies look their fill.

Hell, I'd even let them touch.

"I simply need to pay you for them." I remind Jameson.

"Sure, okay. But only because you were begging for it." She blinks innocently, sipping from her beer cup.

"Sweetheart, begging is something I *never* do."

Beside her, her blonde friends' perfectly groomed eyebrows simultaneously shoot into their hairlines, and for a brief moment, I wonder what else on them is perfectly groomed.

Probably everything.

Eyebrows. Legs.

Puss—

"I'm so confused," Fuck Buddy interrupts. "*What* is going on?"

We ignore her.

"Long story short, Oz won a bet and he has me to thank."

"That's it? What services were you talking about before?" Allison probes, her eyes roaming the room. "Would one of you please explain what's going on?"

Jameson shakes her head. "Sorry Al, but this is between me

41

and Oswald here." She grabs Fuck Buddy by the arm and tugs. "Come on, let's find Parker—that *is* the reason we're here, isn't it? So you can paw at him shamelessly while hopped up on liquid courage?"

Allison blushes prettily. "Yes." Still, her eyes skim the front of my jeans, landing on the bulge there. "Nice finally meeting you in person. I hate doing the walk of shame down your hallway, Oswald."

Shit, that's right. I've only ever seen her ass in the morning walking out the door—and I occasionally hear her moaning Parker's name during their loud, dirty fucking.

Oswald?

Damn if the sound of another girl saying it doesn't grate on my last nerve. I cross my arms and nod, watching as Jameson drags her friends off, her rapid retreat kind of...insulting.

I feel slightly offended that she just left me standing here by myself.

Weird, right?

That almost never happens.

Fine. It *never* does.

Intrigued, irritated, and slightly enthralled, my competitive nature has my senses instinctually tracking her whereabouts throughout the whole goddamn evening.

It's rather inconvenient.

I catch glimpses of her: James and that damn prissy sweater that's somehow come unbuttoned. A sober James with Jack Pryer, a first-year football redshirt, giggling it up in the corner. A sober James with Fuck Buddy near the keg. A sober James tipping her head to tie that silky brown hair back, walking in and out of the front door, presumably for fresh air.

James, James, fucking Jameson Clark and the annoying-as-shit strand of pearls around her neck. The more I stare, the more aggravated I become, especially when I spot her in the living room with my roommate Elliot.

Elliot, who's actually a decent guy. Stable and reliable, he's the serious academic sort—finance and pre-law—and probably a better fit for Jameson than I am.

Better fit for her? Shit, what the hell am I saying?

I *must* be drunk.

The beer flows and so do the shots.

By midnight, I'm shitfaced enough to stop monitoring her every movement all night like a stalker. Shitfaced enough to stop watching every monotonous move she makes. Shitfaced enough to curb whatever possessive instincts are welling up inside my drunk ass—not because I *like* her, but because the poor thing looks so out of place in her boring ass cardigan, and for some ungodly reason, I feel a fucked up sense of brotherly affection.

Affection? A*ffliction*? Affection—horrible adjective, but it's the best I can do under the circumstances.

She spares no such courtesy for me as she continues flirting with Elliot.

Inhaling another beer, my attention wavers only when a hand snakes around my waist, slides over my hard abs. Warm lips meet the side of my neck, and *Christ* if that doesn't feel good. Reaching around, I grab the unidentified round ass behind me, giving it a firm squeeze.

"Oz baby, it's me," a throaty female voice purrs in my ear. "Did you miss me?"

The owner of that voice moves to my front, dragging her talented hands across my middle, over my lower abs, fingers tugging at the denim waistband of my jeans. "Can I get you alone, baby? There's no one in the last bedroom. I checked."

Say baby one more time, I intone sarcastically. *Or better yet, shut the hell up.*

"Maybe." I drag the words out as she toys with the fly of my pants. "If you stop talking."

She nods, red hair and breasts bobbing enthusiastically. We stumble backward, toward the hall, and I back her against the wall, fingers grappling with her tight leggings, stroking the smooth skin beneath her belly button. With an exaggerated moan worthy of a porn star, she shoves her tongue in my mouth with a husky, "I want you to screw me, Oz."

I cup the back of her head, dragging a sloppy kiss across her lips, voice devoid of any emotion. "How about you blow me instead?"

With another eager head bob, she wipes her mouth with the back of her hand and gives me a light shove toward a bedroom door three feet to my right…or is that the closet?

"Not in the hall, though, kay?"

Well, *no shit* not in the hall. I'm more of a gentleman than that. Jesus Christ.

Still, I let her work my zipper, pulling and tugging while I fumble sloppily for the doorknob. She drags it down slowly, right in the hall for anyone to see, her practiced fingers working their way inside my jeans. The door handle gives way just as a shock of emerald appears in my peripheral.

Bright green sweater, gleaming pearls, dark brown hair, and bright blue eyes come to a stunned halt in the corridor. Turn toward us. Stop dead in their tracks, frozen like a deer in headlights.

Or like a virgin in sacrifice.

"Crap, sorry," comes an all too familiar voice.

Shit.

Winter hat back in place, pulled down over that long, silky brown hair, it frames her innocent face and pisses me the fuck off. Too wide-eyed, too inquisitive.

Too sanctimonious.

Nonetheless, she does the last thing I expect her to do:

Watch.

Jameson's perceptive perusal misses nothing as it begins a slow descent down the length of Red's arm, following her grasping hand into the bulge of my pants. Her warm palm vice-grips my hard cock.

With half-hooded eyes, I watch Jameson Clark *watching* me drag my teeth over my lower lip, watching as I groan, watching when Red removes her hand from the front of my jeans, playfully zipping my fly up and down to regain my attention. Down. Up. Down. The metal teeth slide effortlessly.

My alcohol-induced haze remains on Jameson even as Red works over my cock.

James' pale collarbone.

Her flushed cheeks.

"Leaving so soon?" I ask as casually as I can, fly hanging open, underwear bunched up at the zipper.

Jameson never misses a beat. Schooling her features, she takes a relaxed sip from her red plastic cup, staring over the rim with narrowed eyes. "Is this how you're earning the money to pay me?"

What a bitch.

"Maybe," I half scoff, half moan. "Are you calling me a prostitute?"

"No." Back ramrod straight, she arches an eyebrow. "I'm just saying…you might consider charging. You could turn a tidy profit selling that body of yours."

"That sounded oddly like a compliment." Bracing a hand against the wall so my weak knees don't buckle, my eyes rake Jameson up and down. "Interested in being my first paying customer?"

She laughs, the loud sound carrying over both the booming music and the redhead whining in my ear. I ignore her when she gives my arm a tug toward the bedroom.

"*Interested?*" Another laugh from down the hall. "Gross."

Gross? "What the fuck is that supposed to mean?"

"At what *point* do you *stop* using your *body* to prove a *point?*"

Am I drunk or is she enunciating every other word? Groaning, my head dips and my tongue darts out to wet my lips.

"Hey Jim." I sigh, limply pointing down the hall. "If you want to take a piss, you went the wrong way." I moan when Red's hand resumes fondling my balls through the denim. "You went the wrong way," I repeat. "It's by the kitchen. Unless of course you want to join us in the bedroom."

For a few unsettling moments our eyes lock.

For a few unsettling moments her eyes soften, regard me with an unrecognizable emotion and downturned mouth.

She's disappointed.

In me.

I know it as sure as I stand here supporting myself against the wall, sloshed off my ass and twice as turned on. For the first time in almost twenty-one years, a second passes that I'm actually *disgusted* with myself. It's fleeting, but those soft, sober blue eyes—thoughtful and unaffected by all the fangirl *bullshit* surrounding me—make me feel...

Drunk as hell and dirty and chauvinistic.

Self-conscious.

Judged and found lacking.

A minute goes by before Jameson finally spins in her ballet flats and disappears from sight.

I shake my head, disoriented but determined not to give her another thought, and...not going to lie, it's at that moment I pull Red through the bedroom door. Instead of a blowjob, I fuck the shit out of her against the wall.

Because I don't want to care.

Because it feels good.

Because I can.

"You're cute.
Kind of like the nerdy,
girl next door,
but one that likes a good,
hard fuck on your childhood
bedspread."

Sebastian

I sense her before I see her.

Don't ask me how, but when Jameson skirts by my table, determined to avoid me, my bulk sits up straighter.

On high alert.

No greeting, she artfully weaves her way through the tables to the embankment of bookshelves at the far side of the library, firm ass sashaying in tight navy leggings, wearing tall brown boots and a brown leather tote.

Beneath my lashes, I trail her movements—her path direct, marching purposefully to the far recesses of the commons. My hands pause above the keys of my MacBook, pause to watch as she thumps her tote onto the hard table. Eases her laptop out. Plugs it in.

Aligns her pens and pencils, pushing each one into place with the tip of her finger, lining them up as if they each have a rightful spot on the desk. Calculator on the right, computer in the middle.

She takes out a small stack of notebooks, shuffling them. Spreads them out next to the pens.

My brows go up, interested, when she gently peels the rubber band from her dark hair. It shines when she gives it a shake under the dim glow of lamp light on her table then tussles it with her fingers. Black-rimmed glasses get perched on her head.

Fuck if it's not sexy.

Good choice, Jimbo.

Ten minutes later, I'm still watching her from under the brim of my standard issue Iowa ball cap, as if I don't have a crap load of studying to do myself. Oblivious to my surveying, she hen pecks at her computer then lowers her head to write. Scribbles something. Drinks from the straw in her water bottle. Pushes loose strands out of her face before reaching back and quickly braiding her hair.

My knee starts to bounce, on edge.

I look down at my laptop, the curser blinking in the same spot it's been in since Jameson waltzed into the library, flippantly strolling past me like I don't exist and plopping down nine tables away.

Yes, nine.

I counted.

Dragging the curser around my screen, I tear my gaze away long enough to tap out several sentences of my paper, the small black triangle blinking back at me, waiting for a new command. Instead, the calloused pad of my index finger traces a circle around the center mouse pad, uselessly.

My eyes flick back to Jameson, whose slim shoulders are now hunched over an open textbook, face resting in her palms as she reads, the pair of black glasses now perched on her nose.

Huh. Cute.

I count to four before my knee begins its steady, rhythmic bouncing and firmly place my palm there, pressing down to curtail it.

Fuck.

Fuck it.

I snap my laptop closed, grab the cord and case, and spin my ball cap so it's backward. Stand up. Weave my way through the labyrinth of desks, tables, and chairs.

Standing at the foot of Jameson's table, I clear my throat when she barely raises her head to acknowledge me.

"I'm not a tutor, so don't bother," she drones.

"Ha ha. Do you use that line on *every*one?"

Those damn pearls around her neck glow when she stops writing long enough to cast a glance up at me. A smile tips her lips. "Oh, it's *you*. Don Juan."

Smiling—always a good sign.

"Ouch. Careful—my ego is so fragile you might break it." I set my books, bag, and other shit on her table, pulling out the seat opposite her.

A *pfft* escapes her lips. "Fragile? Not likely."

"Did I say fragile? I meant pompous and windbaggy."

"Better." She exaggerates a sigh, fake glaring down at the stack of books I just landed on her desk. "Ugh, what is with you? I didn't invite you to sit down."

Disregarding her lighthearted grimace, I unwind my power cord, plug it into the outlet on the base of the lamp, and give her a low chuckle. "You look like you could use some company."

She volleys back with a low chuckle of her own. "I do *not* look like I want company. You are such a liar."

"Maybe. But you have to admit, the library is becoming our special spot." I pull my lip between my teeth, bite down flirtatiously-ly, and give her a mischievous grin. Instead of blushing like I expect her to—like they *all* do—she rolls her blue eyes and inclines her neck, resuming her studies.

She quickly peeks at me. "Can you do me a favor and try not to make noise? I have a chem test in the morning that promises to be brutal."

"Quiet I can do, especially with a gag in my mouth." I wiggle my brows, even though she's dead set on ignoring me.

Her pen stops. "Somehow I doubt that."

"You could gag me and find out for yourself."

The silence stretches. Then, "No thanks."

"Suit yourself."

I open my laptop, connect to the university's Wi-Fi, and resume research for a business communication logistics paper I've busted my left nut over. It's due on Monday, which gives me four days.

I search a notorious sexual harassment lawsuit from 1997—Johnson v. Olastaire, a case filed by a corporation against one of its own managers—and create notations in the margins of my document.

Opening Excel, I generate a spreadsheet with the compiled information, compare the case with a recent Supreme Court ruling, and set my mouth into a grim line at the article in front of me: sexual assault in a corporate workplace whose PR machine spun the victim into the guilty party.

The whole thing makes me ill and hits a little too close to home, so close it's the reason I've declared human resources as a major.

My older sister Kayla.

Thirty-two, brilliant, and beautiful, Kayla was fresh out of grad school when she became the victim of workplace sexual harassment. A lawyer working her way up in a small boutique firm, she spent countless nights pouring over cases. Endless hours with the paralegals. Never-ending early mornings.

Then, one early evening when she was alone, researching a case, she was assaulted in her office by one of the partners. High powered with clout, he made Kayla the guilty party and human resources turned a blind eye.

The whole thing went public. The media in our hometown painted her as a young, gorgeous corporate climber, censuring her with no ethics and too much ambition.

It ruined the thrill of her first job, future career prospects, earning potential—and her self-worth.

And *she* was the one getting her ass slapped by her dickhead of a boss. Kayla might have won the court case, but she hasn't been the same since.

It's sickening.

The whole thing with my sister makes me ill, so I forge on, diligently copying notes.

Copy, paste. Notation. Copy, paste, notation.

Repeat.

Eventually, I come up for air, lifting my head and reaching for my water bottle. Lift the lid and chug down a thirst-quenching gulp.

Jameson is studying me quizzically. The hands that were furiously pounding away at those laptop keys now hover above her keyboard at a standstill, her pouty mouth twisted thoughtfully.

"What?"

She gives her head a little shake, braided hair swaying. "Nothing." Biting down on her lower lip, she picks up a highlighter and drags it across her textbook, then chews on the end of it.

"Bullshit. You were giving me a look."

Her hands splay. "Fine. Yes, I was giving you a *look*. You've managed to surprise me by actually doing homework."

I scoff. "I told you the other day—I'm carrying a three point seven."

"Yes, but…" The words hang in the air between us. With a shrug, she grins. "I didn't actually believe you."

"I have a scholarship. I can't afford to piss it away."

"Is that why you agreed to that stupid bet with your friends the other day? For the money?"

"Yup, that's why I agreed to that stupid bet. Every little bit helps, yeah?"

Jameson cocks her head to the side and studies me for a second.

"That's it?" I ask.

"What?"

"Aren't you going to grill me?"

She shakes her head. "No. If you had something more to say, you'd say it." Her head dips and she resumes her homework.

"Why do you keep doing that?" I blurt out.

She sighs. "Doing what?"

"Ignoring me." Shit, I sound like I'm whining.

"Look," she says, patiently resting her hands on the table to look me in the eye. "I'm sure you're a real ladies' man and everyone finds you very charming." Her lips purse.

A smile cracks my lips. "But you don't?"

"Sorry." Her head shakes back and forth. "I don't."

I lean against the wooden chair, tipping it to balance on the back legs. Rocking it back and forth, I ask, "And you don't think a guy like me is going to consider that a challenge?"

"A 'guy like you'?"

"Yeah, you know: stubborn, competitive …handsome."

With a laugh, she gives her head another shake. "I can't help *not* finding you charming—you're way too arrogant—so forgive me for not ripping my clothes off and letting you ravish me."

"*Ravish* you." I say it with wonder. "See, that right there fills my head with so many fantastic erotic visuals."

A swipe of the highlighter followed by an undignified *hmph* is her only reply.

"Ravish. *Ravish.* You shouldn't have said that because now I consider you a challenge."

"Be my guest." Jameson laughs again, a soft, low chuckle that sends a damn shiver up my spine. "What you do with that information is *not* my problem."

My eyes skim the top half of her body. Collarbone, graceful neck. Breasts.

"Want to bet?"

"*God* no." She laughs. "Is this your way of trying to get your two hundred and fifty dollars back?" She grabs her pencil and wields it like a tiny sword in my direction. "Which you still haven't paid me, by the way."

"We agreed I'd pay you when they pay me, and I will, Scout's honor."

"Don't you have to have been a Boy Scout to make those sorts of promises?"

"Probably."

"You're terrible."

"But you like it."

An eye roll and a sigh. "You said you weren't going to make noise."

"I know, but I have to know what your deal is."

"My *deal?*"

"Yeah, you know—what's your story? Do you come here to study often? Do you ignore everyone, or just me? Why are you wearing that necklace?"

Her laugh is low and entertained. "Can we save that line of questioning for another day? I have a feeling if I start answering, I'm never getting anything done."

Dammit, she's right.

Now I'm the one sighing. "*Fine.*"

"Do your homework, Oswald."

6

#DOUCHEBAG

"If you were my homework,
I'd be doing
you on my desk right now."

Sebastian

"We have to stop meeting like this."

I look up from editing the text on the screen of my laptop, surprised to see Jameson Clark standing at the foot of my study table with a sly grin. Winter hat pulled down over her hair that hangs in one long chestnut braid over her breast. Jacket in one hand, laptop in the other, her pink cheeks are flushed.

I smile at the sight of those little amber freckles scattered across the bridge of her nose. They're sweet.

I want to lick them.

"You sure do come to the library a lot," I tease. "Here, sit."

My foot pushes out the chair opposite me and she pulls it the rest of the way out before hesitating, laptop poised on the corner of the table.

She drapes her jacket on the chair before taking a seat. "I could say the same about you. You seem to be here as often as I am."

"True, but you know—got that scholarship." I wink at her and she goes through the ritual of laying out her school supplies: pens, notebooks, textbooks, laptop.

Neon highlighter.

Her blue eyes soften. "I still can't get over the fact that you actually study."

"I still can't get over the fact that you find me *resistible*."

"Do your homework, Oswald."

"Why do you keep calling me that?"

"Because that's your name?" She gives me a *duh* look.

"No. It's not."

Genuinely perplexed, her brows furrow. "It's not?"

"Wait. You actually thought my name was Oswald?"

"Um, yes?"

I stare at her. "Wait. You *actually* thought my name was *Oswald?*"

"Do you hear an echo?"

I ignore her teasing. "You're telling me you *haven't* googled me yet?"

"Um, no?"

"Knock it off." I give my head a mental shake, marveling at this information. "So let me get this straight—you have no idea who I am."

She throws her pencil down on the wooden table and crosses her arms. "I have a feeling you're just *dying* to enlighten me."

Damn right I am! "Damn right I am!"

Jameson leans back in her chair with a patronizing expression. "Fine. Go ahead. I'm all ears, hanging on your every word, your majesty."

Shit. Her blatant sarcasm kind of took the wind out of my sail. "Oz. As in *Os*borne."

Jameson stares blankly before scrunching up her cute freckled nose. "Your first name is Osborne? Crap. That wasn't even on my radar as a possibility."

"No." Impatient, my leg begins to bounce under the table. "My *last* name is Osborne."

Her hands go in the air in surrender. "Yikes, don't get all offended. How the hell was I supposed to know?"

Is she fucking serious?

"You know what? Never mind." I reach over the side of the table, dig into my backpack, and whip out a textbook. Cracking it open, I do my best to ignore her.

"Come on, don't be a baby. I told you, I didn't know." She's quiet for a few seconds, and then, "Can I still call you Oswald? I'm sad now knowing it's not your real name."

Agitated, I turn to face her, slamming the book closed with a satisfying thud. "Do I *look* like an Oswald to you?"

She squints, sizing me up. "Hmmm, not really, now you mention it. Now that I'm taking a good look at you, you're more of a Blake. Or a Richard."

"Okay, now you're fucking with me."

"Me?" She points a finger at her chest. "Noooo."

We both start laughing then, the clear sound of her lighthearted giggle doing bizarre shit to my stomach and heart that I can't label—weird, fucked up fluttering and shit.

Annoying.

When we finally stop snickering, she leans in across the table and quietly asks, "So what's your name?"

"I just told you—it's Oz."

"No." Her head gives a little shake. "Your *real* name. It's not like I can't google it if I was feeling motivated, which I'm not." She says the last part with a roll of her eyes. "What did your parents name you?"

For a few quiet heartbeats, I consider not telling her, making her work for it. But then—

"Sebastian."

"Your name is *Sebastian?*"

"Yup." I let the P sound pop.

Jameson studies me then, harder than anyone's ever studied me before, blue eyes searching the rigid lines of my face. The strong jawline. The faded bruise under my left eye from being locked in a chokehold full of elbow.

I feel every stroke of her examination, as if her smooth fingertips are truly caressing my skin.

"Sebastian," she repeats quietly to herself, testing the name. She repeats it several more times, each pronunciation with a different inflection. "*Sebastian...Sebas*tian. Hmm. Who would have thought."

"I'd rather be called Oswald."

"No you wouldn't." Her whisper carries across the table.

My chin rests in my palm, elbow propped on the table.

"You're right. That name sucks donkey balls."

Jameson bites down on her lower lip, her gaze suddenly shy as she glances down at the books opened in front of me on the table. Her throat clears. "We're not getting any work done."

"True." My finger traces the mouse pad in unhurried circles as she begins drumming her fingertips on the table.

"I should probably go."

"Stay. Let's talk for a few more minutes. No harm in that, yeah?"

She seems to mull this over, her teeth still pressed into her bottom lip. "Okay. We'll talk. What do you want to know about me?"

"What's the deal with your roommate and mine?"

Jameson's surprised expression is fleeting. "I think they're just friends with benefits. Why?"

"She should stay away from him. He's a whore."

Jameson laughs. Head thrown back, the cheerful sound fills the room. "That's what they say about *you*."

"Someone said I was a whore? Who?"

"Everyone. After they saw us talking at the party, my friends gave me quite an earful."

I lean back in the chair and it squeaks when I tip it back on its legs. "Any good gossip?"

She mimics my posture and balances herself across from me. "Well, let me think here." The legs hit the ground again and she scratches her chin. "Allison heard you having sex at the party this past weekend and said the door was rattling. So *that* was interesting news."

I pretend to consider this. "Yup, can't lie about that one. I railed that door and the redhead almost off their hinges. Got any others?"

"You date multiple people at once."

"False. I don't date anyone. *Ever*."

Jameson's face is an impassive mask. "Hayley told me you

broke up with your last girlfriend over Twitter."

A grimace twists my mouth into a frown. "Oh, *Hayley* told you, did she? Didn't your mother teach you not to listen to rumors?"

"Yes, but is it true?"

"Yes, but in my defense, she wasn't my girlfriend. She was a pity fuck who turned into a clinger."

"A Twitter breakup?" This time Jameson winces. "That's bad."

"Sorry, but it's the truth. It was the only way to get rid of her. Trust me, I did her a favor."

"How is that doing her a favor? She was probably humiliated!" Then, "Can I ask what the tweet said?"

I chuckle. "Why don't you just go on Twitter and look for yourself."

Those fascinating eyes, which have been judging me for the past few minutes, narrow into bright blue slits as she drags her phone across the table, flips it over, and unlocks the screen.

Gives it a few taps.

"What name am I looking for?"

"OneTapUofI. All one word."

Type, type, type.

Narrowed eyes widen, dark eyebrows shoot up. Her pert mouth falls open a fraction in horror when she finds it. "This is terrible! You are so crude."

I chuckle again. "Read it out loud so I can get a good laugh."

"No!"

"Oh come on, Jim! She had it coming."

"No! You called her a troll—that is so uncalled for." She glances down at the screen of her phone. "This whole tweet is terrible."

"Careful, you're repeating yourself."

"Oh shut up, you—"

"Asshole?"

"Yes."

"Dickhead?"

"*Yes*."

"Douchebag?"

She titters. "You said it, not me."

"No one has ever accused me of being a gentleman, Jim." Casually I regard her from across the table. "Haven't you ever done anything you've regretted?"

She pretends to consider the question. "You mean like letting a stranger convince me to kiss him in public?"

"Ha ha. But yeah, I guess that's exactly what I mean."

This time Jameson *does* think about it, humming to herself as she deliberates on a reply. She inhales, drawing in a deep breath, and says with a straight face, "Once I ate at White Castle. Does that count as a regret?"

"Sure, why not."

"I *call* it the White Castle of Regret."

I laugh, then she laughs, and soon ours eyes are watering tears of mirth.

"Holy shit that's funny," I enthuse, wiping my cheeks dry. "You don't look like you have any sense of humor at all, but you're hilarious."

She's pleased. Smug. "Occasionally I've been known to throw out a few zingers."

"I still want to know more about a girl who wears pearls to the library but willingly makes out with a stranger."

"Willingly? That's a stretch."

"Stop evading the question."

Slumping back in her seat, James rests her head against the chair. "I'm rather shy—"

"You are not fucking shy, but nice try."

"Fine, I'm not shy—but if you really must know, sometimes I wear pearls and cardigans to the library so I look serious and so people leave me alone." She shoots me a pointed look. "Which, obviously, does. Not. Work."

"*Obviously.* It's not a very clever disguise and it makes you look like a kindergarten teacher—and not even a hot one."

"Gee, *thanks*," she sarcastically replies. "My point is I'm having a hard time keeping my grades up. I have to work really hard at it—nothing comes natural to me, especially chemistry, which I hate but have to pass." She sighs. "My major is pre-pharmacy but I'm having second thoughts. One of my biggest regrets is declaring so soon. Sometimes I wish I was more adventurous, although I'm pretty content watching everyone else act like assholes at parties."

"You don't seem to shock very easily." I'm referring to our meeting in the hallway, when the redhead was grabbing my cock.

"No, I don't. My mom does porn, so..." She shrugs nonchalantly, dragging out her sentence. "You ain't got nothin' I haven't ever seen in one of her movies."

The bombshell has my eyes bugging out of my skull and I practically leap out of my chair. "*What!*"

A burst of laughter spills from her lips and before I know it, she's sputtering. Falling out of her seat, waving her hands around, trying to calm herself. "Sit down, sit down, I'm kidding. Oh my god, you should see your face."

"You're an asshole."

"So you keep saying." The smirk returns. "It's like looking in the mirror, isn't it?"

7

#DOUCHEBAG

"My parents are coming for a visit
this afternoon, which means
I have to make the apartment
look like a virgin lives there by 4.
It won't be easy."

Sebastian

S he's the last person I expect to see when I round the corner of the business school, but she's exactly who I see when I bend to tie my shoe. I glance up when her familiar black patent leather ballet flats come into view.

I rise to my full height and straighten.

Jameson is wearing glasses today—black rimmed—and a long, smooth ponytail trails down her back. I can't tell if she's wearing a cardigan under her navy jacket, but I hypothesize that she is—and that it's basic. Buttoned from the bottom all the way up to her throat. Probably in some boring color like gray.

Or dark blue.

"Hey Oz." She greets me with her own onceover, checking me out from top to bottom. "You're not following me around campus now, are you? Cause I'd hate to call security on you."

"Yup. I'm only pretending to tie my shoe so I can look up your skirt."

She's wearing jeans and a smile. "Oz, you met Allison and Hayley at the party—this is our *other* roommate, Sydney."

"Hey." I greet them both with a huge grin because, well, Sydney is almost as good looking as Allison and Hayley. All three of Jameson's roommates are the kind of sexy that hits you immediately, not the subtle, classy kind that sneaks up on you slowly, the way Jameson's does.

The hot roommate's mitten-covered hand shoots out. "Hi. Gosh, you're so... I don't know if you remember me, but we met at Welcome Week in August? I'm on the dance team?"

Shit, have I fucked her already? I got pretty wasted during Welcome Week at a frat's afternoon pre-party and can't remember shit about that weekend.

"You probably don't remember me," she prattles on. "You

were working the information table for the athletic department. You're a football player, right?"

"No."

Not even close.

At Sydney's crestfallen expression, James eases closer to elbow me in the ribcage. I give her a *What did I say?* look and shrug my wide shoulders because honestly, I'm not on the goddamn football team. What does she expect me to say?

"The dance team, huh?" I ask. "Yeah, yeah, that's right. Now I remember. Good to meet you—again." I shoot her a winning smile; I mean, why wouldn't I? Sydney is hot. Flat chested beneath her *Iowa Dance Team* sweatshirt, but still pretty hot.

Jameson grabs her roommate by the arm.

"Anyway, good running into you, Oz." She starts walking, attempting to haul Sydney away. "We're late."

"Where you headed?" I take a few steps forward, slinging my backpack over my shoulder. "Maybe we're headed in the same direction."

"Nope. We're done on campus. A little late getting back to our apartment."

"*Late* getting back to your apartment?"

Jameson clears her throat. "If you must know, our roommate Allison's parents are coming to town, and we told her we'd help clean the place."

"No library?"

"Not tonight."

"Are you sure I can't convince you to meet me in the back corner?" I give her a wicked grin and wiggle my brows.

Sydney's mouth falls open.

Jameson, however, looks dismayed. "*God*, no. I don't have time for that tonight—especially when you still owe me that money."

"Why do you keep bringing that shit up?"

"Because you owe me money."

"*Technically* I owe you money, but think of it this way: you're not really out any actual cash. You just haven't had a gain."

"*Technically* you made a verbal commitment to pay me half of your earnings. *I'm* the one who earned it."

True, but still…

I switch gears. "If you don't come to the library, who's going to help me with my chemistry?"

Jameson squints at me, pushing her glasses up the bridge of her nose with a cute little laugh. "You are *not* taking chemistry classes!"

"Fine, but I like making chemistry, and isn't that almost the same thing?"

Sydney's dark brown eyes volley back and forth between Jameson and me then widen when her roommate lets out an unladylike snort.

"I'll tell you what Jim, since we're *friends*, I'm going to help you out. If pretty little Sydney here has classes that would be helpful for chemistry—"

"Do not listen to him Sydney. He is not taking chemistry."

"Jim, you're hurting my feelings." I place a palm over my heart solemnly. "Sydney, what do you say? You look like the kind of girl who knows her way around a…lab room."

Her toe taps on the ground. "Oz, seriously?"

"My point is, if you're free today, Sydney, why not let me take you for a burger? Are you as hungry as I am sweetheart? Wanna help me study?"

Sydney nods zealously. "I can do that. I've got Bio Chem now so it would be a breeze.'"

"No hard feelings if I take her out, right Jimbo?"

Her face is an impassive mask, the only tell of any indecision her brief nibbling of that pink lower lip.

I gaze back at Jameson, trying to figure her out. Is she seriously going to stand there and let me take out her roommate without putting up a fight for me? Who the hell *does* that? Every chick on campus is dying to date me, bang me, or trap me into a relation-ship—and James doesn't want to do any of those things.

What the shit is *that* all about?

If she's playing a game to keep me guessing, she should know better than to play an athlete.

We aren't deterred that easily.

I make one last-ditch effort, give her one last chance to change her mind and come to her senses. "James, what if we meet for dinner after you're done cleaning? I'll take you for a burger, no strings attached, *and* you can bring your laptop."

"You *just* invited my roommate to go with you instead!"

"Who cares?" I scowl down at Jameson, who cringes.

"She can hear us arguing, you know."

I barely spare Sydney a glance. "So?"

"You're absolutely ridiculous."

"You seriously won't meet me for dinner?" I'll admit it, I'm *this close* to stomping my foot on the ground like a child who's not getting their way.

"I *can't* meet you for dinner. I'm helping Allison."

"I'm not going to beg, Jim."

She laughs. "I don't want you to."

"How about a threesome?" Kidding, not kidding.

"Oz." Her tone carries a warning that I've pushed far enough. We stare each other down until Sydney uncomfortably clears her throat between us.

"A burger sounds great."

"Excellent. I'm starving." I lick my lips for show, both girls following the movement of my tongue with their widened eyes. "In fact, I could eat just about...*anything* right now."

Sydney bites her bottom lip, fighting back an excited squeal, and rattles off some house numbers.

An uneasy feeling settles over me when I look to James for any sign of disapproval, some hint that she's bullshitting. Any sec-ond now she's going to throw her hands up and announce she's kidding—of course she'll meet me at Malone's!

Instead, the large smile pasted on her face appears sincere. Apologetic. Exaggerated, but sincere.

I should be relieved. I should feel ecstatic to have James off my back. No nagging. No bitchy comebacks. No sass.

I shouldn't *feel* anything.

But goddammit if I do.

Jameson

I should be relieved.

I should feel excited for Sydney; Sebastian Osborne is her type one hundred times over. From his broad, firm shoulders to his black tattoos, his dirty mouth to his popularity on campus.

I shouldn't *feel* anything for him.

But…damn if I do.

Crap.

8

#DOUCHEBAG

"If I flipped a coin right now, what would be the chances of her giving me head?"

Sebastian

"So what's the deal with you and Jimmy?"

"Who?"

I tap my index finger on the table impatiently. "Jameson. You know—you two aren't..." I jiggle a limp French fry over the appetizer platter in the center of the table. "You aren't exactly who I'd place together in a lineup."

I take a bite of my fry, watching Sydney intently, chewing slowly while appraising everything about her with male appreciation. In the hour I gave her to get ready for...*whatever this is*...she used every spare minute to get freshened up. Smoky eye makeup, sleek wavy blonde hair, tight pale blue sweater.

Tighter skinny jeans.

At the moment, we're sitting in a corner booth at Malone's, one of the closest bars to campus that serves the best burgers in town. You might reek like deep fryer when you walk out, but the food more than makes up for it. If I'm going to be railroaded on a date—which is costing me what little extra money I have—I'm going to eat a delicious goddamn hamburger, even if it I have to do an extra two miles of running and fifty extra squats to burn off the calories.

"Placed together in a lineup?" Sydney's dark blonde brows furrow in confusion. "What do you mean?" Her long hot pink nail pokes at a mozzarella stick on the appetizer platter, but she makes no move to eat it.

I nab another fry and pop it in my mouth. "Seriously." I swallow. "Conservative Mary and Malibu Barbie? How'd the two of you end up living together?"

Another poke at the mozzie sticks. "Conservative? Who on *earth* are you talking about?"

In a move I'm going to later blame on Jameson, I roll my

eyes. "James."

How can she not know who I'm talking about?

"You're talking about *James?*" she asks, baffled.

I gotta give the girl props: Sydney has the good sense to look affronted. I give her another few points for loyalty, and one for the irritated expression she's trying to mask behind her faltering smile. "Jameson Clark? *Conservative?*"

She says it so incredulously I begin to wonder if I'm starting to piss her off.

Nonetheless...

"Do you know more than one Jameson?" I recline back in my chair and cross my arms. Sydney's eyes, lined in heavy black liner, rake my tattoo-covered biceps, flaring with obvious interest.

Palming my beer bottle, I take a quick pull. "Yeah. Prim and proper. Smart mouth. What's up with that?"

I'm kind of being an asshole, but she doesn't seem to care. Well, she cares, but I don't.

Sydney blushes out a stiff, "James is not boring."

I scoff. "I didn't say she was boring—I know why she's always studying, but what other stuff is she into? She does do *other* stuff, yeah?"

"I think she's just serious about school. She doesn't like to be bothered when she's studying."

I suppress an eye roll. "I know. Has it occurred to her that she doesn't need to wear cardigans and shit to be serious about school or to be left alone?" I ask more to myself than to Sydney. "Does she ever go out and have fun? Let loose? Dress slutty?"

Inquiring minds want to know.

"Yes?"

Yeah, right. My brows rise dubiously. "Really? What *kind* of fun?"

Sydney's arms flail helplessly on her side of the booth. "I don't know! You just saw us at a party—*that* kind of fun. She likes snowboarding and swimming in the summer, so she does that a lot."

"*Snow*boarding?" I ask incredulously.

Sydney nods. "She's *really* good, too. I think she's in the snowboarding club; they're leaving for Utah for spring break soon."

No fucking way. "*Snowboarding?*" I parrot, sounding like an idiot. "There's no fucking way."

Sydney stares at me then, across the table, the most perplexed look on her face. Brows creased into deep lines, her mouth is downturned in an arch. "Sorry? I'm getting really confused."

Her ditzy laugh doesn't reach her eyes, and the air between us gets awkward.

Shit. This isn't cool. I'm a dick, but if I keep overtly acting like one, there's no chance in hell Sydney's going to blow me in the bathroom at the end of this quasi date.

I switch gears and turn on the charm. "You know what? Forget I said anything; I was just curious. So tell me more about yourself."

Now her whole face changes, goes from guarded to animated when she gasps an excited breath. "I'm a senior nursing major originally from Tennessee, I'm on the dance team, and I just *love* wrestling. I'm a huge, huge fan."

A huge fan for someone who thought I was on the football team, I think sarcastically.

"Uh huh." I nod, half listening, and eat another limp fry, chasing it down with a swig of beer while trying to visualize Jameson Clark snowboarding.

I'm fucking sorry, but I cannot for the life of me reconcile the image in my mind. Tiny Jameson, bearer of buttoned up cardigans and pearl necklaces, *snowboarding?* Terrain parks and half-pipes. Boxy jackets and bib overalls.

There's no freaking way.

Sydney's voice drones in and out.

"…and then I transferred last year when I toured the campus

with my cousin. That's how I met Allison, who was already living with Jameson. I have to make up a few classes at the end of this year that weren't accredited at my previous school, which will set me back a semester. That's gonna suck."

Absentmindedly, I reply, "That does suck."

"Right? My parents are going to *kill* me." Suddenly, Sydney's mouth broadens into a huge smile. "So, enough about me. Tell me more about you. What's the famous Oz Osborne's story? I can hardly believe I'm sitting here with you. I feel like we have a lot in common."

Her teeth flash bright white in her spray-tanned face and she gives a tiny squeak of delight.

Great. *Just great.* Jameson tricked me into going out with a sports groupie. I'm going to kill her the next time I see her; maybe she'll let me stick my tongue down her throat as punishment.

I lean forward in the booth, resting my elbows on the sticky tabletop. "I don't know what there is to tell. I'm here on a wrestling scholarship, but everyone knows that. My major is HR, my—"

"HR...like, as in human resources?"

"Yeah."

"Huh." Her response is one I've seen a million times before. "I don't think I've ever heard of a guy majoring in HR. What made you decide to do that?"

I have my reasons, but they're no one's business. I don't know Sydney, don't care to get to know Sydney—so I don't tell her the reason I majored in HR when there were a million other career paths I could have chosen.

"So Sydney, what else do you like to *do* for fun." The tone of my voice is obviously an innuendo, an invitation I'm not quite feeling in my pants.

"Well," she starts slowly. "I like parties...and sports ...and meeting new people...and being *friendly*."

Speaking of friendly: the vision of Jameson rising from her

seat in the library right before she *kissed the shit out of me* has me pausing. The black sweater and pearls she had on. The buttoned up green cardigan she had on as she watched me get a hand-job in the hallway of a house party last weekend. The gray one she wore yesterday.

"Hold up. Does she always wear cardigans? I mean, she wears other shit out of the house, right?"

My date hesitates. "Excuse me?"

"I've never seen her in anything but sweaters. She owns other clothes, right?"

"Er…are we back to talking about Jameson?"

"She has other clothes in her closet, yeah? Not just all that plain crap? Does she own sweatshirts?"

"Uh…yes. I've seen her in other *shit*." Sydney's brow furrows into a pout. "Sorry if I'm coming off as confused, it's just…I've never heard anyone call her *plain* before. I think you need your head examined."

She's probably right because why the fuck am I still talking about this shit?

I grab one of Sydney's mozzarella sticks, dip it in marinara sauce, and swallow it whole. "I just think it's weird. She looks like a fucking kindergarten teacher."

My date shrugs. "She gets that a lot, but that's not how she is. *Trust* me."

9

#DOUCHEBAG

"I finally got her to leave after
dropping hints all morning.
I refused to introduce her to
my roommate or feed her.
The sex was so bad I don't ever
want her coming back."

Jameson

"Well that was the weirdest date I've ever been on." Sydney walks in the door of our apartment, throwing her purse on the end of the couch I'm sitting on. "If you can call it that."

I sit up straighter, my plaid flannel pajama bottoms bunched up around my knees. A piece of red licorice rope hangs out the corner of my mouth as I close my laptop, set it on the coffee table, and lean back into the plush couch cushions.

Trying to appear casual, I slowly drawl out, "What do you mean?"

Sid huffs, banging a few cabinets open and rummaging through them until she finds a clean cup. "He spent the entire time grilling me about *you*."

What? "Shut up."

"For real. The entire time. At first I thought it was cute, you know? I thought he was asking out of polite interest, but then it got *really* annoying."

"Sydney, stop it. That's not funny."

"I wish I was kidding," she says as she fills her cup with water then takes a few sips. "Honest to god, James, that guy is so hot. Like, I could see his hard nipples through his shirt. And his tattoos? Gawd, so hot, but not gonna lie—he killed my lady boner by bringing your name up *every* two seconds."

"Why would he do that?"

She levels me with a stare. "Gee, I wonder."

Rolling my eyes, I follow her when she heads toward the bathroom, padding behind her with bare feet. "I mean, not that I care, but what was he asking? Be more specific."

Sydney puts down the toilet seat cover and invites me to sit. "He wanted to know why you study so much, why you're so serious, do you go anywhere for fun besides the library."

Shuffling past her into the tiny room, I plop down on the toilet, emit an indignant *hmph,* and cross my arms as she drones on.

"I know, right? And here's the crazy part: he was hinting about asking me out again, which I found super bizarre 'cause he didn't seem to give a crap about anything I was saying."

"Would you have said yes if he'd asked?"

Say no, say no.

Sydney's face contorts with an *Are you nuts* look before shifting her focus into the mirror. "Um, *yeah.* I mean, I'm not stupid. It's Oz freaking *Osborne.* He's so freaking hot. I swear, I wanted to pet him. Oh my gawd, James, his tattoos got me so turned on—I could have climbed into his lap. My panties are *so* wet right now."

Tattoos. Wet. *Hot.*

"Right," I deadpan. "Hot."

And wet.

My roommate pulls out a cotton ball, gets it *wet,* and begins taking off her mascara. She turns to me with one eye open. "What is with you? You're acting strange."

"Me? No I'm not!"

But I am—I totally am.

"He asked for your number," Sydney says offhandedly before running the water and bending to splash it on her face. "Honestly, I was surprised he didn't already have it, the way you two carry on."

"He asked for my *phone* number?"

My roommate laughs. "Yes Jameson, your *phone* number."

"Why would he want my number?" I muse, sounding mystified. "That's so weird."

"Uh, no it's not." Blindly, she fumbles for a towel, her voice muffled when she says, "I swear, if I didn't know any better, I'd think…"

I hold my breath. "Think what?"

"I'd think there was something going on between the two of you besides being study buddies." She says it warily, as if she's afraid of what I'll say next, afraid I might tell her to stay away from him.

"*Pfft*, please. That's ridiculous," I object. "I've seen him in the library maybe five times—that's it."

"I'm not so sure-er!" she singsongs. Then, lowering her voice, she teases, "What goes on between the two of you in that library, Jameson Victoria Clark?"

"Nothing!" I protest loudly.

Maybe too loudly, because my roommate's smile widens into a full-out grin.

"*Hmmm.*" Her green eyes scan my ribbed navy tank top and plaid pajama pants. Sid taps a finger to her chin in mock thought. "Come to think of it, he did seem to fixate on your wardrobe. He brought up your cardigans twice. I told him *all* about your cardigan collection."

"Shut up Sydney!" I grab a damp washcloth from the shower and lob it at her. "I do not have a cardigan collection, brat!"

Just one of every color in the rainbow: red, orange, yellow, green, blue... Purple. Pink. White, black, and gray.

And a few patterned ones.

But big deal—who doesn't?

"But you kind of do. Don't bother denying it," she teases, calling off the colors in my closet. "Red, pink, yellow, green."

I stick my tongue out. "I hate you sometimes."

"No you don't." Sydney goes back to removing her makeup. "So you *don't* care if he asks me out again?"

"What? Please. *No.* Why would I? It's not like *I'm* going to date him. Haha. No. Be my guest—he's just some guy I study with at the library."

Seriously, I need to stop talking.

Fiddling with a container of moisturizer, not turning to meet my eyes, she dubiously nods. "All right, if you say so. But...you know, if you change your mind, say something, okay? I don't want it to be weird if Oz and I start dating."

"Oz Osborne *dating?*" I roll my eyes but she doesn't see me. "*Okay* Sydney. Good one."

This time she does turn to face me, her brows furrowed. Hurt. "Why would you say it like *that?*"

"Please. The guy screws *every*one—I saw him getting a hand-job at a party *in the hallway.* It's probably a good idea to stay away from a guy like that, no matter how good looking he is."

"First of all, there is no way he screws *every*one. Every athlete has a reputation simply by being an athlete; they're not all pigs. Oz could be guilty by association. And secondly, why *wouldn't* I want to date him? It's Oz Osborne. If he asks me out, I'd be a fool to say no; do I look like a fool to you?"

No, dammit. She doesn't.

She's not.

I cross my arms stubbornly. "Fine. Just don't let him lead you on—no doubt he's run out of room on his bedpost for notches."

She levels me with a stare. "You don't honestly believe that garbage, do you?"

Well, no. I don't. So why the hell did I say it?

My sigh is palpable. "No. But I also don't think you should get involved with him."

Sydney considers this for a few moments, swiping a hand through her long blonde hair. "James, it's a few dates, nothing more. I'm not going to marry the guy."

Her face turns a suspicious shade of pink—one she tries to hide behind a white terrycloth towel.

"Suit yourself, but don't say I didn't warn you. And make sure you wear a condom."

She giggles prettily. "Him too?"

"That goes without saying," I tease when she sets down the towel to slather on moisturizer.

I wait as she brushes her teeth, braids her hair, and scuttles back to her bedroom.

I wait for the telltale sound of her door closing before I exhale a shaky breath and revisit our earlier conversation.

Sebastian talked about me the entire time they were on their date? Then asked for my phone number?

What does that even mean?

A knot of uncertainly forms in the pit of my stomach, along with a pang of something else.

Jealousy.

I'm jealous that I'm not outgoing in the way Sydney, Allison, and Hayley are. Jealous that guys don't find me sexy because outwardly, I'm conservative. Jealous that I can't just let loose. Jealous that…

Ugh, stop it, James. Stop!

He's not my type, he's not my type, he's not my type, I chant to myself.

Oh god, I'm doing it out loud.

Rising from the toilet, I walk to the counter, bracing my hands on either side of the sink, breathing in through my nose and exhaling out my mouth to curb this wave of nausea.

Nausea at the thought of my roommate dating Sebastian.

Me. *Jealous*.

Is this what that feels like?

This is a new low, and I groan miserably.

#DOUCHEBAG

"Are you the SAT?
Cause I'd do you for three hours
and forty-five minutes…
with a ten-minute break
in the middle for snacks."

Sebastian

"I reserved us a study room."

I stand over James' table, looking down at her open textbook. Her blue gaze hits me square in the gut when she glances up, and I shift uncomfortably on the balls of my feet.

"You what?"

I straighten to my full height. "I reserved us a study room. Upstairs, room 209."

"You *reserved* us a *room?*"

"Yeah, then we can talk and study and no one will hassle us."

Her lips tip into a smile. "Oz, I don't *want* to talk, at all, let alone when I'm studying."

"Oh James. Jim, Jim, Jim…the many dirty ways I could respond to that."

She bites the inside of her cheek to stop her smile from spreading, and a dimple I've never noticed appears in her left cheek. "Haha, very funny."

"You're no fun." I sigh, setting my red and black backpack down on the edge of her table. "Fine, no study room."

"Wait. You're not sitting here."

"Why not?"

She rolls her eyes. "Because you're *chatty* and distracting."

"A good kind of distracting? As in, you spend your time thinking of *all the ways I could fuck you* distracting?"

"Oh my god, no. You are so offensive."

"Fine. No talking. Promise." I make the universal sign for *zipping my lip and throwing away the key*.

She regards me thoughtfully, then lets out a resigned sigh and gathers her things. "Fine. We can go up to the study room."

"Really?" I can't hide my surprise.

"Sure. Clearly your evil intention to wear me down until I'm a shell of a woman is working. You know, like an FBI interrogator beats down a perp, or a toddler begs for candy."

"Or like a fine wine."

"No, *not* like a fine wine. The opposite of a fine wine."

"Whatever you say, Jim." When she rises with her bag, laptop, and textbooks, I reach over. "Here, hand that over. I'll carry your stuff."

"Aww, what a gentleman."

"You're way too petite and delicate to be carrying all this shit anyway. It's bad for your back."

"You…" Her voice full of wonder, James raises her brows up at me. "You think I'm delicate?"

I cast a glance down at her. "Duh."

It only takes Jameson seven minutes to break the silence once we settle into the study room, sitting across from each other in the private, conference-like room. Completely enclosed with only a narrow window in the door, it's isolated at the end of the hall, and quiet.

You could hear a pin drop. Until—

"So. How was your date with Sid?"

I bite back a grin. I wondered how long it would take her to bring that up, and she doesn't disappoint.

"Great," I say jovially. "She's a delight."

More silence. And then—

"So…what did you talk about?" James is the embodiment of composure and indifference, her features passively schooled.

"You know. Stuff."

"What kind of stuff?"

You kind of stuff. "What's with the twenty questions?"

Her shoulders rise into a shrug. "Just curious. Sid was over the moon when she got home. You must have really laid on the charm."

Nope, not even the slightest bit. Instead, I go with, "Or maybe Sydney is just an easy lay."

Jameson stiffens, mouth dipping into a frown. "What do you mean?"

"You know what I mean." My meaning is clear.

Silence.

She ignores me then, bending her head and writing in her notebook, the sound of her pen reverberating against the walls with every punishing stroke.

"No. I don't know." Her voice is quiet, just above a whisper.

I feel like such a dick. "Oh relax, nothing happened. I'm fucking with you."

She's not amused by my antics, or my swearing. "You use that word a lot."

"I do. It's a great fucking word."

She raises her head and her cheeks are red. Blushing. Flaming.

All from the use of a single word. I decide to see how far I can push her.

"You don't like it?" I press on. "Fucking?"

Nostrils flaring, her face gets redder—if that's possible—and her eyes shine bright blue. Clear. Glassing over.

Unfocused. Heavy lidded. Turned on—another language I speak.

"Fucking is my favorite," I soothe gently. "The *word*, I mean."

Clearing her throat, James tilts her head to study me, intense blue gaze falling on my lips. They linger there, watching my mouth as I speak.

"Personally, *Jameson*, I think it's one of the most versatile words in the English language. Don't you?"

One small, jerky nod and I can see her throat contract when she swallows.

"Just listen once: f*uuuu*ck." I draw out the sound in a whimper, pained, the word strained in a slow, tortured moan, like I'd sound if I were about to orgasm.

"Fuck-ing," I coax. "Fuck it. Fuck off."

She shifts in her seat, restless now. "I get the picture, Oswald. You can stop now."

But I don't stop.

"Fuck *you*. Better yet, fuck *me*." The curse rolls off my tongue like a command.

My cock stiffens as I lower my eyes to the chest of Jameson's soft lavender sweater, the buttons now straining against her breasts. The visible skin in the V above her neckline is splotchy and red.

"Oh yeah, fuck me." I quirk my eyebrow. "*Have* you Jim? Fantasized about fucking me?"

"Is it *nec*essary to be so vulgar?" Her question comes out breathless and labored, and it doesn't escape my notice that she's avoided answering my question.

"Necessary? No," I allow. "But it *is* more fun."

"Well it's starting to make me uncomfortable."

"*Really?* It's making you uncomfortable." I rub my chin in thought.

She blows out a puff of what I assume is sexually frustrated air. "It makes me uncomfortable having you sit here and say things like that when we *both* know you're only saying it because you think I look virginal and you're trying to shock me. Too bad it isn't working."

She raises some valid points. Still—

"Don't bullshit me, Jim. Every time I use the word *fuck* you start blushing like crazy. I bet you're blushing everywhere, aren't you?" Her face turns toward the bookshelves to avoid my rebuttal. "Look me in the eye and tell the truth; you're getting turned on."

Her reply sounds small and vulnerable—so unlike her.

"Maybe I wouldn't feel so uneasy if I thought you weren't

playing some immature game. And don't lie to *me*; this is a game. All you're trying to do by saying *fuck* over and over is get a reaction. You don't actually care how uncomfortable it's making me feel."

I ignore all her *feelings* talk and skip to the good stuff.

"Holy shit I can't believe you just said it."

"What? The F-bomb? *Pfft*, please—I swear when the mood strikes me."

I laugh. "Okay badass, give me your best curse. Have at it."

Jameson removes her hands from her keyboard, leaning forward in her chair until she's facing me. Clasping her hands on edge of the table primly, her small but sexy body adjusts in the black leather seat, her back ramrod straight.

She unclasps her hands and drums her fingers on the smooth lacquered tabletop.

My attention is drawn to those hands like a moth to a flame; I look down and study them, pale and fragile, the short nails filed and painted a glossy peachy pink color. I look up at the elegant pearl necklace adorning her slim neck, the lavender of her cardigan sweater with the sleeves pushed up to her elbows.

The gleaming, delicate gold watch circling her tantalizing wrist.

Jameson bites down on her bottom lip, sucks on it a few seconds, then inhales. Exhales a long, exalting sigh as she musters up her courage. "Okay asshole. Sebastian." She breathes my name serenely, the words more a tender caress than profane.

The first sign of my dick involuntary hardening has me at full attention when she continues, voice quiet. "You want a curse word, but I'll do you one better to shock you. Ready? I'm most definitely *not* a virgin. And I'm *definitely* not…wearing…any…" She leans in all the way, her soft breath tickling the lobe of my ear from across the table. "Panties."

She stops breathing the same time I do, the boardroom table in front of us a monolith of epic proportion, stretched wide, separating me from her pantie-less pussy. She shifts in her seat, shooting me a guilty glance; she's wet, I just fucking *know* it.

"Is that an invitation?" I whisper back, palms splayed on the table and coming up out of my chair, ready to pounce. I'd bang her right on this table if she'd let me.

"*No.*" She breathes.

"You sure about that?"

Another whisper. "*Yes.*"

"But not yes as in, '*Yes Oz, yes! Harder! Yes Oz, right there?*" The words come out in an adolescent croak, my voice cracking as I fight the urge to readjust the bulge in my stiff denim.

The entreaty travels across the silent room to its intended target, drifting listlessly, weaving its way into Jameson's black leggings. She shifts again in her chair, lifting her rear off the seat uncomfortably.

"No."

"You know you're breaking my heart, don't you, Jim?"

"Yes."

Yes, yes, yes.

"*Fuck.*"

Suddenly and without warning, Jameson stands, the leather chair falling back and hitting the wall. She collects her things, closing her laptop and scooping everything into her book bag.

"Maybe I should go. I'm not cut out for whatever *this* is, and I didn't come here to get harassed, so clearly I'm not your type of girl."

My mouth falls open, but nothing comes out—no protests, no jokes, no innuendos.

Shit.

"Jim, c'mon—sit down. I'm kidding."

Her bag slung over her shoulder, she drops a pencil to the carpeted floor but doesn't bend to pick it up.

Probably because she's not wearing any fucking underwear.

I groan at the thought.

"Stay—please. God dammit, I'm sorry, okay? I'll stop being an asshole."

"You're a nice guy, okay? I think you're neat. But you're not getting in my pants, so I wish you'd stop wasting your time."

Hold up. Did she just call me… "Neat?"

"Yeah, neat." Her head shakes with a laugh. "I'll see you around, Oz. Do the women of the world a favor and try to behave yourself."

Another heartbeat and she's gone, nothing left but the door slamming behind her and the musky smell of her perfume.

I'm left sitting alone under the florescent lights of the sterile study room. She'll see me around?

Behave?

Yeah, no. There's nothing I love more than a challenge, and Jameson Clark just triggered my competitive reflexes.

I tap a few keys on my laptop before an idea pops into my head.

A genius, totally outrageous idea.

See me around?

You bet your tight little ass you will.

#DOUCHEBAG

"I had to google all of the weird,
kinky sex shit she wants
to do to me. If that's not a reason
to propose, I don't know what is.
Or at least take her
on a second date."

Jameson

"I still cannot believe the *nerve* of him!" I practically shout, slamming out of the campus union, my voice carrying through the courtyard, echoing among the sparse trees and frozen ground. Several students walking down the shoveled concrete path swivel their heads and glare in my direction, curiously. "That... that...asshole!"

Undeterred, I stalk across campus, eyes set on one building, and one building alone.

My day had been going great; after a long, sleepless night, I had finally put Sebastian Osborne out of my mind, aced my chemistry lab test, and scored the last rice crispy treat out of the vending machine in the cafeteria.

All before ten o'clock.

With a whistle and a spring in my step, I'd sauntered into the ski and snowboard office to gather whatever last minute travel information I needed for my trip tomorrow. I had nary a care in the world before Chad Hanson, our president, announced, "Hey James, we have a last minute addition coming on the spring break trip this year. He signed up late last night, paid in full by credit card."

Chad had paused then, shuffled a stack of papers, and cleared his throat, flipping the long hair out of his green eyes before addressing me again.

"James? Did you hear me?"

Shaking my head, I had planted a cheery smile on my face.

"Sorry, I don't know what my problem is. What were you saying?"

"We have a new guy signed up for the trip—Sebastian Osborne, if you can believe it. Why didn't you tell me he was your cousin? He called before I closed the office last night and paid for the trip with a credit card. Weird, huh?"

I'm sorry, what? "I'm sorry, I don't think I heard you correctly."

"I said, we have a new guy signed up for the trip—"

I'd thrown my hand up to stop him. "No, no, I know what you
said, Chad. I just...can't believe that's what I'm hearing. We
closed registration weeks ago. *Weeks.*"

Chad had rolled his lovely green eyes at me—green eyes I'd
lately taken to gazing adorningly at when he wasn't paying attention, stared into the depths of when they widened playfully.

Kind but cocky, after flirting with me tirelessly for the past
year, I was finally starting to reciprocate his affection. Sort of.
Well, in my own special way. Add in the fact that he's an incredibly talented snowboarder?

"I know James, but it's Oz Osborne. You don't just tell that
guy no—"

"Yes you do."

"Dude, I had to make an executive decision; no one else was
here last night." Chad had raised his eyebrows at me, daring me to
argue. "Osborne wants in on the trip, Osborne comes on the trip.
We need the publicity."

"Publicity? We don't need any more publicity! Chad—you
and Patrick went to the X Games last year." Granted, they hadn't
made it past pre-quals, but still.

The X Games.

"Whatever, James, I'm not arguing with you."

"Seriously? That's it? You're letting him come? We had a
deadline, Chad! No one applying for the trip was eligible after the
12th of the month!"

"I know, but dude—since Celeste backed out when her finan-
cial aid didn't come through, we had that one extra spot..."

That one extra spot, my ass.

"Where's he staying, wise ass?"

"We'll figure that out when we get to the hotel. He's your
cousin, so maybe..."

"No!"

"It'll work itself out, so chill."

Chill? Oh my god, snowboarders and their lackadaisical attitudes.

Unfortunately, if Chad Hanson wants Oz Osborne on the damn trip, then Chad Hanson *gets* Oz Osborne on the damn trip. And now *I* was stuck with him for five entire days. Five days and four nights. One thousand eighty-five miles from school. No professors, no roommates, no parents—just us and the mountains and the fresh pow under our boards.

My trip was ruined.

Ruined by the foul-mouthed jock with an appetite for driving me insane. Ruined by a six foot two, sandy-haired Goliath named Sebastian that I was going to *kill* as soon as I could get my bare hands on him.

When I reach the library steps, I glance up at the ivy-covered bricks and four stories, wondering if luck would be on my side, wondering if Oz Osborne was inside.

What does he *want* with me?

I'm not stupid; I know he's coming on this trip to torture me.

But why? He hardly knows me!

Determined, I push through my hesitations, through the heavy doors, and into the lobby. Not bothering to remove my heavy down coat like I normally would, my eyes scan the first floor, taking careful measure of everyone there studying. Ginger guy with the glasses. The girl he studies with who obviously has him in the friend-zone despite his horrible efforts at flirting. The Hispanic kid who's here more often than I am, who always has the same stack of books on the same corner of the same table. The football player and his pretty blonde girlfriend.

And…Oz.

I'd recognize that sneaky sonofabeehive anywhere, even from behind.

Pen poised above a notebook, the muscles in his strong back

strain against his thin baby blue tee shirt, neatly outlined and drool worthy. I mean, I can actually *see* every defined muscle of his damn latissimus dorsi from here.

God that asshole is gorgeous.

Unfortunately, he's not alone; I recognize one of the guys as the idiot from the other night, the one who'd been cheering Oz on and leering at me.

Nonetheless, I march directly to their table, hell bent on a mission and halting so fast I bump Oz in the elbow from behind, noting with satisfaction a black, inky line smudge across what looks like a very important paper.

Smirking, I lean in good and close so he can hear every word I'm about to say, my black puffy coat brushing his rock solid shoulder as I murmur into this ear from behind. "I am *literally* going to kill you."

He rocks back, broad shoulders brushing the front of my coat before cocking his head to the side. "I get threats on the daily, Jim. You have to be more specific."

"Why'd you do it? Are you insane?" I pull away, drawing back to smack him in the arm—his dense, warm, muscly arm. It's rock hard under my palm.

He finally stops writing, puts down his pen, and twists his torso to face me, amused. Cocky bastard.

The hulky guy beside him laughs. "What'd you do to this one, Ozzy? You lay too much pipe?"

The big black-haired guy crudely snickers like I'm a joke. Like I'm one of their little fan club members lining up to sleep with them. Nothing better than a groupie. He must find me *wanting* because his disinterested gaze flares before he redirects his cold, icy blue eyes to Oz. "Get her out of here."

I smack Oz again, the corners of his eyes wrinkling humorously as he makes a show of looking me up and down slowly— exactly how he looked at Sydney and Allison and all the other girls. That redheaded girl giving him a hand-job at the house party.

Callous and cold and dismissive.

"Oh please." I roll my eyes dramatically. "Don't bother pretending not to know who I am you turd. I'm so irritated with you right now I could strangle you with my bare hands."

More chuckles from around the table when Oz replies, "I like it rough as the next guy, Jim, but why don't you wait until we're alone."

"Oh, ha ha. You think this is funny? Is everything a joke to you? Well guess what. Forget it—you are *not* coming on my spring break trip."

"Wait." The blond giant sitting with them grunts out a baffled, "Ozzy man—is this your sister?"

Oz winks at me. "Cousin."

I ignore the idiot, even as my cheeks get flaming hot. "Sebastian Osborne, I want you to get on the phone *right* now to cancel this trip."

"Whoa, Ozzy, she's busting out first names—she must be pissed. Are you sure you aren't banging her?"

Instead of responding to the barb, Sebastian reaches into his bag, pulls out a pack of gum, unwraps a single stick slowly, and pops the piece in his mouth. A few chews and, "Sorry Jimmy, already paid."

My arms cross over my puffy, down-filled chest. "Well, that's too bad, isn't it? Because you are calling Chad Hanson this instant and canceling." I huff, wanting to stomp my foot in protest.

At my raised tone, Oz glances around the quiet library, over his shoulder, to the left then to the right. Conspiratorially, he lowers his voice. "Look, Jameson—can we argue about this privately? *Without* an audience?"

Oh, now he wants to be civil?

Fine. I can do civil.

His behemoth body pushes against the table, chair scraping along the hardwood floor as he stands, rising to his full height.

I'm reminded how masculine and virile he is. And solid.

95

His form towering over me, I fight back an enthusiastic whimper when his hand loosely grasps my forearm. Oz drags me to the far side of the library, dodging and weaving through the tables stealthily, like a maze runner.

Placing my back against the far wall, he braces his arms against it, bending down into me so he can keep his voice low. He smells like peppermint gum, a fresh shower, and woodsy after-shave lotion. Like a lumbersexual.

In a word: *heaven.*

He grumbles near my ear, "Jameson, I'm *going* on that trip."

"Are you insane?" I hiss up at him. "What on earth possessed you to *do* that? You don't even know me. Why would you come on a trip with me?"

I know he doesn't have the money. In fact, I'm pretty sure he's broke.

His blue eyes bore into me and I see his internal debate; he wants to confide something in me—it's there in his creased brow—but what? What on earth is going on inside that big, beautiful head of his?

Big beautiful head? Ugh. What has gotten into me lately?

I give myself a mental slap as Oz gives his head a shake. "I charged six hundred dollars I *don't* have on my credit card last night, James. I'm *going* on that trip."

My lips part. "But *why?* Why would you do that Sebastian? You don't meet someone and then a few days later decide to take a trip with them. It's weird."

His free hand rises and he rakes it through his moppy, un-kempt hair.

"Because." The word rushes out; he has to take a deep, steadying breath to continue. "Because for *once* in my damn life I want to see what it's like being with someone who doesn't know who I am."

My nose wrinkles. "What the heck is that supposed to mean?"

He leans against the wall and stuffs his hands in his pockets, triumphant. "See? Exactly."

I'm so confused.

He releases another breath. "Jim. I'm a wrestler for Iowa; next year I could be training for the Olympics. I could be working in an office somewhere. I'll go where the money is, so who knows, but nothing about me is *normal*."

My mouth opens, then closes. Then, "I'm sorry, is the wrestling thing a big deal?"

I can tell he's trying to school his expression, but he's failing. His mouth barely stays closed, instead coming unhinged and hanging open. "A big deal? James. *Jim*. Thousands upon thousands of fans scream my name on a yearly basis. I've been on television. I was courted by *all* Big Ten schools, and three from the Big Twelve as a high school senior before deciding on Iowa." He looks smug. "So yeah, *kind* of a big deal.

Well goodness, how does one respond to that? "I didn't know."

"I know you didn't know. That's one of the things I like about you—that and your constant need to give me shit." When he smiles down at me, I'm close enough to glimpse a chipped lower tooth. White but imperfect.

Perfectly imperfect.

Ugh.

"Why didn't you tell me who you were?"

"Tell you?" A laughs bursts out of him then, and I catch another whiff of him when he tips his neck back. "You're killing me. It's not a secret. I mean, look around you Jameson. Everyone in here is gawking at us."

I peel my eyes away from his face then; he's right. Heads are turned our way curiously. Gazes, stares, glances—it does seem that everyone is watching us.

Rude.

"What are they looking at? Is it my puffy coat?" I complain, pulling at the zipper, nervously dragging it up and down along its track. "Sue me for being cold all the time."

Oz raises his finger and bops me on the tip of my nose. "You're really something, do you know that? Adorable."

This time, I roll my eyes and cross my arms with a pout. "*Super.*"

He puts an arm around my shoulder and gives me a squeeze. "We're going to have a great time, I promise."

"Yeah, yeah, yeah. I'm still going to be mad at you for not asking me first. Talk about high handed."

"You'll get over it."

Somehow, I doubt that.

12

#DOUCHEBAG

"Hey Mr. Impatient, how about you go down a water slide while it isn't wet. Maybe then you'll understand why foreplay is so important."

Sebastian

"**L**ast night before we leave for Utah. Are you packed yet?" I hand a piece of gum to Jameson across the table. She reaches for it and our fingers touch, sending a volt of electricity straight down my spine. It sizzles.

Weird.

That's never happened before.

I discount it, cracking open my textbook and powering up my laptop.

"I don't have much to pack, mostly just winter clothes and some under layers. No biggie." She taps her pen on the table. "How bout you?"

I nod. "Yup. I have a duffle that's always packed for away matches, so I'll just take out my suit and throw my winter stuff into that. It'll take me a whole three minutes."

"Your suit?"

"My suit. You know—dress pants, suit coat." At her confused expression, I elaborate. "We're required to dress up when we're guests on another campus for wrestling matches."

Jameson giggles. "You keep your suit stuffed in a duffle bag?"

"Sometimes, yeah. Why?"

Her forehead creases. "Doesn't it get wrinkled?"

"Um, yeah?"

Her head hits the solid tabletop with a thud. "Ugh, I can't even with you." She raises it, eyes smiling. "Who irons it out for you?"

"Me, myself, and I." I shoot her a devilish grin. "It's not like I have someone to iron it *for* me, but sometimes I do wear an apron when I press it."

Jameson's head tilts to the side as she studies me, her gaze lingering on my mouth. I can't tell what she's thinking right now, but I can only hope she's picturing me in my imaginary apron.

Naked.

"You do *not* wear an apron."

"No, but now you're picturing me in one, aren't you?"

"I don't know, it depends. Is it one of those old-fashioned frilly ones that tie around your waist, or the barbeque grilling ones?" Her elbows hit the table and she leans in. Her pale blue sweater pulls taut over her round, fantastic boobs.

"Which do you prefer?"

Jameson pretends to mull it over. "On you? The manly barbeque kind, but not with a cheesy saying on it. I wouldn't want it to detract from your—" She clamps her lips shut.

"From my...?"

Her head gives a little shake.

"Come on, say it. You wouldn't want it to detract from my hard...body? My stiff...muscles?" I lean back in the leather desk chair, crossing my arms over my chest. "Would it kill you to flirt with me?"

"That's *not* flirting, that's blatant—"

"Foreplay?"

A jerky nod. "Is that what you're calling it? You're driving me crazy."

"But not the 'I want to fuck you' kind of crazy, huh?"

She looks nonplussed. Chagrined. "Is sex all you ever think about? You're relentless."

"No, it's not all I ever think about, but I swear, something about those goddamn sweaters of yours make me stupid."

"I'm certainly not going to argue with *that*," she says primly. "You *do* sound stupid."

"Does it bother you when I talk like that?"

"Yes." But she's shaking her head no.

I lean in with a chuckle. "Is that a yes or a no?"

"Yes, it bothers me."

"Why?"

Eye roll. "We've been over this."

Have we? I don't remember.

"Well let's go over it again." *Because it's fun bantering with you and it's sexy, and I like to see you squirm in your chair. It gets me turned the fuck on, especially when your breathing escalates and your tits rise inside your cardigan.*

Of course, for once I keep my damn mouth shut.

With a sigh, Jameson closes her laptop with a decisive snap. "I can't decide if I should trust you or not, and it drives me *crazy* that you only see me as a challenge. Crazy."

"You know it's more than that. Why would I be coming on this trip just to try to have sex with you when I could hire a hooker for less than what I paid for *you?*"

"Hire a hooker?!" she damn near shouts, eyes bugging out of her skull. "Would you really do that?"

"Well no. One, because I would never *have* to; I can get laid any time I want. And two, I can't afford it. My point is, I'm coming on this trip because we're *friends*, Jiminy Cricket, not so I can put the moves on you." I manage to keep a straight face when the lie spills out of my mouth, totally convincing.

"*Coming* on this trip? You say it as if you were invited." She snickers. "You're the worst kind of hijacker, and for the life of me, I still can't figure out why." I open my mouth to speak but immediately snap it shut when she continues, "Yeah, yeah, I know—you said it's because you wanted to see what it was like to be with someone who didn't know who you were, but don't you and your Neanderthal friends frequent seedy places like the Florida coast? Beer bongs and bikinis? MTV, loose girls, and STDs?"

Yes, hell yes, yes, fuck yeah, and no.

"Since we're being honest, it seems extremely over the top to come on a trip with a girl you just met to escape the reality you created for yourself. Haven't you ever heard the phrase 'you made your bed, now you have to lie in it'?"

I giggle like a teenage boy at the word *bed*.

Jameson throws a yellow number two pencil at me. "You are so immature."

Immature.

Horny.

Itching for a challenge, and she's just given me one.

13

"Some really good looking guy
just walked into my room
looking for his clothes.
Does he belong to you or
can I call dibs?"

Jameson

"**W**hat the heck are you and your crap doing on my stoop?"

The wind blows, sending snow and frigid cold air whipping past me and into my hotel room.

He's standing in front of my door, letting his red duffle drop to the frozen, snowy ground. A bright lime green snowboard leans against the doorjamb, along with a black boot bag. "My new pal Chad said your roommate bailed on you," he says with a casual shrug of his wide shoulders. Over his tall frame, I see sophomore snowboard club member Beth Lauer staring holes into his ass. Hard.

I don't even want to know what thoughts are running through Beth's head right now and silently will the powdery pile of white snow on the roof to slide down and bury me whole.

Or better yet, bury *him* whole.

Oz chatters on, oblivious to Beth's ogling. "I told Chad we were cousins, remember? So he didn't see a problem with us rooming together. Congrats, Jim! It looks like we're going to be roommates."

"Don't you mean cellmates?" I groan, glancing over my shoulder at the empty bedroom, at the *one* queen sized bed with its *one* threadbare coverlet, the single dresser, and the tiny bathroom with *one* tiny shower.

The Bellagio it is not. It might be a pit, but it was my pit—and mine alone—until thirty-seven blissful seconds ago.

I glance toward Beth as she shuffles past us through the snow; our eyes connect when she lifts her gaze from Oz's fantastic ass. Even in the cold winter weather, embarrassment floods her and she turns, scuttling off hurriedly in the opposite direction like a little pervy rat.

Speaking of pervs…

Having Oz shacked up with me for the weekend is the opposite of what I want. I paid the same six hundred dollars he paid; the last thing I need is my friends gossiping about me while he weasels his way in and out of *my* room.

A groan escapes my lips. "And stop telling everyone we're cousins."

"Come on, what's the big deal?"

"Cousins? Come on, seriously?"

"Should I have told him we were *kissing* cousins?" He gives me a wide, toothy grin. "Unlatch the chain, James, and let me in. My testes just crawled inside my scrot to hide."

Another groan and I'm unchaining the door, grabbing him by his muscular forearm to haul him—along with all his crap—into the recesses of my hotel room. The heavy door slams behind us, the lock automatically clicking into place.

I slide the latch over before turning on him, hands on my hips, sullenly eyeballing him. "First you crash my trip, now you're crashing my room. You can take the floor."

"The floor?" He picks up his duffle bag and suitcase, shouldering past me. Surrendering, I let him pass without an argument, trailing after him. "No can do, Jim. This body is a temple."

"We are not sharing the bed."

"Is it because you don't trust yourself with me?"

"No. It's because I don't trust *you*."

Oz snickers. "Come on, it'll be fun."

"I honestly am going to kill you."

"Why do you keep saying that? *Oz, I'm going to kill you,*" he mimics in a feminine voice. It's actually somewhat disconcerting. "That's the second time you've threatened my life; I'm beginning to think you mean it."

I grin. "What can I say? You make me want to strangle you."

He ignores me, instead hoisting his suitcase to the top of the dresser on the far side of the room and unzipping it. "I've decided if we're not going to be fuck buddies—a bad decision on your part, I might add—then we can be friends of the non-fucking variety. The *boring* variety."

"How magnanimous of you."

He gives me a sidelong glance. "I know, right? I thought so, too."

"That was sarcasm, Oz."

"Sarcasm or not, Jimbo, you'll soon realize the benefits of having me as your friend."

"Oh, you don't say?" I cross my arms. "Enlighten me."

"For example, I'm an awesome wingman. I'll have the ladies beating down our door in no time."

"It was *my* door," I hiss. "And I'm not a lesbian."

"You're not?" He looks dubious.

"No."

"Then why do you keep resisting all my advances?" Oz sits on the foot of the bed, kicking off his shoes. They hit the wall and land with a thud.

His socks follow.

"Uh, because you haven't made any?"

"Wait." He spins around. "Was that an invitation?"

Kind of? "No!"

"See?" He shuffles back to the door barefoot then lugs my suitcase farther into the room and places it on the dresser next to his. "Anyway, as I was saying—the guys will be beating down your cobweb-covered door in no time—or in this case, your cob-web-covered vagina."

Side by side, we begin removing the clothes from our suitcas-es and neatly folding them into the top drawer, his shirts on the left, mine on the right, like we've done it a hundred times before.

"First of all, my vagina is none of your business. Secondly, it's *not* covered in cobwebs."

It's obvious from his expression that he doesn't believe me. "Whatever you say, Jimbo. My point is, with me by your side this weekend, you'll be fighting them off with a baseball bat."

"What if I don't want a wingman?"

Clutching an extra pair of blue jeans against his chest like a shield, he stares at me blankly, his lip curling distastefully. His fingers twirl in the air, directed at my nether region. "Cobwebs."

I stalk to the small nightstand, yank open the drawer, and root around the hollow space for the requisite pen and paper.

"We need to establish a few rules if we're going to be sharing a room this week."

"Fine."

"I'll take the liberty of writing a few of them down."

I hold the little white notepad up for his inspection.

His lip curls up. "Why am I not surprised you're making a list?"

I ignore his question. "One: no sex in the bedroom—"

"So just the bathroom or closet?"

My pen hovers. "I'm being serious. You can't bring girls back here."

"I'm serious too, Jim, serious as a heart attack. I am totally okay banging someone inside the closet."

"I don't doubt that for a second. However, I'd really prefer if you didn't have sex *any*where inside the room." He rolls his eyes toward the ceiling. "Two: stay on your side of the bed, and keep those enormous paws off me."

He places one of said enormous paws over his heart. "Jim, you wound me. Would I jeopardize our budding friendship by feeling you up?"

My eyebrows shoot up into my hairline. "I don't know, Oz—would you?"

He seems to give this question some serious thought, and sighs. "Honestly? Yeah, I would. I'll probably try to touch you inappropriately at least once. Maybe twice if I'm being real. It would be remiss of me considering I've noticed your nice rack. Your sweaters are pretty tight, Jimbo."

Face palm. "I guess I can't fault you for being honest."

He sits up straighter on the foot of the bed. "Does that earn me bonus points?"

A resigned sigh. "Sure, why not."

"Great." He claps his giant hands gleefully, rubbing them together. "Okay, hit me with number three."

"There is no number three. Two is all I have—but we can make them up as we go along."

"Oh goody. That'll be a blast."

I'm standing near the bed, innocently unpacking my snowboarding gear and refolding a pair of my boarding overalls when the bathroom door flies open and Oz comes out, a hazy mist of steam billowing out behind him.

He looks me up. He looks me down.

"How the hell am I supposed to keep my hands to my damn self when you're wearing shit like that?" He waves his bear paws, gesturing wildly up and down, indicating my pajama set.

I glance down at myself, perplexed. "This? It's an old tank top and shorts."

He crosses his arms resentfully, my eyes flying to his broad, ripped chest and elaborately tattooed biceps. *Drool*. "Right, but you're not wearing a bra."

"I'm not wearing a *bra* to bed, Oz. It's also not my problem you're a horn dog."

He disagrees.

"The tank top is *white*, which is practically see-through." For the second time since he's invaded my space, Oz rolls his eyes toward the ceiling, Adam's apple bobbing. He throws up three fingers. "Rule number *three*: no running around bra-less. Cover that shit up, for fuck's sake. I can see your nips and it's giving me a hard-on."

"You're only wearing a towel, you hypocrite! I can see the outline of your—" I stop myself short, a loud, nervous giggle bubbling up inside me so abruptly I actually smack a hand over my mouth to shut myself up.

My eyes drop to Oz's lean hips. I can't help but notice the beads of water dripping down the smooth, tantalizing skin of his sculpted abs...to the well-defined V...the happy trail of dark hair disappearing into the white terrycloth towel barely concealing his—

I cross an arm over my breasts defensively, hiding them from his heated examination. "What do you suggest I wear, smartass? I only packed this and I was planning on rooming alone."

"I don't fucking know, but you can't prance around in that. Go put on one of my shirts."

Prance?

Still, I nod once. "Fine."

"Fine."

"*Fine.* Rule number four: no running around wrapped in nothing but a bath towel. That thing barely fits around your waist."

And it's making me want to do naughty, sleazy things to you. Like pull the towel out of its knot and yank it to the floor to see what's underneath.

Oz stomps barefoot to the dresser, yanks open the top drawer, and pulls out a gray cotton tee shirt. Wadding it up into a fabric ball, he whips it in my direction, sending it whizzing through the air and smacking me in the face.

I barely catch it.

"Please. Just go put that on. And come back uglier."

Sydney: *Has he asked about me at all?*
James: *Who?*

Sydney: *Oh please, you know who. Don't tease me like that! Oz—has he asked about me! Come on, give a girl something to get her through a cold night.*

James: *We've been very busy, sorry.*

Sydney: *I can't believe you're spending the weekend with him. If I'd have known, maybe I would have come along.*

James: *And given up the Florida sun?!*

Sydney: *You're right. I still wouldn't have gone to Utah, LOL. Maybe I should try texting him. Do you think I should?*

James: *I think you should do whatever makes you happy ;)*

Sydney: *Is that a yes or a no.*

James: *Sure. Yes, text him.*

Sydney: *Squee!!!! K, I'm doing it.*

James: *Good luck*

I don't mention to Sid that moments ago Sebastian was half naked and dripping wet, just out of the shower. Or that he was eyeing me up in my white tank top. Or that I just pulled his tee shirt over my head—one that feels like heaven and smells even better.

I set my cell down on the cold, outdated Formica bathroom counter and adjust the contact of the charger. Smoothing down my silky hair, I burrow my nose down into the collar of Sebastian's shirt. Give it another whiff…

Wistfully exhale.

Taking a deep breath before I push through the door to the bedroom, I give the shirt one more quick sniff for good measure.

So damn good I can't stop.

I walk across the room toward the light switch with trepidation, pausing when he sits up in our shared bed. The bed that would have been perfectly acceptable when I was sharing it with

Celeste appears *miniscule* with hulky Oz Osborne resting in it.

A tower of pillows is stacked in the middle, a barrier I erected when he was in the shower, albeit a laughably flimsy one.

Oz is sitting in bed, atop the covers and naked from the waist up. Propped against the headboard, thumbing through a Men's Health magazine, he grimaces when he glances up, greeting me with an irritated, "God dammit Jim, that's worse!"

I look around the room, confused by his angry tone. "What's worse?"

"You. In that shirt."

Well duh. I only threw on his gray Iowa wrestling tee after his ridiculous no-tank-top rule was enforced.

"Is there no winning with you?" I toss my hands up in defeat. "What's wrong with this shirt? You *told* me to put it on. In fact, you wadded it up and threw it at me. It hit me in the face, remember, and almost took out my eye."

"You weren't supposed to take your shorts off!" he accuses, scowling.

My hands go back up, exasperated. "Oh my god, *what* is the big deal?"

"What's the big deal? *What's the big deal, she asks?*" He's grumbling to himself, pounding a fluffy pillow and adjusting it behind his head. I can't help but admire his biceps flexing while he does it. Sorry, but they're amazing to look at. "The big deal is now all you have on is fucking underwear."

"Right," I say slowly, shifting my gaze away from his body to lift the hem of his tee. "But the shirt goes down to my thighs…"

"Are you insane? You keep that shit *on*."

"Uh…"

Oz holds up his hands, halting my argument. "Rule number five: no shaving your legs."

"No shaving my legs?" A burst of laughter escapes my lips and I double over at the waist, giggling hysterically. Tears stream down my cheeks. When I finally catch my breath, I sputter,

"That's the dumbest thing I've *ever* heard. What does shaving have to do with anything?"

He gives me a look that says *duh*. "Hairy legs are disgusting. No dude wants to bang a chick with more hair than he has. Trust me, it's your only defense."

I stare at him blankly, my lip curling distastefully, before wiping away a stray tear. "You're *so* weird."

"You're right. I would totally bang a chick with hairy legs." He karate chops my pillow barrier with his hand, a mocking smile spreading across his stupidly arrogant face. "Is this to keep you on your side of the bed? Cause I gotta say, Jim, I won't fight you off when you decide to cross over to the dark side."

God he's so devilishly handsome.

I shake my head, grinning back as I pull back the covers and climb onto my side of the bed. "That's not going to happen."

"Wanna bet on it?"

"Would you stop doing that?"

"Doing what?"

"Betting on everything."

"Sorry. Bad habit."

I pull back the coverlet and slide in, my bare legs hitting the cool fabric. Reclining next to him in the bed, my body relaxes into the down pillows.

I feel him watching me out the corner of his eye when I reach for and click off the bedside lamp. Sigh. "What?"

A low chuckle comes out of the dark. "Do you really think that pillow barrier will keep me on my side of the bed?"

"Of course not. It's a metaphor for *keep your distance*."

"And my paws off?" He chuckles again, but this time the low baritone has me shivering. He must feel the vibration through the mattress because he asks, "Cold?"

"A little." I hunker farther into the covers, wishing they were feather filled.

"Well, I'm here if you want to spoon. My mom used to say I

was a hot box—you'd be hot and hopefully sweaty in no time."

I bite back a smile in the dark. "Thanks for the offer."

"I'm a giver, Jimmy."

I don't doubt that. As I lay there in the dark, listening to his steady breathing, my mind wanders. I mean, would anyone blame me? Lying here next to this big, broody, sexy, warm-blooded male, naked from the waist up?

I'd have to be nuts not to fantasize—or dead from the waist down, which I'm not.

I clear my throat, the sound filling the dark. "Tell me about wrestling."

"What do you want to know?"

"Are you any good?"

His answer is a deep, gravelly rumble. It booms and shakes and reverberates the bed. Even without the lights on, I know he's clutching his stomach.

"Don't make fun of me!" My arms stretch out and I poke what I'm assuming is a thick bicep. My fingers sink into his hot skin and I quickly pull them back.

"I'm not making fun of you; you're just so damn cute."

I hesitate. "Well? Are you any good?"

"Yeah, I'm *good.*"

"*How* good?"

"I'm *real* good. Not just real good—I'm the fucking best." The mattress dips and he turns to rest on his side, facing me. "Know what my favorite part of wrestling is?"

"What's your favorite part?" I gulp down a whisper, then a sigh.

"The moments before I finally get that pin, the anticipation when you both know it's coming. The buildup, the back and forth leading up to that point." He is positively humming, and my nerves hum right along with him. "My body stretched out, sweaty from the effort, my opponent laid out underneath me."

Why does it sound like we're not talking about wrestling any more? A throbbing heat forms between my legs, and I wiggle around uncomfortably to avoid having to rub them together.

"Oh." This time I do whisper and sigh.

"Yeah." The mattress dips again as he rolls toward me. "*Oh.*"

"Is it a power trip thing?"

I can feel him considering the question. "Not at all. For me, the thrill is all mental, knowing I can calculate how someone is going to react before *they* do in order to gain the upper hand physically." Then, as an afterthought, he adds, "It's more about controlling my own body and its movements rather than someone else's."

The room is silent.

"Does my size...scare you James?" His voice is reluctant and full of worry, as if the thought just occurred to him.

"No. No, your size doesn't scare me." Quite the opposite; it doesn't scare me—the sheer size of him thrills me and my traitorous body. I don't mention how it's become harder and harder to breath when we're together. How I've begun fantasizing about him when we're apart. How lying here in the dark is a test of my resolve.

I want to touch him.

I want to let him touch *me.*

Whisper his name as he...

"I might be big, but I don't ever want you to be afraid of me, James. I would never hurt you."

"I know." He would never.

"My dick would never hurt you either. He's very gentle."

Great. Now I'm going to be lying here thinking about his penis.

"*Oh my god, Oz,* you are so—"

"Good in bed."

"Why must you do that?"

"I'm just stating the facts, Jim."

"Go to sleep, Oswald."

"I don't always make
an ass of myself
while I'm snowboarding,
but when I do,
it's under the chair lift."

Sebastian

Holy shit, Jameson is good.

No. Scratch that.

Not good. Fucking. *Great.*

I'll be the first to admit: when I heard James was a good snowboarder...I didn't believe it. Granted, all my assumptions were based entirely on her conservative looks. Her preppy sweaters. Her pearl necklace. Those classy, demure, diamond earrings. The leggings or whatever those pants are that she's always wearing.

None of those things scream, "I shred it going down a mountain riding a snowboard."

But shreds it.

She does.

She really, really fucking does—and watching her today was unbelievable. I couldn't take my eyes off her: dark brown hair in two of the sexiest braids I've ever fucking seen, peeking out from underneath her black helmet and sleek goggles. I happily trailed down the mountain after her, chasing every movement of her blue tie-dye coat and bright blue snowboarding pants.

Struggled to keep pace as she nose crailed a 360 in the terrain park. Marveled when she banked it off the slider. Cheered when she slid skillfully on the down rail.

I consider myself a decent snowboarder, but even *I* can't do an Ollie. Jameson nailed three of them.

She removes her bright blue coat as we walk into the warm ski chalet and my eyes browse around, noting all the people inside escaping from the frigid cold: several youngsters that are obviously siblings, a married couple sipping coffee, and the same MILF with huge silicon tits and botoxed lips that accidentally bumped into me this morning when I was putting on my lift ticket. She may or may not have been giving me *come fuck me* eyes.

Scratch that—she definitely was.

The black straps of Jameson's snowboarding pants draw my attention; they're pulled taut over her shoulders, running up the front of her tight, black wool under layer, showcasing her boobs. They're not huge or fake—not like the MILF's—and I admire their size and their smooth, round shape beneath her sweater.

An entire handful.

Next comes the helmet. Jameson reaches up and unsnaps the strap cradling her chin before sliding it off and shaking her two brown braids so they hang over those gorgeous tits, stray hairs flying haphazardly around her flushed face.

Fucking sexy.

I close the distance between us, reaching for her coat and helmet. "Here. Let me go put these in our locker. You have the key?"

She glances up at me, surprise widening her pretty eyes. A smile widens her mouth, and she bites down on her lower lip to keep it from spreading. A faint blush tints her cheeks that wasn't put there from the cold. "Sure. Yes. Thank you."

Reaching into the pocket of her jacket, she produces a small silver locker key. It dangles between us on the ring.

"Oh! Would you take my pants, too?" Jameson pulls the straps of her pants down, sliding them down her arms until they fall at her side. "I don't want to roast when we're in front of the fire; I'll die of heat stroke."

I watch as she pops open the front buttons, glides down the zipper, and thrusts the black vinyl pants down her hips with a seductive little shimmy. Underneath, she's wearing nothing but tight, black wool tights.

Oddly, I find the whole thing incredibly erotic.

Stepping out of them, she bends at the waist, sticks her perky ass in the air, and picks them up off the floor, handing them to me with an appreciative smile.

Naïvely. Like she wasn't just shaking her ass in the general direction of my junk.

I hold a hand up to halt her. "Wait. You're not seriously going to run around here in just that *under*wear, are you?"

Jameson bends her head, glancing down her torso at her stocking clad legs—her gorgeous, long legs—before looking up at me.

"Uh, you mean my itchy *wool* leggings? Yeah. This is what I'm running around in." Her laugh is full of humor. "Why?"

"They're not decent."

Her hands go on her waist and she juts out a hip. "What do you care?"

I stare down at her inner thigh. "I don't. I'm just picturing you naked, and so is everyone else. If you can live with that knowledge, then I guess we don't have a problem."

"I highly doubt everyone is picturing me naked." Jameson laughs dismissively. "But I guess I'm okay with it if they are."

I cross my arms over my broad chest in disagreement. "You don't think Chad over there is checking you out? And that Blaine kid?"

Her face screws up, bewildered. "It's *Brandon,* not Blaine."

"Same thing," I argue, because I honestly don't give a shit what the kid's name is.

"You know what, Oz? You're really weird sometimes. No one is checking out my goods, so you can lay off the big cousin routine."

"The feelings in my groin are hardly familial," I joke, finally reaching for her gear. "Suit yourself if you want to date them, but don't come crying to me later."

Another soft laugh and she's giving me a little pat on the arm. The brief contact sends heat straight to my—

"I think I'll manage, but thanks." She pats me again, running her fingers up the sleeve of my cotton under layer. "And thanks for taking my stuff to the locker room. I'll go find us some seats."

So off I go like a good little Boy Scout, transporting Jameson's pants, jacket, and helmet down to the locker area. I insert the key into the metal door and toss everything into our rented locker, including my own coat, pants, and helmet. I chuck all our shit in before locking it up and stuffing the key into the pocket of my loose athletic pants.

Turn from the locker.

Across the warm locker room, I'm not terribly surprised to discover MILF leaning against the far wall, appraising me. A coy smile tugging the corner of her red lips, her bleached blonde hair is braided underneath a black knit skullcap. The rest of her outfit is pure white: white turtleneck, white ski pants, white socks.

If she's going for the virginal look, it's not working—and let's face it, she knows she's not fooling anybody.

I pass MILF and shoot her my sexiest smirk, knowing she'll be around later if I get bored.

Taking the stairs two at a time, I make my way to the main lobby, sans boots, and search the cavernous, rustic lodge for those thin black leggings. I find them propped on the large, gray stone hearth of the blazing fireplace. James' cute little toes and cute little feet are in gray wool socks that are yanked up her calves.

Catching me watching them, she wiggles her toes when I approach. Patting the seat on the massive leather couch, her feet hit the ground as she makes room for me to sit.

"Here, I got you a hot chocolate," Jameson announces, handing me a white, steaming mug. Whipped cream is dolloped on top. "This is for taking my things downstairs."

Our fingers brush when I slide my palm around the cup to remove it from her grip, and with an easy grin, I plop down next to her on the couch. I settle onto the well-worn leather, spreading my legs wide so our hips and thighs touch with satisfying heat.

"So, Oz man, how's your season goin'?" asks some kid in a red Burton sweatshirt. Stocking cap pulled low over his forehead, his goggles still rest on his head.

"It's a bitch. I'm lucky I was able to get away for the weekend." It's partly true; the truth is, I had to lie like a mother to get the weekend off from my trainer. I concocted some bullshit about my left hamstring being too tight and not wanting to pull it before our next meet.

Which is in exactly six days. Against the powerhouse Penn State.

Contractually, D1 athletes like myself aren't *technically* allowed to participate in other sports, especially "dangerous" ones like snowboarding.

Fine. There's nothing technical about it. We're not supposed to be doing anything that could get us injured, and that includes playing beach volleyball with my annoying cousin Brielle, or oh, I don't know—snowboarding down a freaking mountain.

If I were to break, sprain, or pull something, there'd be a huge possibility I'd cost my team their season.

Which means, I'm royally screwed if I get injured on the ski hill.

"How much can you bench press?" a boarder in an Iowa hoodie asks. His hat is backward and like James, he's only wearing wool leggings, and his aren't nearly as nice as hers. Even from my spot on the couch, I can see the bulge of his junk—I mean Jesus, is it hard to put pants on in the company of ladies?

"About four hundred."

"Holy shit," he mutters, suitably impressed.

"Sorry, I didn't catch your name."

"I'm Scott—my friends call me Striker." Scott lifts himself from his spot on the fireplace hearth to extend his hand toward me for a fist bump. "I play soccer."

I muster up a limp tap. "I might have heard of you," I admit begrudgingly, narrowing my eyes. "Does your coach know you're on this trip?"

Scott studies me back, the red hair under his cap sticking out in spikes. The little shit has the balls to volley back with, "Does yours?"

A pointy little elbow stabs me in the ribcage, and I look down into Jameson's angry blue eyes. Wordlessly, she sends me a silent message: *Stop it right now.*

I lift my chin a notch. *Simmer down.*

"So what's the deal with you two?" one of the girls asks. Her light blonde hair is piled in a messy bun atop her head, and despite the fact that we just spent the entire day outside, she has a face full of expertly applied makeup. "Are you dating?"

"They're cousins," Chad explains with authority.

"No we're not." Jameson furrows her forehead, her pert little nose wrinkling.

"You're not cousins?" Chad eyeballs me. "Dude, that's what you told me on the phone."

Oh shit, that's right. "Right…" I drawl out the word, adding, "Cousins that kiss," with a laugh. "Sometimes."

No one thinks it's funny.

Especially not Jameson.

She gasps—a surprised, horrified gasp that sounds so surprisingly orgasmic it plays on a loop through my mind.

"Oh my god, he's totally kidding!" She jams her pointy-as-fuck elbow deeper into my ribcage. "Oz, tell them you're kidding," she hisses through clenched teeth.

"Fine. I'm kidding about the cousin part," I deadpan. "But we've *definitely* kissed and we're definitely *not* cousins." I take a casual gulp of hot chocolate to occupy my mouth and feel the whipped cream coat my upper lip. I lick it. "I lied. I'm trying to get into her pants, but if you want the truth, it's proving rather difficult."

Beside me, Jameson groans, head falling back against the leather sofa. "Oh god, my life."

Chad sits back against the stone fireplace chimney, studying me: my flip flops, the athletic pants, the thinning wrestling tee shirt. His eyes take in my black tattoos, the hard set line of my mouth, the scars above my brows and across the bridge of my nose.

Finally, "Why would you lie, dude?"

I shoot a sidelong glance at Jameson that only he and Scott can see, then raise my heavy eyebrows, sending the silent message, *Isn't it obvious*? Slowly, they both nod in understanding as my arm goes up on the back of the couch, resting behind Jameson's reclined head.

I give my forefinger a soft tap on the leather, toying with the silky ends of her hair, wrapping the loose strands around my finger.

She lets me.

"Hey, what are we all doing later?" a dark-haired girl asks. I think her name is Sam or whatever, but regardless, her shocking black hair is piled high on her head in an untidy knot, the ends messily sticking out everywhere. It's kind of cute, actually. I wonder if she's single; my body is desperately seeking vagina. "My boyfriend wants to FaceTime. I just want to know what time to tell him."

Never mind.

Chad, obviously the leader of this crew, rubs the scruff on his chin. "Tell him whenever. I think tonight after dinner we'll just chill."

"Speaking of dinner, I could eat the ass out of a dead skunk," Scott announces, to the mortification of all the girls. Sam, Jameson, and two blonde girls make faces, calling him a disgusting slob. "It's almost six. Let's go eat."

"Cab it downtown?"

"Sounds like a plan."

#DOUCHEBAG

"Last night the girl
I was having sex with
slapped me because
I shouted the wrong name.
But then she remembered it was
the fake name she gave me."

Sebastian

"What did you think you were you doing back at the restaurant?" Jameson starts in as soon as we're back in our hotel room following the group dinner. I shut the door behind us, sliding the deadbolt into place. "Were you cockblocking me?"

"Cockblocking you from *who?*" What the hell is she talking about? I toss our coats and shit on the bed, spinning on my heel to face her. "Who the hell were you hoping was going to ask you out? Scott? Cause that guy is a douche."

"Scott is *not* a douche," she argues feebly. "He's a nice guy, unlike *some* people! And no, I don't want to date him."

I snicker. "He'd *love* knowing you called him *nice*. Nice guys heart that shit." Not. "So who do you have a lady boner for?"

"None of your business."

"Then how the fuck am I supposed to know if I was cockblocking you or not? I'm a wrestler, not a freaking mind reader."

Jameson strolls to the dresser, tugs it open, and pulls out her white tank top and sleep shorts. "Well you're a *shitty* wingman, too."

I furrow my brow, disgruntled. "Do I look like a goddamn wingman?"

Her mouth hangs open. "Yes! You *literally* said you were going to be my wingman!"

A snort escapes my nose. "Not with those snowboarding guys! I thought you meant other guys staying at the hotel!"

"Fine!" In defeat, Jameson throws her arms in the air. "Then let's get dressed and sit in the hotel bar."

I squint at her skeptically. "Are you even twenty-one?"

"Oh my god, I hate you right now." She taps her foot on the

carpet in a tiny huff, pretending to be mad. It's kind of adorable. "Rule number six: no cockblocking. And yes I'm twenty-one. Can we go now?"

"Uh…have you *seen* the idiots staying here?"

"Yes, I'm staring at one," she deadpans, keeping a straight face for a few seconds before her face breaks into a grin.

"Ha ha, very funny." I smirk. "Lucky for you, *I* don't count."

"If you would have at least let Erik give me his phone number, we wouldn't be having this conversation. You were really freaking rude to him."

"He was wearing a *yellow* sweatshirt!" I hardly manage to keep the disdain out of my voice.

She stares blankly. "So?"

"So? So! You can't trust *any*one wearing a yellow sweatshirt."

Her brows rise and she points to my yellow sweatshirt. "*You're* wearing a yellow sweatshirt."

"Thank you! I just proved my point." I flick an imaginary piece of lint off my hoodie. "Besides, Erik had small hands." No reaction? Fine. I prompt her, "Small hands? Small…"

"Dick."

"See? You get it."

"No—*you* are a dick."

God she's adorable when she's argumentative, all in a snit. Blue eyes blazing bright, alive with interest, James clutches her sleep clothes in one hand, propping her fist on her hip with the other. "Are we going down to the bar or not?"

"No. Not until you calm down. You're being really irrational for someone who doesn't plan on hooking up with anyone." I look her up and down. "And what the hell are you doing with that tank top?"

Her blue eyes roll to the back of her head. "If we're staying in, then I'm getting ready for bed."

I point to the offensive tank top. "Not in that shit you're not.

No. Jim, we established this on day one; that shirt makes me want to bone you. Hard."

An unladylike snort leaves her nose. "Remind me again how that is my problem, because right now I'm not really in the mood to take orders from you."

"If you wear it, you're breaking rule three: no running around bra-less."

"Try and *stop* me from wearing it, Neanderthal." Jameson postures with bravado, backing into the dresser, eyes darting to the open bathroom door. Her bare foot inches toward it.

She's going to make a run for it.

I'm remarkably calm for someone about to strike. I bear down on her.

Mouse, meet cat. *Meow*.

"Don't even think about it, Clark."

She'd roll her eyes at me if they weren't glued to the bathroom door. "*Pfft*. Think about *what?*"

"That innocent act isn't going to work on me, but nice fuckin' try." Tsk, tsk. "You're not going anywhere with that tank top, either, Jimbo." I extend my arm, palm up, and wiggle my fingers. "Hand it over."

Jameson huffs, crossing her arms over her chest, blue eyes sparkling. "You can't tell me what to do."

"No, but I can pin you to the ground and take it from you." The thought gets me excited and my blood surges. "How about I give you a two-second lead. One—"

I don't even finish the count because Jameson lunges toward the bathroom, light on her feet and quicker than a track team sprinter. I lunge for her but she switches trajectories, makes a quick right, dodges my outstretched arms, and dives for the bed.

Falling a few inches short, she scrambles on top of it then rises to stand in the center, waving the threadbare tank top above her head like a victory flag.

"Yes! Suck it!" she bellows, fist pumping the air and jumping up and down on the cheap, shoddy mattress. Arms outstretched, I wince at the sight of her remarkable tits bouncing with the motion. "Suck it, Osborne."

"Aww, aren't you just the cutest." I cross my thick, tattooed arms over my chest. "Don't be so damn quick to celebrate, Clark. You're stranded up there now."

That wipes the cocky smirk from her face.

"Dammit," comes her breathy curse. She bites down on her bottom lip before removing a stray hair from her mouth. "I loathe you right now."

No she doesn't.

"You're kind of fucked." I'm catlike in my approach, creeping across the carpet like a predator stalking its prey. "Which is too bad, because I'm really enjoying this."

Meow.

"What are you going to do with me?" she whispers. Her flimsy white tank top is clutched to her chest, providing zero protection.

"What would you *like* me to do?" Because I can come up with a million different ideas, all of them involving legs, tits, and ass. And nudity. Lots and lots of nudity.

"Um…" Her eyes dart from me, to the bathroom, to the dresser. Me. Bathroom. Dresser.

Me.

Poor thing is planning her exit strategy, but it's clear she's failing miserably because she's still standing in the middle of the bed; I give her an A for effort, but a big fat *F* for execution.

"You could make a run for it," I start, altruistically spreading my hands wide. "Or…"

"Or what?"

"Or I'm going to come over there and—whoa! What the hell do you think you're doing?"

I watch as she drops the white tank on the bed and reaches for the waistband of her black wool leggings. Balancing on the squishy mattress while she shoves them down past her hips, knees, and ankles, she steps out of them and they get tossed listlessly to the floor.

My eyes hit the skimpy baby blue underwear covering the patch between her smooth, sexy legs.

Lace. My weakness.

"You put those goddamn pants back on *this instant*," I thunder, taking a step forward.

"You sound like someone's father." Jameson laughs, reaching for the hem of her thick, wool ski sweater. "And I'm *not* going to be calling you Daddy any time soon."

She pulls the sweater higher, exposing a pale expanse of well-toned abdomen.

"Stop it. What the hell are you doing?"

"What does it look like I'm doing, genius?" Her muffled laughter taunts me. "Payback's a bitch."

She lets out a shriek then a gasp when my arms go around her bare waist and I plow her into the mattress, flipping her down onto her back, pile-driver style.

"Oz!" She belly laughs. "Get off me!"

"Say the magic word," I tease, hovering above her. Like magnets to metal, my fingers find the bare skin of her thigh and land there by gravitational pull. Skimming lightly, they don't stop until they find the wooly bottom of her sweater.

Tug. Tug that shit down so it covers up her taut stomach, because God forbid I have to look at that shit right now and keep my hands to myself.

Easier said than done.

I lean into her until I've lightly nudged her delicate shoulders flat on the mattress, hook under her legs until they're cradled in my arms, and stare down at her.

"Say the magic word," I repeat, my voice raspier than intended and far more serious.

"The magic word." Little smartass.

My head dips low, whispering in the hollow of her neck. "Nope, not it. Try again."

Burning hot, my hand moves from the backside of her knee. It tracks unhurried up her smooth, shaved thigh, imprinting its searing hot *need* on her skin. Spreading my palm wide, my thumb strokes that intoxicating indentation of her bikini line.

She lets me.

It's smooth and completely hairless and now I'm fucking dying to know: "Do you wax your pussy, Jameson?"

A little whimper and a whispered, "*No, I shave it,*" has me aching to see it. Touch it. Taste it.

Under the plain cardigan sweaters, the prim pearl necklace, the refined black patent leather shoes, Jameson Clark is sporting some prime, Grade A hairless pussycat inside her pants.

And I want to play with it.

"Goddamn that's sexy." *She's* sexy, all of her. Every last conservative inch.

My thumb brushes the seam of her panties and she gasps like a good girl. I angle toward her, wanting to press my mouth on her visible bare skin.

Jameson licks her lips. "Oz, please."

"Please? Please what?" *Please beg me to bang you.*

"Let me up?"

She doesn't sound convinced that's what she wants, not in the least. Not with all the *panting*. Not with her chest rising and falling with each labored breath. She sounds like she's relishing the press of my hard body, the contact of our pelvises as I gently pin her to the mattress in a classic wrestling move.

I inch away, giving her space, help her rise by taking her hand and pulling her up. Those high cheekbones flush and she looks away with a huff when she's back on her feet. Hot. Bothered.

Flustered.

"Fine. I won't wear the tank top. You win," she mutters, avoiding my dark eyes. "Give me your shirt."

I stand, adjust the raging hard-on inside my pants, and cross the room. I grab the shirt that's been folded into a neat cotton square off the dresser, and, lifting it to my nose, I give it a whiff. "Mmm, smells like you. I'll probably never wash it again."

Jameson's trembling hands reach for it. "Just give it to me."

"See? Now that's what I'm talkin' about…"

#DOUCHEBAG

"The girl I was banging last night
stopped me in the middle of sex
to take off her purity ring
and lob it in the trash can."

Jameson

Oh my god, I have to pee.

Bad.

In total darkness, I ungraciously slide out of bed as quietly as I can so I don't wake a slumbering Oz—who, it turns out, is a total bed hog—and feel my way along the wood-paneled wall in the general direction of the bathroom.

Thankfully, the light is already on, the overhead light above the tub emitting a dull glow. I have to pee so bad my fingers are already inside the waistband of my underwear when I beeline for the toilet in a squat. Shoving them down around my ankles, I lower myself with a relieved groan.

I pee, eyes squeezed shut to ward out the glow, only cracking them open when I fail to find the end of the toilet paper.

I shimmy my sheer, blue underwear up my slender thighs.

Turn to flush.

Raise my head to check myself in mirror as I wash my—

"*Fuck* Jameson." My name is drawn out in a husky, forced moan.

I gasp, scared shitless.

"Holy shit!" I yell, swatting a startled hand toward Oz. If I had a weapon, I'd club him with it. "You asshole! You scared the crap out of me—"

"*Fuck* Jameson."

"Wh-what…I'm so sorry. I thought you were in bed!"

I spin toward the sink, our eyes meeting in the mirror, mine widening in shock, his in pleasure, then I finally let them trail down his thick, bent, pumping arm. Red mesh athletic shorts pool around his ankles, his large hand wrapped around the length of his hard—

"Oh my god."

I do a swift check, just to be sure. Yup. Sebastian Osborne is masturbating in the bathroom, and I just peed two feet from him.

Now that I've seen it, I can't *un*see it.

And if I'm being honest, I don't want to.

Sebastian

"**O**h my god Oz, *what* the hell are you doing!" The high-pitched indignation is completely unnecessary as Jameson meets my aroused, half-lidded eyes in the mirror. Hers are round with shock and horror and *something else entirely* as she casts surreptitious glances down at my stroking palm.

Twice.

Three times.

"I would think it was pretty *obvious* what I'm doing," I grunt out, words catching with each even stroke. "Besides, this is your fault."

"*My* fault!" She stands frozen at the sink, back to me while water drips from her wet hands. "You're *masturbating* while I peed, you freaking creeper! What the hell is wrong with you?"

"Maybe you should have thought of all this before you stripped down to that skimpy underwear and got me hard with that shaved pussy of yours."

"I-I...how..."

Another slow stroke up and down the blunt tip of my dick and my eyes flutter shut. "Everything about you makes me hard. I don't know what my fucking problem is." *Goddamn this feels good.* "Jesus Jameson, the door was closed. Who'd you think was in here?"

"I... You didn't lock it, jackass! Plus, it's one o'clock in the morning! I thought you were in bed!"

"I was. Now I'm not."

For the fourth time, her eyes stray, landing on the hard, pulsing cock in my hand. I pump it once while she watches and let out a satisfied groan as it gets harder while I fist it.

"You disgust me."

Such a pretty little liar.

"Do I *really?* Then why are you...*ugh fuck me...*" I pant. "Why are you still standing there? You like it, don't you?"

Shit, I've never been one for exhibitionism in the past, but having her watch me jack off gets me even harder.

Holy hell, that little she-devil fucking likes it.

Seconds go by before she remembers herself, before she spins on her heel and slams out of the bathroom, pulling the door shut behind her with a bang. It rattles on its hinges but I don't hear her footfalls walk away.

Instead, I recognize the sound of someone slouching against the door. A few more seconds, and a throat is cleared.

"Hey Oz?"

I stroke myself slowly to the sound of her voice, teeth raking my bottom lip. "Yeah?"

I stop myself from adding *baby*, an instinctual reply I somehow don't think she'd appreciate.

Another rapid stroke. *Shit. Fuck.* I'm so close to coming.

"Sorry I busted in on you."

My thumb caresses the tip of my cock, spreads the pre-come, and I suck in a labored breath to control the inflection of my speech when the first tell of my balls tightening makes them ache.

Somehow, I find my voice. "Are you sure? Because I'm pretty sure you wanna watch...*oh fuck this feels good.*"

The sound of her labored breathing comes at me muted and I imagine her, forehead pressed to the cool door, listening.

She *is* listening to me jerk it—I just fucking know it.

"Say something."

Speech wavering, she complies. "Rule number seven," she gulps. "No masturbating in the bathroom."

"James? Amend rule number seven to read: no masturbatory emissions with the door *unlocked,* and you have yourself a deal."

Unable to control it, I moan.

"Fine."

The silence is almost deafening, until I hear the sound of her finally moving away.

"*Fine*." I come in my hand, in the dim bathroom.

Alone.

"You either have a dog
in your room,
or you brought a girl home.
I can't tell from all the weird
sounds which one it is."

Jameson

I can't fall back asleep; I'm pretty sure he can't either.

I'm pretty sure he was moaning my name.

Sebastian was moaning *my* name—and the last thing I need is to be the porn star in some jock's nocturnal emissions.

Both of us wide awake, the weight of the mattress dips when he shifts, moving closer toward me.

"Hey James?"

He's rarely called me James since the day we met—it's always Jim or Jimbo—and I like the sound of him whispering my name.

Rolling toward him in the dark to seek out his voice, it sounds a mere inch away. Sharing a bed was probably a horrible idea, but there's no turning back now, and it beats the hell out of having one of us sleep on the bodily fluid-soaked hotel floor.

Just the thought of what's on the carpet below gives me the heebs.

"Yeah?"

His voice falters, drumming the mattress with built up energy. "What's the real reason you let me kiss you in the library?"

It's a good question, one I haven't stopped thinking about since. I think of all the things I could say to him right now. I can tell him it was for the money (which I don't need). I could tell him it's because I felt sorry for him. I could tell him it was out of some humanitarian effort.

Instead, I go with the truth.

"I told you, I was curious."

"Curious about what?"

"I've never kissed anyone like you before."

"What do you mean?" I *hear* the pleased smile; the bastard is gloating.

Except he knows exactly what I mean, the cocky bastard; he just wants to hear me say the words out loud—not that I blame him. Don't we all like hearing flattering things said about ourselves? Compliments. Flattery.

Gorgeous hunks of the male persuasion being no exception.

"Well, I wasn't kidding when I said you weren't my usual type." I speak in his direction. It's dark and I can barely make out the shape of him on the bed. "The guys I date are usually less..."

"Hot?"

Yes.

I let a sigh escape my lips. "No. That's not what I was going to say."

"Less shredded?"

Yes. "No. They're usually less—"

"Popular?"

Yes. "Would you stop interrupting me?" Then, "Wait. Did you just call yourself popular? You know we're not in high school, right?"

"Babe, if you think I'm cool now, you would have been really impressed with how badass I was in high school. I was the *shit.*"

I don't doubt that for a second. Closing my eyes, I conjure up an image of high school Sebastian Osborne: tall, cocksure, and a total hottie. If I had to guess, I'd imagine he probably screwed his way around school in the back seat of his parent's car starting freshman year, racking up first place wrestling medals and trophies after making varsity sophomore year. Going undefeated the following three years. Missing his graduation to compete in the state wrestling tournament...

Fine. I *might* have accidentally google stalked him.

Accidentally.

And no, it didn't say anything about him having sex as a freshman—that part I made up.

"I never said I thought you were *cool.*" I laugh, snuggling into my blankets and pillows with a shiver. "Cool. Who even says that any more?"

Oz's scoff comes out of the dark. "Cool or not, I totally would have fucked you by now if this was high school."

Is he for real? Thank god the lights are off, because my cheeks flush and I can feel my neck getting hot. I burrow deeper. "Um, no, you totally wouldn't have."

He scoffs again, this time louder. "Oh come on, give me a break; you *so* would have let me bone you. No way would you have been able to resist the big D. All the chicks dug me."

He's so utterly ridiculous I chuckle, but sadistically, I also find him completely charming.

Ugh.

"Bad news, Oz: if you think I'm a killjoy now, you should have seen me in high school. I was worse. Brace yourself for the plot twist: I was *saving* myself."

"Saving yourself for what? A convent?"

"No idiot, for someone who respected me. *Loved* me. Marriage. I don't know, I was young—or maybe I just knew I didn't want to give it up to a fumbling, inexperienced high school kid."

"So who'd you end up giving the cherry to?"

I lie silently a few seconds, ignoring the fact that he just referred to my virginity as 'the cherry', and contemplate my answer with a snicker. "I finally gave it up to a fumbling, inexperienced college sophomore because I was tired of waiting for a good guy to come along."

His chuckle comes out of the shadows. "Did you have an orgasm?"

"I'm not answering that question."

"So that's a no."

"Why do you... Ugh. Yes, that was a no, but I've made up for it since." I shrug my shoulders in the dark.

He hums out an, "Interesting..." Then, "So what do you consider a *good* guy?"

"Are you using air quotes in the dark?"

Oz laughs, shaking the mattress. "Yeah, how could you tell?"

"You're kind of a goof." Nonetheless, I consider his question. "A good guy? Hmmm. The answer is…I have no idea. Someone respectful, I guess? Who does what they *say* they're going to do. Is reliable. Who doesn't cheat… doesn't bullshit me."

"That's a lot of negatives."

It does sound like it now that I'm saying the words out loud. "When it comes down to it, I'd like someone who makes me laugh."

"*I* make you laugh."

Giggle. "You sure do."

"And I'm respectful," he adds helpfully.

Hmmm. "That's debatable."

"I do what I say I'm going to do."

Rolling over on my back, I stare toward the ceiling. "No offense, but I don't know why you're telling me all this. Are you applying for the job?"

"Probably because I'm trying to fuck you?"

I roll my eyes heavenward, ignoring his vulgar answer. "Okay, what about you? Who did you give it up to your first time?"

"Ah, I remember it like it was yesterday: I was fifteen and her name was Penny VanderWahl. She was my friend's older sister and she let me screw her in the hayloft of a barn. Definitely was not a virgin. Does it count if I blew my load putting on the condom?"

Gross. "I don't think so."

"Yeah, you're probably right; there was no actual penile penetration. It was just the tip."

"Oh my god. Filter! Filter!"

His entertained snort cuts through the dark. "I hate to break it to you, Jim, but if you think that's bad, you don't even want to know what's going on inside this head right now."

You're so wrong, I can't stop myself from thinking. *So so*

142

wrong.

I do want to know.

"You're as deep as a puddle, Osborne. Of course I know what's going through your head right now. You make no secret of being what my grandmother would call a skirt chaser."

"Skirt chaser? Shit, I haven't heard that one in a while. I like it though."

"It's *not* a compliment, Sebastian."

He chuckles. "If you say so, Jim."

We lie there in silence, but I can hear him thinking. Feel his even breathing beside me. Feel his hand slide across the firm mattress, slide under the wall of pillows, and grasp my hand.

Fingers entwined, he squeezes. "I'm glad I'm here."

"I…" I swallow the lump in my throat. "Me too."

And I am.

I'm glad he's here with me, however high handed his antics were in getting here. Goofy, good-looking, and oddly kind-hearted Sebastian Osborne. My friend.

"Thanks for the invite. I needed a vacation."

In the dark, I roll my eyes.

"Did you just roll your eyes at me?"

"No?"

"You're a terrible liar, do you know that?"

"Go to sleep, Oswald."

He gives my hand another squeeze. "Sweet *wet* dreams, Jim."

"She was stripping
for me on video chat,
but I had to keep it on mute
because my coach was giving
the team a lecture.
That took most of the fun
out of it."

Jameson

We snowboard the rest of the weekend, packing up on a Sunday afternoon for the one thousand eighty-five mile ride back to campus. Gray clouds linger overhead, threatening to snow, an occasional chunky snowflake falling from grace down to the ground.

As I'm heaving my duffle bag out of our room, dragging it across the resort parking lot, a lone snowflake hits the tip of my nose and rests there. My eyes cross and I watch it momentarily before the heat of my skin melts it and it disappears into a tiny drop of water.

One by one, the rest of them begin falling. Wet, silent, and beautiful, like millions of tiny wisps dancing through the sky.

I draw in a breath, and as I inhale and exhale, the warmth of my breathing turns to a puff of smoke. Out of nowhere, Oz appears beside me, bending at the waist and reaching for my bags, swinging them over his shoulder as if they're weightless and nudging me toward the bus.

I trail along behind him, nothing to carry except my laptop bag and a small tote. Oz carries it all.

Once the bags are stored in the lower level of the bus, he patiently waits while I fumble with my carryon tote. Waits while I climb each step, hand poised on the small of my back, guiding me. Follows behind me down the long, narrow aisle of the bus. Waits while I choose a seat.

The bus isn't full—not even close—so I can be choosy, and I head toward the back where it's private, deciding on the third to last row, near the bathroom.

I stow my bag under the seat and take the window.

Oz tosses his duffle on the empty seat across the aisle, sliding in beside me, his head hitting the seatback with an exhausted thump. He spreads his legs as wide as his giant frame allows.

"Tired," he grumbles irritably. "Jim, can I lean my head on your shoulders? I just want to sleep for a bit."

"Uh, sure."

Oz sits up then, reaching for the hem of his hoodie and pulling it up over the top of his head then rolling it up. His intended target? My chest.

He comes at me, attempting to jam the wadded up sweatshirt under my chin.

I dodge the bundle headed in my direction, toward my face. "Whoa buddy. *Whoa.* Um, what are you doing?"

He gives me a look. "Uh, making a pillow. Sometimes shoulder bones are lumpy."

I can't help it; I laugh. "Fine, but I don't necessarily want to be suffocated by you *cramming* your sweatshirt under my neck. Here, let me do the honors; I don't need you crushing my trachea."

Oz hands over his makeshift pillow and I refold it then roll it up. Reclining against the seat, I fold up the armrest to make more room and fit the hoodie in the crook of my neck.

Ahh, perfect. "I'll close my eyes, too, I guess."

A short nap can't hurt.

"Thanks, Jim."

His large frame shifts to get comfortable, long legs stretched, feet under the seat in front of us. It's like fitting a square peg into a round hole; he just doesn't fit.

More flip flopping, more disgruntled sighs, and his body gets twisted into a fetal-like position—no small feat for a man of his size in the cramped space we're given.

I pause at that word: man.

Oz is a *man*. A solid, sexual, funny, clever, smart man.

Whose cheek is buried in the crook of my neck, the silky strands of hair on his gorgeous head tickling my nose when I tilt my neck to accommodate him.

He really *is* huge.

I gasp when his torso twists and he flips to try to find more room, shifting positions, nose buried in my chest. Slips his bulky, tattooed arms around my waist to get comfy, my arms shoved uselessly above his back for lack of place to put them.

"Relax Jimbo. It's just a nap," his lips murmur into the hollow of my neck, arms giving my waist a squeeze. His hot breath strokes my collarbone. "And it's okay to touch me."

He's right; I need to relax.

I allow myself a brief moment to appraise him, curled up in his seat, leaning into me. Embracing me, really, cuddling me like his favorite teddy bear. The smell of him assaults me: peppermint breath, masculine shampoo. Clean. Male. The scent of him makes my mouth water and my body ache.

The smell of him makes me *thirsty*.

Soft cotton short-sleeved shirt bares his powerful arms. Black and flesh-colored tattoos cover the entire left bicep, wrap around his forearm, and end at the wrist. His hands are large, calloused. Working hands.

Those hands tell a story. They're solid. And …dependable.

They cause pain.

Bring pleasure.

Slowly, of their own violation, my palms find purchase on his deltoids, sliding up the smooth fabric of his shirt in one languid motion, memorizing the hard planes beneath. The pads of my fingertips trace each curve curiously, learning the shape of him.

Those same fingertips dig into the corded muscles of his thick neck. Kneading. Massaging.

Memorizing.

"Damn Jim, that feels good," he croaks into the wadded up hoodie still jammed between us.

"Go to sleep, Oswald," I croon into his hair, feeling more for him at this moment than I've allowed myself to admit.

I know better than this. This guy is an energy-filled livewire of testosterone; he's the opposite of what I'm looking for despite not really knowing what *that* is.

He sleeps around. He's callous. Crude. Rude. Insensitive.

Totally inappropriate.

Pensively, I stare down at the crown of his hair, resisting the urge to inhale. Regardless, I catch an intoxicating whiff of his shampoo—actually, it's *my* shampoo because he stole it—and close my eyes, savoring the differences between us.

His hard to my soft. His outspokenness to my tact. His virile to my…

Holy crap, I need to get laid.

But Sebastian Osborne is the *last* thing I need. The last person I need to…*lay* me.

There was a time I used to worry about never finding *the one*. Worry I was going to be alone forever with no one to come home to at night but the dog. Or cat. Or fish. In fact, most of my friends were happily single. Wanted to be.

On purpose.

Free to do whatever and *whom*ever they wanted.

I think I woke up one morning and decided it didn't matter any more; not having a man in my life wasn't going to define me, wasn't going to make me feel less whole or undesirable.

Undesirable. What a ridiculous thing to say at the age of twenty-one.

Undesirable—maybe it's too strong a word because men did desire me; I just didn't desire most of them back. Sure, I was up for the occasional meaningless one-night stand; I probably had my hand down my own pajama bottoms more often than Oz did down his.

But maybe a hookup to take the edge off wasn't enough.

Not any more.

Or maybe not a hookup with him.

Although I sit here, wrapped in the arms of a guy who wants to screw my brains out—a guy who'd screw me into a twelve-hour coma if I let him—I couldn't make myself say the word yes.

Yes.

What was stopping me from letting him?

The heat pooling between my legs has me fidgeting in my seat.

"I can hear you thinking," Oz murmurs. "Babe, relax."

Babe.

He's called me that a few times before, but this time it's almost like he *means* it, if that makes sense.

It's then that I feel his large mammoth palms begin their ascent, wandering up my back. Up and down, straying from my waist in what little room they have to roam. They feel so warm and *good* I arch my spine to give him more access, arch it just a little, because…*oh god that feels good…*

"You *can't* hear me thinking," I argue weakly with zero conviction.

"Yes I can. I read body language as a sport, remember? Relax, James—I can't sleep with all this nervous energy."

Body language as a sport.

Pining down an opponent in nothing but that singlet wrestlers wear, hot and sweaty and hard. The catalogued image of him in that tight spandex unitard—the pictures I'd googled when curiosity finally won out—have me uneasily squirming in his hold.

I wonder if this is what it's like to be pinned down by him.

Wonder if this is what it's like to be beneath him in bed.

Not in it, on top of it.

No covers. *No clothes.*

Oh god.

"James. Relax." He tips his face up then, our lips a fraction of an inch apart. Full, pink lips that I've tasted. Sucked on. Stuck my tongue between.

"I'm trying," I breathe. "But it's hard."

"It's *going* to be hard if you don't stop moving around."

I can't even summon up the energy to lecture him on propriety, so focused on his lips. Before I can flop my head back against the window, before I can shut my eyes and pretend to sleep, warm lips press firmly against my mouth. One. Two kisses. A wet tongue quickly darts out and flicks the corner of my mouth.

His large palm supports the back of my neck, pulling me down, pulling me in and resting his lips on mine. My heartbeat keeps time with the seconds our lips bond. One, two, three, four...

Lids briefly close and Oz pulls away, settling his cheek onto my chest.

Peppermint lingers on my gaping pucker.

"What... Why'd you do that?" Even to my own ears my voice is barely audible, throaty. I want to press a finger to my lips, but my hands are otherwise occupied, pressing into the solid, corded muscles in his back.

"Because I wanted to. Now chill out and take a nap with me. Be my calm."

Be his calm? Be his calm.

"I'll try," I say breathily.

Oz's head angles up and our drowsy eyes meet. "You're cute."

He's always saying that.

Cute.

I hate it.

Feminist or not, I still hate that I'll never be *hot*, or *sexy*, or *coy*.

Inept at flirting, I say nothing, let the moment pass until his gentle snores fill the small space we're occupying for our ride home.

The first to wake, I'm able to sit up when Oz shifts, his legs spread wide and arms crossed as he rests.

I study his profile, eyes faltering on his handsome face, letting them travel the fine line of his nose, up his strong jawline, my perusal tracing his earlobe with every sweeping pass.

His lip twitches. "Are you watching me sleep?"

Ah, so the beast is awake.

Yes. "No."

"Liar." A smile tips his lips but his lids remain closed. "You've been watching me sleep all weekend, haven't you, you little creeper?"

"Did you watch *me* sleep all weekend?" I tease, not expecting him to agree with me.

He pauses, cracking an eyelid open and studying me. For a second I don't think he'll answer honestly. "I might have once or twice."

Seriously? "Seriously?"

His head lolls to the side, toward me. "Seriously. You're gorgeous when you're asleep."

Okay then.

"So wait. You *didn't* watch me sleep?" His demand jars me from my slumber and he gives me a nudge with his elbow. "Hey, wake up."

"Leave me alone." I don't even crack an eyelid, just swat blindly in his direction. "I already told you this at *least* five times."

"Right, but I just assumed you were full of shit."

A groggy smile. "You're ridiculous."

#DOUCHEBAG

"She had one of those clap-on,
clap-off lamps.
I fucked her so hard,
every time I rammed the
headboard into the wall,
the lights turned on and off.
It was awesome."

Sebastian

Is it weird that I miss her?

She's not a fuck buddy. Not a girlfriend. And if I'm being perfectly blunt, she's not even a *friend*.

And yet...

I want to see her. Talk to her. Give her shit just to see her face turn red with embarrassment.

I sent her the first text at dawn this morning after a conditioning jog around campus, knowing she was probably still in bed but wanting to message her anyway. Not having a legit reason to message her, I went with:

Did you make it home okay?

I stop running when the phone in the pocket of my athletic shorts buzzes, pacing around the cement jogging trial to keep my muscles warm but wanting to see if it's her.

Jameson: *We got home two days ago, weirdo... But more importantly*

My phone buzzes again.

Jameson: *DO YOU KNOW WHAT TIME IT IS?!?*

Oz: *Yes. 5:47 and I wasn't expecting you to actually answer, so you can't get mad. Don't you have your phone on silent when you sleep like a normal human being?*

Jameson: *NO!*

Oz: *Since you're up, want to join me for a run? I know where* *you live...*

Jameson: *Don't even think about it. I will murder you if you show up at my door. Murder.*

Oz: *Or I could climb into bed with you. I've gotten used to sharing a bed with you and your tower of cockblocking pillows.*

Jameson: *Those pillows did their job. Wait. Why am I awake? Why are YOU awake?*

Oz: *I'm standing on the jogging path near campus, texting you.*

Jameson: *The sun hasn't even come up yet...*

Oz: *It's just coming over the rise. I should keep moving. I have to get to the gym in 5*

Jameson: *When's your next wrestling meet? Match? Rumble? Throw down...? WHY DID YOU WAKE ME UP*

Oz: *Lol it's called a match, and it's Thursday, so we leave late Wednesday night.*

Jameson: *Sigh. Where is it?*

Oz: *Pennsylvania—Penn State*

Jameson: *WOW! I mean, I'm really tired so all I can say is WOW but... WOW*

Oz: *LOL. Will you be at the library today?*

Jameson: *Yawn. Who wants to know?*

Oz: *Me*

Jameson: *Well in that case*

Oz: *Yes? I'll text you after class tonight, yeah?*

Jameson: *Sure, but only because you caught me at my weakest. I'd say yes to anything right now to be left alone.*

Oz: *ANYTHING?*

Jameson: *Dream on pal. Anything but THAT*

Oz: *One of these days you're going to change your mind Jameson Clark.*

Jameson: *I'm going back to sleep.*

20

#DOUCHEBAG

"When I asked her how
flexible she was,
she told me she once threw
her back out putting in a tampon."

Sebastian

"**S**o you leave tomorrow night, huh?" James asks while tapping on her keyboard, her lithe fingers flying over the small black letters at a rapid pace.

I look up from the ethics textbook flipped open in front of me. "Yeah. We have to be on the bus at nine. Which is going to suck. We lose an hour with the time change."

The room is quiet as we both go back to our homework. But then...

"Do you ever get nervous?"

My eyes stop running along the rows and rows of text, and I pause to consider her question. Do I ever get nervous? Hell yes. All the time in fact—the adrenaline rush before a match combined with everything I have riding on my wins has had me nauseous on more than one occasion.

But no one has ever asked me, so I consider how I want to respond. I go with a simple, "Yes."

"When?"

I pause again. "When my opponents are the same weight class but bigger. Bulkier. Or smaller. Or come at me with a chip on their shoulder I can see when they come onto the floor." And now that I'm on a roll, I stare absentmindedly at the painting hanging on the far side of the room. "Some guys are so desperate to win you can see it in their eyes. The hungry ones with everything to lose with each loss."

Like me.

The unspoken words hang between us.

"What's your record?"

"This season? We just started, but I'm eight and oh."

Undefeated, badass mother.

Impressed, Jameson's pretty blue eyes get wide as fucking

saucers and a small gasp escapes her lips. "Sebastian, that's *amazing*."

Sebastian.

My name sounds like praises from her lips.

I sit up straighter in my chair, a little more cocksure than I was ten seconds ago. I mean, it's not like people aren't telling me on a regular basis how fucking amazing I am, but a compliment coming from Jameson Clark somehow feels like winning at life.

She doesn't dole out compliments on the regular.

She doesn't suffer fools, and she's not easily impressed.

"It really is amazing." I puff out my chest and posture. "You should see me in action sometime."

"I have."

This is news to me. "You have? When?"

"I mean, there's a chance I googled you—after you *demanded* that I google you, of course."

"You actually stalked me online? I'm in shock." Why am I having such a hard time imagining her at her computer searching for shit about me? Possibly in the dark, hopefully touching herself inappropriately, preferably wearing something lace. And see-through.

The thought has my dick twitching.

"Would you stop it? It was *not* stalking. You told me to google you.

I don't stop.

"Yeah, but when was this *alleged* stalking? Be specific." I tease, using air quotes.

She looks horrified. "Please stop calling it that." Hesitates. "And it was right before we left for Utah. I wanted to know what level of egomaniac I was dealing with."

I push the textbook across the table and out of my way, reclining back in the chair my ass has been planted in for the past hour. "So what, pray tell, did you discover during this *research*?" Again with the air quotes.

A grin widens my face when her face turns scarlet, the skin beneath her sweater a bright, furious pink.

"Well," she begins deliberately, clearing her throat, each syllable measured. "I know you're from Illinois—same as me. I know you have a sister, and that in high school, you were a star."

James hesitates, blowing out a puff of air. The long, wavy hair hanging in a cascade lifts off her face. "You're here on a full ride. I know you're a heavyweight wrestler at six foot one, but you're two twenty-eight pounds of solid muscle with a body fat percentage of seven."

"True facts."

"You're considerate—and as much as I hate to admit it, you're funny. And you care more about grades then you want people to know, but for the life of me I can't figure out why."

I grab my yellow Iowa water bottle as she sucks in her bottom lip and nibbles nervously before raising her blue eyes to study me across the table. "Um…you smell good. Like fresh air and peppermint."

My brows shoot up.

Yes. This. *That's* the shit I'm talking about.

I lean toward her, interested, but otherwise sit perfectly still, longing to hear her speak.

"Go on."

"You…have the strongest arms I've ever seen."

Yes.

"You have a leg fetish."

I nod, water bottle poised at my watering mouth. "Fact."

"You knew I wasn't a tutor the day we met but you came over anyway."

"Twice," I confirm, chugging on my water, the room-temp liquid pouring down my throat.

"You like working with your hands, and despite what everyone thinks—what *I* thought when I first met you—you're not a *total* man whore."

I sputter, choking on the laugh, spitting out a mouthful of water in the process until it dribbles cold and wet down my chin. Yanking up the hem of my cotton tee, I wipe my face with a few swipes.

"How do you know I'm not a man whore?"

"I didn't say you weren't, I said not *totally.* For one, you didn't make a move on my roommate Sydney when you had the chance and she probably wanted you to—and for the life of her she can't figure out why. And two, you didn't make a move on *me* in Utah even though we shared the same bed."

"And you weren't wearing pajama bottoms."

"Correct."

"Why would you do that, by the way?"

She sighs, loud and long and breathy. "Ugh, are we back to that?"

"Fuck yeah we're back to that!" I'm indignant. "You knew damn well what you were doing. Cunning femme fatale. Not wearing pajama bottoms was shady and ruthless."

She giggles a soft, tinkling laugh, sweet and delighted, toying with the buttons of her pale pink cardigan. "Femme fatale?" James rolls her eyes. "Hardly."

My gaze lowers, settling on that second glossy button where her long, lean fingers push it in and out of the buttonhole, right in the center of those round, fantastically full breasts—the breasts I tried to get a sneak peek of *at minimum* one dozen times on the trip.

"Please." I snort, crossing my arms over my broad chest. "Don't tell me you didn't know what you were doing flouncing around with no pants on."

Her grin spreads wide. "You're crazy."

"I call bullshit. You knew that was driving me nuts."

"Well yeah, but...it could have been anyone running around pants-less and you would have tried to sleep with them."

"Did we *not* just establish that I didn't make a move on your roommate what's-her-face?"

"*Sydney*. Right, yes, but—"

"And I *did* make a move on you."

"You did? When?"

"Remember when I said I was trying to fuck you?"

She rolls her eyes. "That's not making a move on me. That's blatantly telling me you want to sleep with me."

"Not sleep. *Fuck*. Huge difference, Jim."

"You know, just when I think you have some deep-rooted sensitivity just dying to get out, you ruin it by talking."

I shrug my broad shoulders. "You can't blame me for being honest."

"No, but jeez, Oz, sometimes a girl doesn't want to have it shoved down her throat like that. She'd like to have an actual conversation. Be romanced."

The phrase 'shoved down her throat' makes me want to giggle like a thirteen-year-old. I manage not to, but *barely*, although I *cannot* resist mentioning it. It's too damn good.

"Do you have any idea what you just said? You said *shove* and *throat*, and I immediately thought blowjob. So don't even— hey, sit down. Where are you going?"

She's packing up her laptop with a roll of her eyes. "Home. As much as I'd love to stay, I really do have some serious work to do."

"You get so fucking huffy. Would you sit back down please?"

"I do not get huffy!" James sets her bag back on the table and crosses her arms. "I'll stay if you can give me one good reason why I should sit back down and let you continue to distract me. *One*. I'm pretty sure you can't do it."

"Wanna bet?"

A decisive nod. "Yes. Absolutely."

"Terrific." Because *I got this*. "You're on. What are the stakes? Make 'em good."

"How about you choose mine and I choose yours."

Bad idea, Jim.

Horrible, horrible idea. So horrible, in fact, I'm practically rubbing my hands together with glee.

"Good. Ladies first."

"If you can't come up with one legitimate reason to keep me in this room, you have to..." Jameson furrows her brows in concentration. "You have to..." She makes a little humming thought. "Hmmm. Let me think."

"Take your time," I coax, leaning back in the study room's big leather office chair. I spin around a few times, watching her scrumptiously from the corner of my eye as she bites her lip, thinking hard. "I have all night."

She's quiet for an entire two minutes then snaps her fingers. "All right, I've got it! If you can't come up with a reason I approve of, you have to cook for me."

Is she fucking serious?

I try not to yawn at her mind-numbing idea, but it's so lame I let one slip out.

"Cook for you? That's it?" To say I'm disappointed is a gross understatement, and it must be palpable because she nods with a smirk. "Cooking as in *Let's eat!* or cooking as is *You bring the chocolate body drizzle, I'll bring the tongue?*"

"Cooking as in home-cooked meal."

I lean forward in the chair, the smooth leather seat and wheels creaking and straining under my weight when I give it one more spin. "All right. My turn."

I let the silence drag before slapping my hands together with a satisfying clap, rubbing them together gleefully. "If I win—*when* I win—I get to pin you down again. Get you down on the mat. Get you sweaty."

On the mat, in the gym, in the dark, when no one else is around.

Jameson rolls her eyes, but I can see the doubt materializing behind her flippant gaze. It becomes tangible when she swallows apprehensively. "Uh, okay. You can pin me down again, I guess."

I begin ticking off reasons she should stay with me; they spill from my tongue like the sweat dripping off my forehead during a match. Fluid, molten, and drenched.

"One reason for you to stay? I want you to. Second reason: you're driving me to distraction and I can't concentrate unless you're with me. Three: I want to pop the buttons on your damn sweater. Fourth: glasses. Five: I might need your help with an answer; you seem really smart."

Her mouth forms a straight, unimpressed line at that last one.

"But the real reason I want you to stay?" I draw out the sentence, emphasizing the last few words. "You're the only girl on this campus I have any respect for."

I push back on the table and lean back in my chair, crossing my arms and letting those factoids sink in.

"Well." James gulps. "That's—"

"That's the truth. I respect the hell out of you, and if you leave, I'm leaving too, and then I won't get anything done. I'll fail my homework, fall behind, and flunk out, thus making me ineligible for my scholarship. Do you want that hanging over your head?"

That cheeky smile I love returns. "No, certainly not."

"Good. Then sit down and get out your calendar."

"For what?"

"I win, which means I'm going to pin you to the mat and you're going to like it, so we need to pick a date." Her mouth falls open, incredulous. "Now sit back down and do your homework, Jimmy."

"I've faked almost every
single orgasm I've had,
so I'm pretty sure I can fake my
way through this tragic
blind date."

Sebastian

I don't know how I find myself outside Jameson's house, on her street. On her lawn. On her front porch, knocking. But by the grace of God, the universe decided to grant me a favor, and for the first time in my collegiate years, my classes were done by late morning.

Practice ended early. I don't have to work.

The team bus doesn't leave until late.

So here I stand on Jameson's porch, fist raised to knock.

I give it a few brisk raps and wait. Footpads approach the door and I straighten to my full height, paste a smile on my mouth, and wait for the deadbolts to slide free. The knob turns. Door gets cracked open a sliver and a giddy twitter emerges.

It's not Jameson.

My smile falters, but I quickly recover. "Hey Sydney. What's up?"

I stuff my hands inside the pockets of my lightweight winter jacket and bounce on the balls of my feet.

"Oz! Hi!" Sydney exclaims, all blonde hair, tits, and excitement. "Did you get my text? I texted you!"

Yeah, no shit. Ten texts, all of them annoying and unanswered. I try to act startled by this revelation. "You texted me! Weird. None of them came through."

Lies, lies, lies, and they roll off my tongue like honey.

She screws up her heavily made-up face into a pout. "Really? Shoot. There must be something wrong with my phone. I'll have to take it in to have it looked at."

"Yeah, good idea. So..." I cut to the chase. "Is Jameson home?"

"Jameson?"

"We didn't have plans but I thought we'd hit the library or

something."

Mostly *or something*.

Anything.

"She's not here and I don't know when she'll be back, but I happen to be free." Sydney coyly twirls a blonde tendril then flicks the entire curl over her shoulder. "Come on, let's get ice cream. Lucky you! It'll be fun."

Yay, lucky me.

I stand idle, debating about whether I should go for ice cream or not while Sydney slips back inside, emerging a few seconds later with a jacket and purse as if the whole thing was settled.

Shit.

She spins on her heels, calling back into the house before shutting the door behind her and stepping out onto the porch. "Allison, Oz and I are going for ice cream! If James comes back, tell her we'll be back whenever!"

Or don't, I almost groan out.

Cause the last thing I fucking want is Jameson finding out I went out with her damn roommate again. I don't know jack shit about women, but I *do* know she's going to hear about this and get the wrong impression.

Sydney hauls me to my truck—the truck I worked my ass off to own and paid off in full last month—hopping into the passenger seat with delight.

In a hurry to end this ice cream social as soon as possible, I make short work of the trip. Order a cone—chocolate, hold the sprinkles. Grab it to-go. Get back in the truck. Drive back to Jameson's place at warp speed with Jameson's roommate blathering nonstop beside me.

Touching my leg. Giggling. Trying her damnedest to be funny and engage me in conversation.

Instead of drawing out the excursion, I dump Sydney off in her front yard before reaching the bottom of my cone.

If she notices the hustle, she's too polite to let on, smiling brightly the entire, hideous time, until the very moment we pull back in front of the house.

"Oh look! James is back!"

Oh, goody.

Sydney is out before I can object and yanks open the driver's side door, yanks on my arm, and drags me out. "Come inside and say hello."

Every step up the walkway is like being marched to my execution with cement blocks chained to my ankles. A pit forms in my stomach, and I feel...

I attempt to pinpoint how I actually fucking feel, and...it's shitty.

I feel shitty.

Kind of sick.

We're on the stoop now and Sydney is marching through the front door, chatting away. I hesitate, feet rooted to the concrete steps on their covered porch, not wanting to proceed any farther.

"Aren't you coming in?" Sydney asks, holding the screen door open when she notices I haven't stepped into the house behind her.

I shake my head. Negative. "I should get going."

"But..." Pause. "Should I get James for you?"

No. "Sure."

Her disappearance into the dimly lit living room is followed by voices, a few doors opening and closing, and the appearance of—

"Jim."

She's standing under the entry, hand braced against the doorjamb. "Hi."

The first thing I notice about Jameson is that her hair is down, hanging around her shoulders, kind of windblown and messy, like she's just been driving with the windows down. It's sexy.

The second thing I notice is that she's not wearing a cardigan, a sweater, or a cardigan sweater. Snug jeans hug her curvy hips, and I can't help but linger on the threadbare V-neck shirt with the plunging neckline.

"Hi."

Jameson rolls her eyes, nothing but passive aggression etched across her pretty face. "What's up?"

"I came by earlier to see you."

"Mmm hmm."

"You weren't here."

"Nope." She looks me up and down warily. "I was running errands. Got back right after you left. With Sydney."

With Sydney.

With *fucking* Sydney.

Goddammitall.

My hands plunge immediately into my pockets. "I had free time today, so I thought…"

"You'd get ice cream?"

Yes. "*No.*"

"No you *didn't* get ice cream?"

"Yes. Yeah, we did."

Her sad smile is forced. "How nice. Was it good?"

I study her then, gauging her mood. I mean, clearly she's pissed, but calm, cool, and collected Jameson doesn't fool me. Scares me a little, yes. Fools me, no.

Too bad I have no idea how to proceed without getting myself into trouble. I mean, she's jealous, right? That's what this is?

She's upset and now she's going to trap me into admitting that leaving with her roommate was a dick move.

Shit, shit, shit.

I proceed with caution.

"I came here to see *you.*" Not your freaking roommate, who I'll admit is smokin' hot, but whom I have zero interest in. Not even for a quick lay. "And maybe take you out."

Jameson spreads her arms wide, gesturing into the open doorway. "And here I am."

"Like I said, I have a bunch of time. Not much homework, no papers due." I shuffle my feet on the stoop. "Practice ended early. Our bus doesn't leave until later."

"Lovely."

Her short answers are throwing me off. I inhale and push on. "Anyway, since I have all this time, I thought we could, you know, do something—"

"Wow, that is *soooo* weird," she interrupts.

Yup. It's a trap; I can hear it in the way her voice suddenly became too chipper. Too bubbly. Too fake happy while shooting stabby daggers of death my way.

"What's weird?"

"Well, you *say* you came here to see me, but…gosh, I don't know. You left here with *Sydney*, so…I'm a bit confused about how this whole thing works."

"I *did* come here to see you." How many times do I have to explain it? I remove the phone from my pocket and check the time. "I'm already packed for my trip, and it's still early if you want to…"

Jameson picks an imaginary piece of lint off the front of her tee shirt then stares over my shoulder off into the yard. "No thanks."

"Are you sure?"

A short laugh that does nothing to conceal the hurt shining in her eyes. "*Oh yeah*—I'm sure."

"But I'll see you on Monday at the gym when I get back from my meet, right?"

She throws me a curt nod. "A deal is a deal. I promised I'd let you pin me to the mat, so I'm going to let you pin me to the mat."

"Eleven fifteen?"

Jameson sighs. "I'll be there, Sebastian. Quit nagging."

"Wearing a singlet?"

A soft chuckle. "No, I won't be wearing a singlet."

"But they're the required uniform."

"How about I don't."

I think about this for a second, the mental image of Jameson wearing nothing but a basic black leotard too much for me to resist. All that exposed, smooth, creamy skin. "Rule number eight: we both have to be properly attired if we're doing this. Do the best you can to find something black." And tight. And fitted.

A loud, drawn-out sigh. "*Fine.*"

"Good."

"*Great.*" She pushes away, a smile threatening to crack the thin line of her lips.

"All right then, we agree. Oh, and James?"

"Yes, Oswald?" This time she *does* give me a smirk, a plastered on, shit-eating grin at the use of her nickname for me—one I plan to wipe off with my next pronouncement, raking her body up and down with my dark, hooded eyes.

"We don't wear anything under our singlets."

Her worried brows shoot up. "Nothing?"

"*Nothing.*"

I leave her there, standing on the porch with her mouth hanging open. Turning, I strut to my truck, whistling the entire way.

"Did you know that when
a female sloth is in heat,
she screams and the males
follow her sound and sometimes
fight each other to win her—
yet I can't get one guy
to text me back."

Jameson

Nothing—*nothing*—could have prepared me for the sight of Sebastian Osborne in his wrestling singlet—not the google search images, not the marketing shots from the university's athletic department, not even the vivid visuals fueled by my overactive imagination.

Last week's drama with Sydney evaporates, replaced by the sight of him in that sleek, body-hugging spandex—it is nothing short of a miracle.

God's gift to women.

A dreadful poly one-piece constructed solely to plague my estrogen levels.

It shows off. Absolutely. Everything.

Black with the school's mascot in the center, the low cut straps over his shoulders hug his muscular pecs, dipping down to showcase his lower body. His abdominals. His sternum. From his hard nipples to the valley of his well-developed chest...

His *everything*. I can see every gloriously well-defined detail.

Ugh.

I watch him stretching on the balls of his feet before he sees me emerging from the locker room of the wrestlers' designated practice gym. I examine the padded center of the room, feigning interest in the gleaming hardwood floor and the freshly painted school logo painted on the concrete cinderblock walls.

Oz stands, hands on his lean hips, grin spreading across his face when he catches sight of me walking out of the locker room dressed only in a plain black ballet leotard—one I raced around town like a *madwoman* to hunt down, realizing too late there are zero dance stores in this college town. The only place selling anything remotely close to a leo is Target, and theirs?

Theirs are for children.

So yeah. I'm wearing a kid's extra large, which doesn't exactly fit. In fact, it doesn't fit at all.

Black, sleeveless, and extremely tight, I try to ignore it and force myself across the cold wooden floor, pulling at the fabric riding up my butt crack. All because Oz is an asshole who insisted I wear one.

A single light shines above an azure mat in the center of the gym floor, a hanging light bulb, just like you'd see in the movies.

Darkness shrouds the recesses of the room.

I point to the light above. "Uh, did you plan this? It's way creepy."

He smirks. "I may or may not know the custodial staff, and now I owe them a favor." He looks me up and down. "You look hot by the way."

Insecurely, I pull at the straps barely coving my breasts. Because I. Am. An. Idiot. "Hot as in 'cheap stripper'?"

"No. Hot as in 'cheap *ballerina* stripper'. Where did you get that thing, anyway?"

"Target, because I didn't have time to order one from one of those online dance stores and it was the only place that had them."

His beautifully sculpted lips slide into a knowing curve. "Don't you have Prime? That would have only taken two days to ship."

I want to face palm myself because he has a very valid point. Instead I ignore the question completely. "I'm freezing here; can we get this over with? I feel like I'm about to be put under a microscope."

Advancing farther into the room across the shiny, polished hardwood floor. Conscious of my bare, colorless legs. My pale, freckled arms. My pink painted toes that could use a fresh coat of polish.

Hyperaware of Sebastian watching me pad barefoot across the room, I try not to stare at his masculine glory. His taut broad body. His lean hips. His massive thighs. His sinewy, rippling biceps. His bulging…

Oh god.

I can't look.

But I *have* to look.

My depraved eyes travel wantonly from his defined collarbone down to his hard-as-rock pecs and flat, toned abs, every inch of his long, thick dick visible under his thin, tight singlet.

Lord bless the designer of that horrible outfit.

My eyes widen when they settle on the length of him, glaringly obvious in the spandex fabric that leaves *nothing* to the imagination because he is wearing *nothing* underneath.

Not even a jock strap.

I swallow.

Take a few more cautious steps.

Hesitate.

"Scared?" his voice inquires, not really in a taunt. I'm surprised when he sounds…sincere. Caring. "Excited?"

"It's hard to get excited when you don't know what to expect." I cross my arms over the breasts I always considered porcelain; they haven't seen the sun in months and now they just feel…white. White, white, white.

"So you *are* scared."

I give a single nod. "A little."

"Don't be. I'm going to take real good care of you." He moves under the single dim light. "You might even like it."

I gulp down my nerves. "Not likely."

"Don't knock it 'til you've tried it."

"You've been pissing me off lately." I give a little indignant huff. "You're lucky I showed up."

"We had a deal."

"I'm here, aren't I?"

His hooded gaze drifts up and down my person so excruciatingly unrushed that goose bumps develop *all* over my skin, over my entire body.

I shiver.

"Uncross your arms, Jim." He gives his hands a clap. "Let's get this party started."

I can't help it—I let a nervous giggle bubble out of me, drop my arms to my sides, and stand there awkwardly, fidgeting. "When you call it a party it doesn't sound so horrible."

His enormous palms rub together gleefully. "I haven't been able to think of anything but pinning you down all day. Having you under me." He takes one deliberate step toward me at a time. "Not studying." *Step.* "Not practice." *Step.* "Not work."

He stops, the barest inch of space separating us.

Barely.

"And here you are. Jameson Clark, in my gym." The heat radiating between us is combustible. "So. What are we going to do about this, Jim. Any suggestions?"

Two black leotards. Two sleek figures.

One hard, one soft.

Raising my eyes to meet his, I manage to shake my head back and forth, mouth dry.

"Nothing? *Really* James? No suggestions, not even one? Good thing I have a few for the *both* of us."

He makes the simple statement sound dirty and pervy and hot.

My estrogen levels skyrocket, ovaries tingling on vibrate.

Sebastian's warm hand grips my arm, sliding gradually up toward my elbow. I shiver while my lady bits do…other inappropriate things.

"Okay Jimbo." His voice is low. Erotic. "This is what we're going to do: I'm going to show you how to get in position, then I'm going to flip you on your back. Okay?"

I stare at his pecs.

"Jim, nod if you understand."

I bob my head up and down.

He smiles down at me, all testosterone and sex appeal, cupping my chin in his huge hand. "God you're fucking cute."

Cute? Ugh.

"Bend your knees like this and mimic my stance." He releases me and steps back, squatting and separating his legs slightly, knees bent and back arched. "The point is to center your gravity."

I mimic his stance. "Like this?"

"*Just* like that Jameson." His voice is a gentle stroke, soft and sexy and low, and I blush at the sound of it, my ovaries giving another sigh. "Now. Spread your legs—yeah, spread them like that—and step with your lead foot, like this. We call this the power leg."

With my quivering right foot, I step forward.

"Now raise your hands to a guardian stance." He nods his approval when I do it correctly, eyes scanning my body. "I'm going to lower my head and aim at your hip, okay? Because I'm bigger, I'll be able to maneuver you into the position I *need* you to be in so I can lift you."

I'm just barely able to nod my consent. My breath is labored and I can scarcely stand the thought of him touching me, let alone manhandling me, without getting hot and aching all over.

Hot and aching and *wet*. I'll have to suffer through it…

He regards me, leisurely and cool, taking his sweet, sweet, tortured time studying me. Gauging. Calculating. Painfully slowly.

Under his veiled gaze, my nipples harden and his nostrils flare when those same heated eyes graze my breasts, land and stay there.

"No pearls today?" he asks.

"No pearls," I whisper.

"*Damn shame*," he whispers back.

He lowers his stance again, legs bent at a low angle, on the balls of his feet to find his center of gravity. Advances toward me with his palms outstretched, hands reaching low. Reaching until those large mitts skim the inner thigh of each leg.

My breath hitches when his thumbs stroke that clean-shaven valley between my legs before slipping his hands over my hips to cup my butt cheeks.

"That is not a wrestling technique." I gasp when he gets a little too close to my crack for comfort, glides his hands up my back and presses with light strokes.

"It should be," he mutters. "This is more exciting than the first time I had you under me, probably because this time I can see your boobs—they're fantastic."

Before I can protest, his large hands are under my thighs, grappling my ass.

My feet are hoisted effortlessly off the ground.

Lifted.

Flipping.

Back flat against the cool plastic, I'm unexpectedly sprawled out on the mat, staring at the ceiling, my loose hair fanned out around me.

My breath hitches when Oz shifts the arm he has hooked under my left leg, the calloused pads of his coarse hands gently gliding up the pale skin of my calf. He strokes it up and down until my breath comes hard.

"There, there," he soothes. "That wasn't so bad, was it?"

"You make it look so easy."

"That's because I'm good at it," he teases, hovering above me, arms cradling my head in his large palms, caressing my hair. "And because you're tiny."

"I only feel tiny because you're so big."

Everywhere.

His right eyebrow rises, mouth quirking into a smirk. "True. I am big."

Everywhere.

Those coarse fingers float deliberately over my leg, lingering at the baby fine skin near my crotch, palm flat, his thumb stroking my bare bikini line. My intake of breath is sharp; Sebastian's thumb hooks the fabric at the seam of my leotard, drawing it away from my skin, flirting dangerously close to my…to where I want it most.

Oh lord.

His touch is the barest tremor from a sigh and I feel...*so good I could orgasm from it if I let myself.*

I feel the heat rising up my chest, resisting the urge to fan the blush on my cheeks. I've never found it this hard to breathe, have I? Never found it this hard not to wiggle my hips. It takes all my willpower not to squirm beneath him. Rub. Wiggle.

I bite down a moan.

He's not my type, he's not my type, he's not my type.

"Was it really necessary for me to wear this stupid leotard?" He needs to take his hand out of it before I embarrass myself.

"No," he purrs. "Of course not, but I also didn't think it was fair for *me* to be the only one showing off the merchandise."

"And I fell for it."

"Hook, line, sinker. There's a sucker born every minute," his lips say while his fingers finally travel to stroke my hipbones.

"Are you calling me naïve?"

"No, but I'm hoping you're a sucker—because *I* am."

"Well *that* was a tad pervy."

The air around us is as thick as the cords of his neck, as the rigid length of him that's pressed against my inner thigh, straining inside the spandex singlet.

"*One.*" He hums out the count, pounding the mat with the flat of his palm. "*Two.*" His head dips. "*Three.* To the victor go the spoils."

Head bent, his tongue does a leisurely, wet glide between the valley of my plumped breasts; from the scooped neckline of my spandex, he licks all the way up to my clavicle. Slow. Sexy. Nips my collarbone and sucks.

Wet. Hot.

Wet.

Oh sweet baby Jesus holy mother of—

"Stop." I gasp when he licks my neck. "Sebastian, stop." I gasp again. *God, it feels too, too good.* "Rule number nine: don't do it if you don't mean it."

"Oh, I fucking mean it," he growls into my neck, his tongue declaring warfare on every cell in my body. Behind my ear. Across my collarbone. My aching, desperate body.

"That's not what I mean. I don't think I can do this. Not with *you*. I'm sorry; as much as I…"

As much as I want him, want his body and want the feel of him on top of me—I can't do it. I just can't do what he's done with countless other women that came before me unless I've thought it through. Spontaneous hookups aren't my thing anymore.

He pulls back to look at me, face an unreadable mask. "Don't apologize. I get it. I'll stop."

I don't even realize I'm holding my breath until I let it go, air expelling from my lungs in a disappointed puff. Stupid, stupid James, thinking maybe he'd say something different. Thinking maybe he'd try to change my mind.

Thinking maybe…

Nope.

He doesn't.

Instead, he gazes down at me, taking my measure. Taking me in. Lowers his head again and brushes the corner of my lips with his mouth. One side then the other, way too lovingly for my heart not to sob out its regret. Plants a soft kiss on my temple. Cheek. The corner of my eyes, causing them to flutter closed of their own accord. Fluttering, fluttering closed with a sigh.

That. *That* right there—my favorite spot to be kissed: the tender skin just beneath my lower lashes.

"You might be saying you can't," he hums near my ear. "But you like that, don't you, Jim?"

I muster a brutally honest and breathy, "Ugh, *yes*."

God yes.

"Should I do it again?" Purr.

Yes please, says my nod.

He does. Rains tiny kisses onto that delicate skin. Soft kisses. Caring. One at a time, the pitter patter of my beating heart keeping time with the rhythm of his gorgeous lips.

Warm *full* lips cover my mouth gently, and for the barest hint of a second, my eyes open, wanting to glimpse this tender moment between us. Remember it.

Sebastian's eyes are closed. Cheekbones high. Lips—oh those lips—resting upon mine, waiting. Seeking. Asking.

I answer, slowly parting my pout, tongue hesitantly exploring his. They mingle. *Suck.* Twirl until we're both moaning into each other.

"God, James, I want..."

His large hand rubs my inner thigh tenderly, runs the length of my hip and over the cheap polyester of my ill-fitted black leotard while his lips work my mouth. Up toward my sensitive breasts. Dragging an index finger along their undersides, he drags it languidly back and forth against my sensitive flesh until I'm arching my back, wanting him to touch me.

Do anything—*anything*—to me. Wanting more. Wanting more than a few quick strokes on a sterile gymnasium floor.

I whimper when his mouth breaks contact. "Yes Sebastian? What do you want?"

Me. Say you want *me*. Say you want to date me and spend time with me and get to know me. Not just have sex with me on a cold gym floor.

Say the words and I'm yours.

"James baby, I want you to ride me all the way to sex town."

Wait.

What?

He did not just say that. "*What* did you just say to me?"

A deep chuckle rumbles his chest. "I've always wanted to get laid on these mats. Call it a crazy kid fantasy. You up for it?"

It's official: he's a douche and the moment is ruined.

"Honestly Oz? I have no idea what to say but no. No, I don't want to have sex on these wrestling mats. I—that is not what I was expecting you to say."

His fingers brush a few errant hairs out of my eyes. "What were you expecting?"

I give a short, sardonic laugh. "I thought you liked me."

"I do like you."

"No Oz. I thought you *liked* me. Enough to, *you know...*" Oh god, how do I say this. "Enough to want something more. Last week when you went out with Sydney, it kind of hurt my feelings."

Now he's pulling away slightly, his long, firm body still hovering. "Shit, I knew you were jealous."

I count to three. "I didn't say I was jealous; I said it hurt my feelings."

"Are you asking me to commit to you James? Because I don't think I'm ready to be tied down by one person."

We lie still. Unmoving, breathing heavy, consumed by the ice-cold bucket of reality he just dumped on us both. Moments go by—I'm not sure how many—before I try shoving him off.

It's such a pitiful effort his solid mass doesn't budge.

"Tied down? No. All I said was, I thought you liked me more than some screw on a dirty gym floor. You've never even taken me out, and you've gone out with my roommate twice."

"That second one was an accident."

I cringe, not realizing until this *very* moment how much I actually care for him, how much I like him. And not just like him— I'm talking *like* like. An old-school, playground-style crush on a boy. Butterflies, sexual fantasies, daydreams, caring, emoticons.

All the feels.

All of them.

I am developing the world's biggest crush on him, developing aches for him in ways I didn't imagine were possible.

"We shouldn't even be here right now," he groans into my hair, caressing it with his mammoth palm, breathing life into my temple. My eyes flutter shut, tears threatening to spill from the corners as I listen to him carelessly natter on. "This was a mistake. If anyone from the team finds out, I'll never hear the end of it."

"Then why did you bring me here?"

He shrugs, still on top of me. "You lost the bet."

"That's the only reason?"

"What other reason would there be?"

What other reason indeed.

Jerk.

"I slapped her ass after
we had sex and left a hand print
on her butt cheek.
I told her it was like leaving
a five-star review."

Sebastian

"Heard you were in the practice gym the other day with that librarian chick."

One of my teammates approaches, dripping wet from the shower, one towel dragged over his shoulders and another wrapped around his waist.

"Yeah." I turn my back to rifle through my borrowed storage space in the visiting team locker room. "How'd you hear that?"

"Gunderson."

Gunderson? He's a freshman and team PITA (AKA Pain In The Ass), and apparently a kiss-ass snitch with his nose jammed high up Cannon's asshole.

"What else did fucking *Gunderson* tell you?" The little *fuck.*

"Nothing." My teammate laughs, tossing his towel on the bench. "Just that you had the janitor unlock the practice gym and pull out a few mats. What were you doing with her in there anyway, breaking in the new floors?"

With the funding from a generous alumna donor, the wrestling gym recently had a complete overhaul of flooring, murals, and some of the bigger equipment.

"No. I wasn't breaking in the new floor."

"So what were you doing—playing fucking Twister?"

"You know what Cannon? It's none of your business."

The short sophomore stabs a finger into his chest. "You're right—it's not *my* business, it's *all* of our fucking business. That's our gym, too, bro; you don't see me bringing chicks in there. Get your damn head in the game."

"He's right, Ozzy. You know girlfriends aren't allowed in the practice gym. Fucks with everyone's heads."

Shit, they're right.

I haven't been focused.

184

I haven't been training as hard because I've been preoccupied. This thing with Jameson has a guilty knot forming a pit in the bottom of my stomach.

The look on her face when she walked away has haunted me all week.

"She's not my girlfriend."

"Then I don't understand why you went on that snowboarding trip when you could have gone to Daytona with the team. Man, there was so much pussy it's a miracle I'm able to walk straight," a bronze Zeke calls out from a shower stall. His booming declaration echoes off the tiles and bounces off the ceiling. "My dick is still numb."

"I told you, I wanted to relax."

A snort. "Oh. Snowboarding is relaxing now, huh?"

"Well, no. But the scenery was pretty." Jameson was pretty.

Jameson *is* pretty.

"Pretty." Zeke's voice is flat, unimpressed. I hear him pause. "The *fuck*, dude."

"Wait," Aaron Bower cuts in. "At least tell us you got laid on that trip. I mean, there had to have been snow bunnies somewhere, right? MILFs? Bored housewives with Hoover-like suction?"

He makes a sucking sound with his mouth, pumping his fist against his cheek, mimicking a blowjob.

"Right?" Zeke agrees, still inside the shower. "Last time my mom went on a trip during spring break, she fucked some douchie Ivy Leaguer hanging out by the hotel pool."

"Daniels, your mom sounds like a lady slut," comes a taunting shout.

"Up yours, Santiago."

The water in the shower cuts off and Zeke steps out, dripping wet, toweling off. Undeterred, he wraps the towel around his neck, letting his balls air dry as he turns to me.

"So. Did you at least get laid?"

I roll my eyes and make a show of digging through my cubby.

"What do *you* think," I posture, neither confirming nor denying the claim.

A hand claps me on the back. "That's my boy. Who was it?"

"Please tell us it was the slutty librarian chick I keep hearing about," John begs. "That is who you went with, right?"

Someone lets out a loud, sardonic laugh.

Zeke.

"Yeah right. That bitch? She's wound up tighter than Betty the actual librarian."

I ease myself down onto a nearby wooden bench and sit ram-rod straight while they hassle me, mock Jameson, and shoot the shit.

"Have you tapped that yet?" another teammate asks, referring to Jameson again.

"I don't know, Santiago—do people still say *tapped?*"

"Tapped. Fucked. Screwed. Banged. Shagged. You like any of those better, pansy? You're starting to sound like your virgin girlfriend."

"She's not my girlfriend." Not even close—I saw to that on Monday.

The guilty pit in my stomach churns.

"Oh yeah? You seem to be spending a lot of fucking time at the library these days *studying* with someone you claim not to give a shit about." Zeke uses air quotes around the word studying.

What a douche.

I pull my socks on, the impulse to defend Jameson strong. Defend myself. *Us.* "I never said I gave a shit about her."

"So then why are you always at the library, dude?"

"Just tryin' to maintain my average."

Zeke, always confrontational, stares me down hard. "Your average."

"My GPA," I clarify. "Grade point average."

"I know what a fucking grade point average is, dickhole."

My dark eyes bore into him. "You seem really pissed off for

some reason. Did someone take a dump in your oatmeal this morning? Didn't you blow off any steam locking Rogers in that half nelson an hour ago?"

"Maybe I *am* pissed. Maybe I don't want you dating a prig. It gives the rest of the bores false hope."

"You're a dick."

He laughs, almost maniacally. "Never said I wasn't."

A loud, roaring shout carries over the locker room, echoing from the office. "Osborne. Daniels. This isn't a pissing match. Get your goddamn asses dressed and on the bus. You have eight minutes."

Zeke grunts out his disappointment, leveling me with an icy glower before going to his own cubby. He yanks out his duffle bag, calling out over his shoulder, "This isn't over Osborne. Far from it."

"My dream, late night booty call would live right next to a McDonald's so I could bone her, then grab a burger."

Sebastian

I stumble into the house, exhausted from the long bus ride and Zeke's continued badgering during the five hours it took to get us home. He criticized. He fumed. He bitched until my head rolled to the side and I popped on my Beats to drown out the sound with music.

I'm tired.

I'm starving.

I'm ready for warm food and a soft bed.

It's quiet when I drop my bags in the laundry room, first one back at the house. Hanging my duffle and removing my jacket, I make quick work of taking my shoes off and setting them aside.

I flip on the kitchen light and pad, sock footed, to the fridge. Yanking it open, I stare into it, blinded by the bright light, contemplating the slim pickings: three-day-old spaghetti sauce, a half-eaten hamburger, yogurt. There's a gallon of orange juice left, some filtered water, and an open bottle of Dr. Pepper.

My choices suck dick.

Bemoaning the fact that I didn't stop and grab something fast on my way home, I grab the leftover Malone's hamburger and yogurt, slap them both on a plate, and lean against the counter.

Where the hell is everyone? I grab my phone and tap out a quick text to my roommate.

Oz: *Where are you?*

Zeke: *Stopped for food.*

Shit.

Oz: *Grab me something would ya. Starving.*

Zeke: *Yup. Back in thirty.*

He might be a total dick, but he's a dick that's going to feed my hungry ass.

Satisfied that a meal is on its way, I dump the burger and yogurt in the trash, grab my bag, and head down the hallway for a hasty shower.

It takes me a total of six minutes, beginning to end.

Throwing on mesh shorts and a ratty old tee shirt, I head to my room and down the carpeted hall, pausing in front of my roommate's door. Giving it a few short raps of my knuckle, I don't hesitate to turn the handle.

Not wanting to wake him if he's sleeping, I push the door open slowly, the dim light from within an indication that he's home and awake.

"Hey, Elliot?"

My eyes stray to the bed, lingering on two entwined figures, namely my roommate humping the *shit* out of some girl, humping her into his mattress like it's his last chance at a lay.

Their moaning fills the air.

Momentarily stunned, it takes me a moment to recover. "Oh shit! Sorry man."

I should have shut the door then, should have backed away and gone to my room, but the sight of my roommate's white thighs driving fervently into whatever chick he's railing has me staring incredulously.

Conservative Elliot never brings girls home. *Never.*

Not once.

Well, I shouldn't say never, but the occasions are so rare I can't remember the last time it happened. It's not his style, so I'm going to assume this isn't some fling.

This must be a girl he's been seeing but hasn't introduced us to.

Someone he probably really likes.

So I should shut the door and walk away, be happy he's getting his rocks off.

But I don't.

Shame on me.

My eyes stray to the floor, to the discarded undergarments. The sheer lace bra. Lavender satin thong (nice choice). Jeans. Black patent leather ballet flats. White car—

Wait.

Black ballet flats?

White cardigan.

White fucking *cardigan?*

My eyes shoot to the bed, the tangle of sheets. Male moaning. A female gasp I'm all too familiar with.

Long, glossy hair spills over Elliot's navy pillow, his arms braced on the sides of the brunette's face as he frantically pumps and pumps and rails his hips into her while she gasps in pleasure.

Fucks her.

Fucks *fucking* Jameson.

It's her, I just *know* it.

In a rage, my mouth opens and I take a few steps toward them, intending to—to what? Pull him off her mid-thrust? Start a fight? *Fuck!* My squeak of outrage must alert them because Jameson opens her eyes, lifting her head listlessly off the pillow in a groggy, sex-induced haze.

Elliot's fingers cup her ass, digging in near her crack, and I see red when he squeezes. See red when she giggles and moans.

"*You're so amazing,*" she whimpers, and I watch in stunned horror as she licks my name off her lips. "You're the best, the best…*right there…yes!*"

I watch, speechless, as she pants. Coming.

Coming.

Our eyes meet, hers glassy with ecstasy and she smiles, head rolling back in a sated, drunken state. Elliot sucks her neck, his dirty tongue running up the length of her throat.

Fuck, fuck, fuck me hard.

I smash his door shut so hard it cracks, shuddering on its hinges, and thunder down the hallway. Throw open my door. It bangs against the wall, bouncing back from the force. Pacing, I walk back and forth in the confinement of my room like a goddamn caged tiger, counting to regain my composure.

One, two, five. Ten.

I stalk back out into the hall, breathless like I've just sprinted eight miles, and fight the urge to punch the fucking wall separating Elliot's room from the hall.

I wait.

I'm leaning against the wall outside his door when she comes out, wearing nothing but his tee shirt. His fucking tee shirt. I'm reminded of our trip to Utah—of her wearing nothing but *my* gray wrestling shirt—and almost lose my shit all over again.

I count to five, noting with satisfaction her startled gasp when she sees me, a gasp not unlike the one I heard a half-hour ago when she was screwing me over.

Screwing my roommate.

"*Hi!*" Spiteful, my high-pitched and cheerful greeting is anything but pleasant. "What's up?!"

I'm sure I sound psychotic, but I'm just so fucking pissed.

She looks left, looks right for a rescue. Sorry honey, no one's coming to save you. "If you have to take a pee, or gee, I don't know, *toss a condom in the trash*, the bathroom is down the hall to the left."

Aren't I just the goddamn welcoming committee? Tone it down a notch, Osborne.

Instead of making her way to the bathroom, Jameson leans against the wall, mimicking my stance. Ramrod straight, back against the wall, left knee propped up, foot touching the drywall.

"You're back early," she says pleasantly. "How'd the wrestling meet go?"

Arms crossed, I study her. Flushed cheeks, tousled hair, eyes a little wild...the post-gasm look is unbelievably sexy on her.

I cut to the chase. "How long has this been going on?"

Her head hits the wall behind her with a soft thump. "Just this once. But it was our second date."

"Since *when*?"

"We've been casually texting since the house party."

Sonofabitch. That was at least two weeks ago. *Or has it been three?*

"When were you going to tell me?"

An ironic laugh leaves her throat. "I wasn't."

"Why? I've been chasing you around for weeks; you'll fuck *him* but you won't fuck me?"

"This isn't a contest, and please lower your voice."

"Why."

"Why what?"

"Why would you let him..." I swallow, unable to get the words out. Goddammit if this whole thing isn't making me feel like complete and utter shit.

Her answer is a dry laugh. "Oh please—don't tell me this *bothers* you. *You* who won't commit. *You* who get hand-jobs and blowies from anyone with a pulse." An unladylike snort. "Give me a flipping break."

I stab a finger in her direction. "You're fucking nuts if you think I'm going to be okay with this."

"This has nothing to do with you."

"Bullshit. This has everything to do with me! You moaned my name. My. Name."

Her only response is a nonchalant shrug that makes me want to pin her to the wall and show her what she really means to me.

"Did you sleep with him to make me jealous? To bring me to heel? Because I'm telling you right now Jameson, it won't fucking work. All it did was piss me off."

A long, soft sigh. "He's a nice guy, Oz. I like him. We might not be dating or a couple, but at least he's not going to make me feel used and cheap in the morning. He won't make me feel like a number. I'll still have my dignity when I walk out of here."

"What are you fucking talking about?" I poke a thumb into my chest. "I treat you with respect."

"Calm down and *lower your voice*," she hisses. "God, Sebastian, everything isn't always about *you*. Did it ever occur to you that maybe I don't want to be with someone who wants me to *ride him to sex town?*"

I silently count to ten and take a deep calming breath, clenching my fists at my sides. "Why won't you let me *fuck* you?"

She studies me, cool, calm, and collected. Shoulders back and dignified, as if she's already thought this through and knows the answer. "Because you say things like 'why won't you let me fuck you.' You think I don't *want* you? You're wrong. I do. I lie in bed thinking of you every night; I *dream* of you Sebastian. But I'm not a fool. You will *break* my heart."

"So this is your solution? Sleep with someone else? My freaking roommate, of all people."

"I didn't do this to hurt you."

"It's too late for that! How could you do this to me, Jameson? Tell me! I didn't screw *your* roommate when *I* had the chance."

Her face falls. Shoulders sag. "I guess I...wanted to feel good. I wanted pleasure. I wanted an orgasm. I haven't had sex in forever, and Elliot was the safe choice."

"Oh my fucking god." My fists clench, wanting to punch the wall behind me. "This is such horse shit."

Jameson crosses her arms. "I've made up my mind."

"I've never lied to you about who I am."

"And I *love* that about you, but—"

"But what?" I can't keep the bitter taste out of my mouth.

"Wonderful and awful," she whispers. "Beautiful and forgettable. *That's* how you make me feel, all at the same time."

"How can you stand there and say that? I adore you! I think you're beautiful. I can't go a minute without thinking about you, the way you smell and the way you're always pulling your hair back, or tapping your pen when you're concentrating. You drive me crazy."

"It's not enough."

"Don't do this Jameson; don't say that shit. Please, you're breaking my heart."

She backs away, stepping toward my roommate's door. "You won't do it on purpose, Sebastian, but you're just going to end up breaking *mine*."

I swallow the hard lump in my throat. "And I suppose Elliot won't."

She gives her head a sad little shake. "Elliot won't."

And that's the pisser of it all, right there. Elliot won't, because Elliot is a great fucking guy who actually deserves a girl like Jameson Clark; I guess that makes me the asshole with no time, a shit ton of debt, the busted up body, and the crude temperament. The guy who sleeps with too many women, who gets sloppy drunk and receives blowjobs from strangers.

Fucking Elliot and his goddamn golden halo.

I'm going to beat the shit out of him. First, I'm going to grab him by his saggy balls. Then, I'm going to sucker punch him right in his fucking face. Then—

I shove off the wall and paste on a fake smile. "Fine. I'll just leave you to it then. Have funsies."

She looks devastated, shoulders falling. "It wasn't supposed to be like this."

I walk away, toward my bedroom at the end of the hallway, pausing when I reach my door. "Hey James?"

She's still standing where I left her, rooted to the spot. Her chin quivers. "Yes?"

"I want you gone by morning."

I don't have to wait that long.

Fifteen minutes after our confrontation in the hall, I hear Elliot's bedroom door open, the sound of muffled voices, and footfalls outside my door. They hesitate before moving down the corridor toward the entryway.

The front door opens and clicks closed. I numbly listen to every sound, still trying to figure out what the hell just happened here.

What in the actual shit happened?

Hands behind my head, bedside lamp still glowing, I stare up at the ceiling fan and—call me a sadist—do my absolute best to recount every detail of what I walked in on: *Jameson moaning. Elliot's white farmer's-tanned ass pumping into her. Jameson's half-hooded eyes as she comes. Her mouth forming the shape of my name as she gets banged by another dude.*

I try a dozen times to piece it all together—then a dozen more, failing miserably time and again.

Jameson having sex because she wants to feel good. Having sex with someone else, because it feels good, with someone who isn't me. Cause she wanted an orgasm and pleasure. Naked in the room next to mine, in a bed that's not mine, in my house.

Did I mention naked?

Jameson getting railed by my roommate. In my house.

Jameson.

Elliot.

Jameson and Elliot.

Elliot finally getting laid, by Jameson, whose pants I've been trying to get into for weeks. Elliot, my friend, who deserves a girl like Jameson, who banged him because she wanted to feel good.

I wonder if life is going outside to have a smoke right now, because it just got done fucking me.

Fucking me hard.

Logically, none of this makes sense.

Yes, I might have come on a little strong with Jameson, but

she doesn't even *know* Elliot. How do you jump into bed with someone you've met at a party *once* and flirt with in a few freaking texts? Who does that!

Fine. I do.

I toss and turn, pounding my pillow into a useless lump, aware of my own hypocrisy. And yes, I might be a hypocrite, but at least I'm not exhibiting uncharacteristic behavior. Not like *she* is. Sleeping with strangers is what *I* do, what I've always done. It's easy, fast, and doesn't involve any effort.

No follow-through or emotions required.

Jameson might not be a virgin, but I can god*damn* guarantee she's doesn't sleep around. She can't.

Not the way I do.

Did.

Do.

Shit, shit, shit, my mind is a mess.

I can't even form my thoughts straight, thoughts that have me sitting up and climbing out of bed and storming down the hallway to Elliot's room. I bust through his door, not bothering to knock.

"Why did you do it?"

He's seated on the bed in nothing but his boxers, flipping through Netflix, and the sight of his hairless bare chest pisses me off.

"Do what?"

"Don't be obtuse," I spit out. "You had *sex* with Jameson."

"So?" Elliot's sandy brown hair sticks up around his ears and he swipes the unkempt locks from his brow. "Since when is it a crime to have sex with a hot, willing female?"

The words 'hot' and 'willing' have the hairs on the back of my neck prickling. My fists clench at my sides, wanting to strike.

"Watch it," I threaten as Elliot looks toward me like I've lost my damn mind—and maybe I have. "You watch the way you're talking about her."

His brows rise. "I can't call her hot?"

"No."

He gets up off the bed and makes his way to the closet, pulling out a sweatshirt. "Look, I don't know what your fucking problem is, but spit it out already. It's late and I'm spent."

Spent?

Spent?

"I want to beat the shit out of you so fucking bad," I growl, still rooted to my spot by the door, watching him pull the sweatshirt over his head. "Please give me a reason to beat you senseless."

He pulls the hem down and his hands go up in surrender. "Whoa dude, I have no idea what you're talking about—are... Shit, man. Are you dating Jameson? Is that what this is about? Did—holy shit—is she *cheating* on you? With me?"

His eyes widen in horror as the idea takes root in his brain. "Holy shit, she is, isn't she? She's cheating on you. Holy shit. Oh my god. Don't hurt me."

Elliot looks like he's about to hyperventilate or piss himself—or both—so I take pity on him.

"No, she didn't cheat on me with you! Jesus Christ, we're not even dating."

His shoulders sag and he breathes out a long sigh of relief. "Thank fucking god!" Confused brown eyes meet mine. "Wait, then why are you so mad?"

"I..."

I don't know.

"I...have no idea."

Elliot's head tilts as he studies me, takes measure of my stance and expression. "Hold up. Oz, do you... Are you in *love* with her?"

"Love?" I scoff a little too loudly. "No. Hell no." But I find myself hesitating on my next words just the same. "She's just my friend."

My friend.

Just my friend? The words make me ill and suddenly I want to vomit.

"Dude. You should see yourself right now; I can't freaking believe this."

"What?"

"You *do* like her. Like her, like her."

"Shut up Elliot, this isn't fifth grade."

"Don't let your lobster get away, man."

My lobster? What the hell is he talking about? "Please don't ever say shit like that in my presence again or I *will* have to punch you."

"Wow, I can't believe this; Oz Osborne, Iowa's prodigal wrestling legend, actually has a heart."

"I said shut up, asshole."

But he doesn't shut his hole. Not even close. "You have actual feelings for someone. You don't just want to bang her."

"Didn't I just tell you to shut up?"

"Look man, I really don't even know what to say. I'm sorry. Shit. If I'd known, I never would have…"

He never would have slept with her; I know that now.

How do I know?

One, because he's loyal and isn't ruled by his dick—unlike the rest of us. Elliot is ruled more by emotion. So if he slept with Jameson, it's because he genuinely likes her. Two, because he knows if he fucks me over, I'll beat the fucking shit out of him.

So the simple fact remains…it sucks more knowing *she* chose to sleep with *him*.

I just don't get it; I'm *awesome*—how can she not see that? Where the hell did I go wrong with her? Was I too pushy? Did I scare her off? *Don't hate me*, I hear her pleading. See her tears. Jameson is weeping, wet drops dampening her beautiful face. My eyes water, too, and I reach for her, grasping as tears stream down my cheeks, but there's nothing there to hold. *I didn't know it would hurt you,* she sobs. *I didn't know… Please Sebastian, I'm falling for you.*

"Then how could you fucking do this to me!" I cry. "I'm fall-ing in love with you and you ruined it. You ruined everything."

Sebastian, I love you. Sebastian, I love you.

Sebastian. Oz, can you hear me?

Oz.

Oz.

"Oz, dude wake up."

I gasp out in a sob, jerking myself awake. "Holy shit!"

A large, meaty palm is clamped down on my shoulder, squeezing hard and, startled, I jolt, the back of my head hitting the cold window of the bus, my temple cracking against the hard glass. *Sonofabitch that hurt!*

"Oz, is everything okay man?'

I become aware of the sensation of damp, streaking tears staining my cheeks, and I briskly wipe them away with the back of my hand, embarrassed.

"It's fine. *I'm* fine."

Freaked the fuck out—but fine.

I rub the spot where I just clocked myself, fingers grazing through my sweaty hair, and glance around at my oblivious team-mates, most of them still asleep, save Cory Phillips playing on his phone and Tanner Frank reading on his Kindle under the overhead light.

I exhale, leaning back in the seat, and swipe at another stray tear.

"You sure you're okay?" Jonathan Powell's head reappears over the seat behind me. Lights from the campus parking lot come into view, illuminating the interior of the bus. "Sorry to wake you up and freak you out, but we're pulling in."

"Yeah." I massage my scalp. "I'm good. Thanks for waking me."

It was just a dream.

The whole thing was just a dream. A shitty, messed up dream.

200

In a trancelike state, I stumble off the bus. Go through the motions of dressing, storing my gear, and checking in with the coaching staff. Get my schedule for the upcoming week.

Barely remember the car ride home.

By the time I'm falling into the house, I'm exhausted. Zeke's continued badgering the five hours it took to get us home has taken its toll, coupled with my emotionally taxing dream. Zeke criticized. He fumed. He bitched until my head lolled to the side and I popped on my Beats to drown him out with music.

I lumber into the kitchen, glancing around cautiously.

I'm tired.

I'm starving.

I'm ready for warm food and a soft bed, but being here, in this house after that wacked out dream feels way too fucking weird.

This all feels way too real.

Just like in my dream, it's quiet when I drop my bags in the laundry room, still the first one back at the house. Just like in my dream, I hang my duffle and remove my jacket, make quick work of taking my shoes off and setting them aside so no one trips on them.

Flipping on the kitchen lights, I walk to the fridge, yank it open, and bend at the waist to peer inside. Three-day-old spaghetti sauce and no noodles. A half-eaten hamburger from Malone's. One yogurt. Ketchup. Beer.

A half-gallon of chocolate milk (perfect to help prevent a hangover). There's also a gallon of orange juice left, some filtered water, and an open bottle of Dr. Pepper.

Having no appealing choices, I settle for the leftover Malone's hamburger, the yogurt, and the gallon of milk, slapping everything onto the counter.

Where the hell is everyone? I grab my phone and tap out a quick text to my roommates.

Oz: *Where are you?*

Zeke is the first to respond: *Stopped for food.*

Okay. That's weird as shit and kind of freaking me out.

Oz: *Grab me something would ya. Starving.*
Zeke: *Yup. Back in thirty.*

This whole thing is just way too bizarre to be real.

I lift the lid on the garbage can and dump the burger, grab my bag, and head down the hallway, wavering in front of Elliot's door. I stop. Take a deep breath. Give it a few short raps.

"Yeah?" his voice answers from inside.

"You awake?" I hesitate to open the door.

"Uh, *yeah.*"

Gradually, I turn the knob. Give the door a gentle push. Stick my head partially inside, like a father not wanting to walk in on his teenage daughter. "You decent?"

"Dude, what's your problem?" Elliot laughs. "Yeah I'm decent." He's sitting at his desk staring at me like I've sprouted two cocks and a vagina. "What's up?" He spins in his desk chair, resting his arm on the back of it, idly waiting for me to respond.

"Letting you know we're back." Obviously.

"*Okay.*"

"Everything good?" I can't help it; I throw several shifty glances into the recesses of his bedroom, browsing for a glimpse of...

My eyes land on the bed and stay there.

And stare.

Everything appears to be in order. Navy blue comforter pulled into place. Pillows at the headboard. A short stack of clean, folded clothes at the footboard.

No black patent leather shoes. No white cardigan. No naked Jameson.

No fucking has taken place here, I'm sure of it.

After an awkwardly long silence, Elliot clears his throat. "You're being really weird. Are you sure you're okay?" He pauses. "Do you want to, uh, talk or whatever?"

His appalled tone says it all: *please say no.*

"No, I'm good." Elliot's shoulders drop in relief. "I just thought I saw...nothing."

Visibly relieved, my roommate continues to regard me curiously loitering in the doorway. "So...anything else?"

"Huh? No. We're good."

He's not convinced but he's not going to press. "All right, *welllll.*"

And that's my cue to leave.

"Right. Well. G'night."

Stoically I trudge down to my bedroom, close the door behind me, and flop down, face first, on the bed.

25

#DOUCHEBAG

"She's really hot but sounds like a Saturday morning cartoon. Can you imagine what it would sound like fucking her? I'd rather stick my dick in a bowl of Captain Crunch."

Sebastian

Here's where it gets really shitty: I can't even look at her. Sitting across from me, Jameson glances up and nails me with that cute little smile, her top front teeth playing peekaboo beneath her pretty top lip when she bites down.

Instead of smiling back at her like a normal human being, the image of her face when she climaxes fogs my mind and I glower.

"Wow." She grins. "Such a sourpuss today."

I fixate on the word puss, because it sounds like *pussy* and I can't keep my mind out of the damn gutter—but I don't dare tell her I'm crabby because thoughts of her kept me awake all night, because I've been daydreaming about her during the day, on the bus between matches, during practice—and every minute since.

I can't stop thinking about her.

The smell of her gorgeous hair.

The way her sweet, conservative sweaters cling to her fantastically round boobs.

Her smile when she finally catches sight of me walking into the library toward our table.

That delightful way she ignores me when she's trying to study.

The cute way she piles all her crap in my chair so I can't sit in it without a hassle.

God she's adorable.

Oz.

Oz?

"Are you listening to me? Hey. Oz, are you listening? Oz. Is everything okay?"

I glance up and realize she's staring at me expectantly, has been asking questions and probably expecting a coherent response.

Say something, jackass.

"Everything is fine."

But it's not fine. *Not any more.* Not even close.

She knows enough not to push, and for once, because I have no idea how to handle these feelings brewing inside me, *I* ignore *her*.

"Why on earth would
I ever need a boyfriend?
I have a huge bed all to myself,
a drawer full of vibrators,
and I'm smart enough to change
my own motor oil."

Jameson

Oz is acting strange.

Again.

Just because my head is bent and I'm seemingly concentrating on my studying doesn't mean I don't notice him watching me, doesn't mean I don't notice his labored breaths, his restless ticks, and the fact that he's analyzing me so closely it turns my cheeks a hot, blushing pink.

I ignore the heat, desperately fighting the temptation to press my hands to my face. I keep my nose to the grind, feigning interest in my textbook.

I've read the same sentence six times.

Seven.

Eight.

And counting.

He's been like this for the past two days, sitting with me to study but avoiding anything resembling an actual conversation. Giving me one-word answers. Watching me under that baseball cap with dark, broody eyes. Hasn't made a single attempt to sleep with me, flirt, or move us to a private study room.

Like I said: strange.

Across the table, I let him look his fill an entire ten minutes before I can't take it any more. I raise my head slowly. Meet his intense gaze. Push my glasses up the bridge of my nose, perch them atop my head.

Set my highlighter down and cross my hands primly in front of me on the table.

"*What.*" No beating around the bush for *this* girl.

"What?" he parrots, playing dumb.

"I know you have something to say. So *say* it."

He gives his head a stubborn shake, lips pursed. "Nope.

We're good, Jimbo."

Liar.

But if that's how he wants to play it… "Fine. Never mind then."

He frowns, lines etched across his angry, handsome face when I unfold my hands, grab my highlighter, and resume reading.

Pretend to anyway.

Oz continues to gape, silently taking inventory of my movements. Sullen eyes trail the long strokes of fresh pink marker ink across my paper. Follow my hand when I slip the glasses back down onto my face. Skim over my shoulders when I brush away a strand of hair.

He's done this all before, gawked at me—many times in fact—but somehow this is different. His gaze is more thoughtful. More penetrating. More engrossed.

I'm not sure why, and I'm not sure when, but something has changed. The air between us has shifted. It's thick. Heated.

Serious.

I try again, eyes still locked on my textbook. "*What.* Out with it."

I don't mean to sound so annoyed, but this odd silent treatment coupled with those dark eyes boring into me is making me mental.

"Would you please say something?" Once again, I set down my highlighter. "I don't know what's going on with you lately, but I'm over here *not* getting anything done. You and your heavy breathing are weirding me out and driving me loco."

He tears his gaze away and looks to the opposite side of the room before responding.

"Nothing is going on." He removes his hat to run the tips of his fingers through his glorious hair. It sticks up on end, disheveled. "It's just been a rough few nights, that's all."

Ahhh, a rough few nights; that information I can work with.

"How so?"

"I…haven't been sleeping the greatest." He sounds reluctant to admit it, but I press on.

"Why?"

Oz shifts uncomfortably. "Just some fucked up dreams. No big deal, but it's the same one every night."

I pause. "What are the dreams about?"

Oz shifts again. "Nothing."

"Nothing?" I ask skeptically. "Dreams about nothing don't keep you awake every night, Sebastian."

"*These* dreams about nothing do." He winces.

"So they're not about nothing—they're about *some*thing."

His nose scrunches up. "Are you purposely trying to confuse me?"

"Is it working?"

"Yes."

"So you'll tell me what they're about?"

"Sure, why the hell not."

"Wait, wait, wait!" I put my hand up. "Stop! Before you blurt it out, let me guess; are they about the zombie apocalypse coming to melt your face off and you can't escape no matter how fast you run?"

His mouth tics. "Nope."

"Does this have anything to do with your parents or your sister?"

"Nope."

Tapping my chin with my highlighter, I pretend to think long and hard. "You're falling into a dark hole, a place with no Netflix and chill, no wrestling, and you can't get a single girl to shag you."

"You're a smartass, do you know that?"

"I'm right though, aren't I? This somehow involves sex."

His heavy brow lifts a tad. "You're getting warmer. Yup. I'd say you were warm."

I roll my eyes. "Of course it involves sex. How predictable of you." A sigh escapes my lips. "Did someone use too much teeth giving you a blowjob?" I ponder before instantaneously slapping a hand over my mouth. "Oh my god, did I just say that out loud?"

He's turning me into a pervert.

"You sure did, but no worries; no blowjobs were harmed in the making of my dream."

"So it wasn't a nightmare?"

"Oh no, it was—it definitely was."

"I wasn't in it, was I?" I joke. "Star of the show, that's me! Ha ha."

He doesn't reply. Just sits there, and…

"Oz." My eyes close momentarily and I speak slowly. "*Please* tell me I'm not in your pervy sex dream."

"Tsk, tsk—I just said it was a nightmare," he clarifies. "Not a dream."

"Semantics." I wave him off. "*Please* tell me I wasn't the star your perverted sex *nightmare*."

"Fine. I won't tell you." Oz rolls his eyes skyward really dramatically; it's overdone because that sorry bastard is lying and we both know it.

I clear my throat. "This wasn't a…um…*fantasy*, was it?" I struggle to get the words out, cheeks flaming.

"Hell no. It was definitely a nightmare. How many times do I have to say it?" He downs some of his water bottle and I watch the thick column of his neck raptly when he tips his head back to swallow.

"*But*," Oz begins, sagging his shoulders and casually studying his fingernails. "Would it be so bad if it was?"

Would it be so bad if I was his fantasy? No, it wouldn't. It wouldn't be bad at all.

In fact, I bet it would be *stupid* good.

And that's part of the problem, isn't it? The *good*ness. Earth-shattering, life-altering sex with Sebastian would be good. Great. Phenomenal. Those pecs, those hips, those thighs. That incredible dick he has snugly tucked into his jeans.

But at what cost? Am I willing to give up a small chunk of my heart that I may never get back? I'm not a commitment-phobe by any means; I've never had my heart broken. I've never been cheated on. I've never been in love.

So what is my damn problem?

Fear of the unknown. The intensity I feel when I'm with him. The uncertainty of what he feels for me besides physical attraction. Falling in love with him. Him not falling in love with me. Unrequited love. Infidelity.

Embarking on something he may start but never want to finish.

I've never wanted to pursue more of *something* before.

And now maybe I do.

See there?

I just figured out my own problem.

Now   what?

"I can't remember what happened
last night, but this morning
I found his underwear wrapped
around a pack of hot dogs
in the fridge."

Jameson

Oz: *On the bus to Ohio.*

Jameson: *Really? I didn't realize you had games—I mean, matches—in the middle of the school week.*

Oz: *Yeah. Midweek, weekend. This match is against Ohio State. I can get you a printed schedule if you want one?*

I stare at the phone, not sure how to respond. He'll get me a schedule? For what? Doe he seriously want me keeping tabs on him? For me to know where he is?

Kind of like a girlfriend, and we both know he doesn't want one of those.

Jameson: *Um, okay. Sure. A schedule would be cool. For my fridge? LOL*

Oz: *Yeah, for your fridge. Or desk. We have a match at home next week against Indiana. You could come if you wanted. The action is slightly better than a single light bulb in the middle of a gym floor.*

Jameson: *That one light dangling above the mats was super creepy. It had a decidedly rapey vibe.*

Oz: *That wasn't a RAPEY VIBE—that was mood lighting; I was trying to be romantic.*

Jameson: *YOU WERE NOT. STOP IT*

Oz: *Lol. So you're saying the romance was a fail?*

Jameson: *I doubt that's what you were doing, but in any* *case, it was a fail. LOL*

Jameson: *I mean, you had me by the crotch and flipped on my back onto a dirty, plastic mat.*

Oz: *I'll have you know, those mats are brand new and get wiped down daily…*

Jameson: **throws hands in air* I stand corrected*

The phone sits silent for a few moments before it pings with a new notification. My heart races uncontrollably as I sit on the edge of my bed to open the new message.

Oz: *Hey Jameson?*

Sitting up straighter, I'm instantly on alert, because when a guy uses your full name in a text message, shit is about to get serious. Even I, who hasn't had a date in months, know this as fact.

Me: *Yes Sebastian?*

In my mind, that yes is breathy and wistful, and comes out on a sigh. Too bad it doesn't translate via text.

Oz: *When I get back in three days, I think we should*

The message is cut off, and nothing follows.
I think we should.
I think we should…
What!
What do you think we should *do?*
Dying a slow death, I wait impatiently for the second part to come through. *I think we should…*what? *I think we should* make out again? *I think we should* meet in the library? *I think we should*

date?

What. What *for the love of god* should we do!

"Sweet Jesus, where's the rest of the text? Where is it!" I shout to the walls of my bedroom, shaking the crap out of my cell and thanking God my roommates aren't home to witness my incessant grumbling as I jiggle the phone back to life.

I wait, and wait—then wait some more—for him to finish that short sentence, for the little blue light in the upper left hand corner to blink.

Finally, sick of the torture, I grow a pair of lady balls and text him back: *What should we do?*

Two minutes pass.

Then three.

Then eighteen.

Then two hours.

Then ten.

And still, nothing. I get nothing.

It's agony.

28
#DOUCHEBAG

"I have an amazing penis
and an average personality."

Sebastian

"I thought I asked you not to wear that tank top to bed, especially when I'm not allowed to touch you." I watch Jameson from across the hotel room from the center of the bed.

She pulls the fabric away from her form, glancing down at the sheer white garment. "What is your obsession with this shirt?"

"I'm not obsessed with it. I just don't want you wearing it."

"That makes no sense. My boyfriend loves this shirt; when I wear it, it reminds me of him."

"Boyfriend?" Since when does James have a boyfriend who's not me, and why am I just finding out about it?

I watch her cross the room to stand in front of the large sliding glass door; heavy snow falls in sheets across the windows, our Utah snowboarding trip blessed with several inches of fresh powder.

"Yes, my boyfriend." Jameson rolls her eyes. "Elliot? Remember him? Your roommate and the love of my life?"

The love of her life?

I laugh, frowning when it sounds foreign and forced. "Since when?"

"Since you're too busy for a girlfriend, that's when. Wrestling, friends, studying, your job—remember when you told me you weren't ready to be tied down? Well we all have our priorities, Sebastian." Her smooth, delicate hands find the hem of her threadbare tank top and she tugs it up past her flat stomach. "I'm not yours."

Up and over her bare, taut breasts.

My mouth waters and my hand flies to the burgeoning bulge in my gym shorts, stroking.

"No touching. No looking. All this is just for Elliot." She

pushes down the waistband of her pajama bottoms. "You won't be tied down to one person, remember?"

Remember? "I never said that."

I would never say that. Would I?

Did I?

"You did. And now you're going to lose me."

Jameson pushes the sliding glass door open and the curtains billow like clouds around her ankles. A gust of wind carries in thousands of cold, shimmering snowflakes; they stick to her hair, glistening before melting into her warm skin.

She turns her back, stepping out into the frigid winter storm.

"Where are you going? James, come back!"

"You're losing me, Sebastian," her voice whispers. *You're losing me. You're losing me.*

Gasping, I open my mouth, but no sound comes out.

Somewhere in the hotel a door slams. Water from a faucet. Light streaming in from the bathroom on the far side of the room.

"Wake up, fuck stick. Time for warm ups."

Huh?

"I'm not covering for your ass if you're not outside by five."

I crack an eye open and peer over at one of my teammates— my roommate for this trip to Ohio—who's lacing up his running shoes.

"Did you hear me?" he asks. "Get moving."

"Yeah, I heard you." I roll with a moan toward my cell. "Jeez, what time is it?"

"Four forty-five. Time to grease the tires." He lobs a damp bath towel toward the bed but misses. "You look like shit, by the way. Get any sleep last night? You were mumbling all night, whining like a little bitch."

"No." No, I didn't sleep, because I did nothing but toss and turn, sweat and moan, and talk in my sleep.

"What was I saying?"

My teammate laughs. "You were calling out some dude's

name and begging him not to leave you. When you started to cry, I had to put a pillow over my head."

Shit. "Sorry man."

"Whatever. You're lucky I didn't put the pillow over your head instead." He grabs a pair of dirty shorts from the floor, tossing them at my head. "Time to hustle."

"Stop throwing shit, I'm up, I'm up."

I rise from the bed to quickly move through my morning ritual—piss, brush my teeth, get dressed—mind on one thing, and one thing alone: Jameson Clark.

#DOUCHEBAG

"Nothing says regret like the dick
of someone you don't know,
yet slept with, poking you in the
ass crack the next morning."

Jameson

Something is ringing.

One eye pries open, head flops to the side, and fuzzily I ogle my nightstand. My phone buzzes and rings, doing a happy little samba across the flat wooden surface. It's loud, obnoxious, and annoying—exactly like it's supposed to be.

I slap at my phone and snatch it up with a groan when it's in the palm of my hand.

I blink at the unidentified number calling, but nonetheless swipe to accept, letting the call connect.

"Hello," I rasp groggily.

5:37 is not a good look for me.

"James?" The voice is vaguely familiar. Masculine. Deep and sexy and familiar.

"Huh?"

"It's me."

God I'm tired. Am I even awake? What day is it? "Me who?"

Deep chortle. "Sebastian."

My eyes pop open in a panic, because why on earth would he be calling this early unless there was an emergency? I struggle to sit up. "Oz? Sebastian! Is everything okay?"

"Yeah, no—everything is *great.*"

I am literally *going to kill this guy when he gets back.*

"You're calling me at five in the morning cause everything is *great?*"

"Yes and no. It took me this long to find a phone to use."

"But it's still dark outside."

Pulling the phone away from my ear, I gaze down at the number, dazed and confused. Not his number. Not his phone. "Wait. Whose phone is this?"

"I borrowed one from the team manager. Mine died last night

and I don't have a charger."

He borrowed a phone to call me? "You have my cell phone number *memorized?*"

"Mind like a steel trap, Clark, remember? Three. Point. Seven." He's breathing hard and it sounds like he's pacing.

"Are you out for a run?"

"Yeah. Sorry it's so early but I felt like a huge dick leaving you hanging last night. None of my teammates would let me borrow me their fucking phones, and I couldn't charge a phone call to the hotel room."

Assholes.

"Oh," I respond dumbly, still unable to form an articulate sentence.

"Yeah, so sorry bout this—I know you're still in bed—but I won't have a phone until Friday when we get back. Left my charger at home and no one will let me borrow theirs."

"Assholes."

He chuckles through the line, low and good. Good and *oh my god*, I'm so tired I want to smush his adorable face. The sound of his delicious laughter sends a *hum* of pleasure careening down my spine…rocketing through my pelvis…and tingling my ovaries.

I snuggle down into my sheets and imagine that smooth, silky breath of his trailing across my stomach.

"You weren't dreaming about me again last night, were you?" I joke, the early morning light just now beginning to peek through my drawn curtains.

"Maybe." I can hear him smiling.

"Mmm, that's weird." My voice drawls. "Before I was rudely interrupted from my deep slumber, I was dreaming about dipping my toes into the warm Caribbean sand on a beach somewhere. A cabana boy was about to bring me a sippy sippy." I yawn, stretch like a feral cat, and make a mewing sound. "*Mmmmm.*"

"Wait." It sounds like he's stopped in his tracks. "Are you wearing that white tank top?"

Disoriented, I mumble, "Huh?"

"The white see-through tank top you had on in Utah. It's what you were wearing in my dream last night—this morning."

"Isn't it a bit early for this line of questioning?" Careful to keep the vibe flirtatious and not a prelude to phone sex, I tease, "I can't even form a cohesive sentence."

"Yes or no?"

"No." I flop down on my back to stare at the ceiling as he grunts, disappointed.

"Bummer. That visual was the only thing getting me through this run. I'm freezing my balls off here, picturing you in that shirt, but it's worth it."

"Um…"

He grunts again, this time frustrated. "Shit, babe, I thought I'd have more time to talk but Coach just walked outside. Gotta go. Let's do something when I get back. I'll text you tomorrow, yeah?"

Babe? Did he just *babe* me? What on earth is happening right now?

Isn't it a little early to be drinking the Kool-Aid?

"Um, okay."

I hear his decisive nod. "Tomorrow."

"I want you to sit on my face.
It's Sunday, so we might
go to hell, but at least you'll have
a comfortable chair on the way."

Sebastian

Oz: *You there?*

Jameson: *Of course ;)*

Oz: *I charged my phone.*

Jameson: *I can see that! Who lent you a charger?*

Oz: *No one. I broke down and bought one at the Walgreens across from the hotel. Dodged traffic to cross the intersection, I'll have you know. Didn't realize how fast I could sprint until last night.*

Oz: *There was one point I thought I was going to be hit by a car. Just sayin.*

Jameson: *WHAT?! Why would you DO THAT?!*

Oz: *Because I was sick of waiting.*

Jameson: Sick of *waiting for...?*

Oz: *It's a 9-hour bus ride home—do you really think I wanted to wait any longer to text you?*

Oz: *James? You there?*

Jameson: *I'm here.*

Oz: *Does it bother you to hear that?*

Jameson: *To hear that you...*

Oz: *Miss your sarcastic mouth? Yeah. I do. Is that some freaky shit or what?*

Jameson: *Where is this all coming from?*

Oz: *It's a long story, but I think we should talk when I get* *home.*

Jameson: *"We should talk." Cause that always ends well.*

Oz: *I just pulled a Jameson and rolled my eyes—don't be so dramatic.*

Jameson: *Me? DRAMATIC?!*

Oz: *Me, Oz, you, Dramatic.*

Jameson: *Cute. Very cute. Where are you right now?*

Oz: *Seat 12D, driving past some very picturesque cornfields somewhere between Ohio and Iowa. You?*

Jameson: *You know—the library, at my usual table.*

Oz: *Shit, that actually makes me jealous.*

Jameson: *Why?*

Oz: *I kind of consider the library "our thing" now and you're there without me.*

Jameson: *Really? Because you've been acting really weird lately.*

Oz: *I have? lol*

Jameson: *I just rolled my eyes, are you happy? Yes, you have. Are you finally ready to tell me why?*

Oz: *Yeah, but I'd rather do it in person.*

Jameson: *Can you at least give me a hint?*

Oz: *All right.*

Oz: *It does have something to do with you.*

Jameson: *Not THAT kind of hint! Be more specific.*

Jameson: *Hey Sebastian? Can you actually call me to talk, or would that be weird?*

Oz: *Yeah, I can call you. Since I haven't seen you in a few days, how bout FaceTime instead?*

Jameson: **blushes* Yes, that works, too. Give me fifteen minutes to pack up and dash home. And fluff my hair. Haha.*

Oz: *Fifteen minutes. Got it.*

Oz: *And for the record, I love it when you say shit like 'dash'. It's so ducking cute.*

Jameson: *LOL, ducking.*

Oz: *Autocorrect won't let me say ducking.*

Oz: *Not ducking. Ducking.*

Oz: *DAMMIT*

Jameson: *I am laughing so hard right now.*

Oz: *Lol. Starting the clock. Ready. Set. Dash.*

"Are you in bed?" I ask, hunching down in my seat, farther inside my hoodie, grateful to have the entire row to myself.

"Just laying on it." On cue, I hear her sheets rustle, and I imagine they're crisp, clean, and smell like fresh air and sunshine.

Heaven.

Jameson looks back at me through the camera on her phone, long hair framing her face, all innocent eyed and sexy.

"When will you be home?" She bites down on her lower lip timidly, like she's just broken out with a case of nerves, like she's embarrassed to ask.

Those five little words and the way she's asking—man, they do some unexpected and weird shit to my stomach, make it flip.

I clear my throat. "They have us scheduled to pull in around eleven."

"Eleven isn't so bad, early enough to go out and…or …what?"

"*Well.*" I drag out the word. "*Then* I was hoping to see you."

Her eyes get wide. "Tonight? But it's Friday."

"Right."

"Aren't you going *out?* To party?"

"I mean, we *can*. If that's what you want to do."

"We?"

"Yeah. You and me."

"Together?"

"Unless you don't want to. I just thought—shit." I run a hand through my hair then drag it down my face. "Never mind what I thought. I'm an idiot."

"No! No. Sorry, I just. Gosh, Oz, I just assumed you'd be with your friends."

"*You're* my friend," I point out, giving her a lopsided grin.

This pleases her and a smile brightens her face, one that makes me want to kiss her through the damn phone.

"I am, aren't I?"

"You are," I enthuse quietly into my phone. "Am I yours?"

"Yes."

"I love it when you say yes like that and do it with an eye roll. So sexy."

Jameson laughs, tipping her head back until it hits the white pillow propped against her headboard. "I know you do."

"Know what else I love?"

"What?"

"I love your hair," I blurt out.

Her eyebrows shoot up, surprised, and she touches the long gleaming locks self-consciously while holding her phone with the other. "You do?"

"Every time I see you, I want to touch it, run my fingers through it."

"You *do?*" She looks back at me apprehensively.

"There's a lot about me you don't know."

"I can see that." Jameson fidgets on the bed. "What else are you hiding from me?"

I wanted to wait, tell her all this in person, but since she's asking—and so fucking adorably—I reluctantly say, "Those dreams I was telling you about the other day?"

"The nightmares? Yes, I remember."

"I wasn't kidding when I said they were about you."

"Oh?" Her mouth forms a tiny circle.

Clearing my throat, I glance around, checking the bus for anyone who's awake, making sure my teammates are otherwise occupied before I continue pouring my damn black heart out into the small screen on my phone.

"What was so horrible about them then?" she teases, attempting to make light of this tension-filled conversation.

"I dreamed that you…" I exhale. "It was really fucked up."

"It's okay if you don't want to tell me Sebastian. I'm sensing it makes you uncomfortable, but it obviously changed how you're seeing me." Does her voice sound throatier than usual? "We've been off the past few days, and…if there's something we can do to fix it, I'd like you to tell me."

"No, we're fine—that's just it. Maybe I don't want us to be fine any more."

Jameson juts out her bottom lip, pouting. "I'm not sure what you mean. Are you breaking up with me?"

"See? That's just it. This is why I need to see you in person."

She furrows her brow. "Oz, you're kind of weirding me out."

"It's just not something we should be talking about over the phone."

"Right. That does me no good, because for the next few hours I'm going to be freaking out," she says.

"Don't. It's nothing horrible."

Jameson sticks out her tongue. "Says the only one of us who has a clue what the hell is going on."

"Can you come over later?"

"To your place?" She tucks an errant hair behind her ear.

"Yeah, my place."

"Um, yes. Of course."

Pretty sure a goofy grin crosses my face. "Great. I'll text you my address."

"Okay."

"It's two blocks from campus, a barf pink color—you can't miss it."

She giggles. "Okay."

"I'll be back around eleven thirty. We have to unload and shit when we get back to school, then I can take off. Give me a few to get home and change. How does eleven forty-five sound?"

"Uh, sure."

"James?"

"Yeah?"

"Unless you want me to come to your place?"

Is that crossing a line with her? The last time I showed up at her house, it didn't work out so well.

"No, your place is better. My roommates are nosy, and… I'm not sure what they're doing tonight. Plus, Sydney was planning on staying home, so...I mean… Unless you *want* to see her."

Sydney.

Right.

Best to avoid that shit.

"I don't want to see her. I just want to see *you*."

"I went down on her
while she was eating a box of
chocolate truffles.
I honestly don't have a clue
which one gave her the
screaming orgasm…"

Sebastian

Jameson is in my house.

In my room.

On my bed.

Planted near the headboard of my king size bed, she's wearing a fitted white tee and a pretty pink cardigan. Tight skinny jeans. Her heels? Those are on the floor by the door.

Heels from those sexy, petite little feet of hers.

I watch her dangle them over the side of my bed, toes painted a neon purple, then tuck them under her legs when she curls up, moving closer to the center.

She looks fantastic.

She beams up at me from the bed, urging me to, "Sit down, would you? Your pacing is making me nervous."

"Sorry, I can't help it." I lower myself to the edge of the bed and wipe my sweaty palms across my jeans. The impulse to bounce my knee is strong. I crack my knuckles instead. "I have all this pent up energy from sitting on the bus all night."

"Do you want to go for a run?"

"Do *you?*"

Her nose wrinkles. "Um no—I was just trying to be supportive."

"You would go running with me to be supportive?"

"Um…no, but I would hold the stopwatch while you ran around the block, throw a cup of water on you when you ran past?"

God she's perfect.

Clever and beautiful and smart. With perfect lips and perfect tits, she's got me all kinds of fucked in the head.

We're friends and anti-lovers, with sexual tension chucked into one fucked up non-relationship relationship that's all my doing because I said I couldn't commit.

I suck so hard at this.

"Hey Jameson?"

"Yes, Sebastian?"

God, she's been using my name nonstop lately, and I don't think I'll ever get sick of hearing my name slip from her lips.

"I've..." I gulp down my nerves. "I've been dreaming of you."

Her face turns fire engine red in the same instant a sigh escapes her lips. "You've said as much."

"You cheat on me."

Her brows shoot up. "Say *what?*"

My back hits the mattress and my arm flops over my face to conceal my eyes. "In my dreams, you're my girlfriend and you're cheating on me. With one of my roommates."

The room is silent except for the ping of a Facebook notification on my laptop.

"Which one?"

"Which one what?"

"Which roommate am I cheating on you with? Please tell me it's not that asshole Zeke or whatever the brute's name is, because no way would that happen. Not even in a dream."

"It's not Zeke." My chuckle rumbles the mattress. "It's Elliot."

"Elliot?" I hear her smiling. "*Aww*, he's the quiet, nice one?"

Aww?

I uncover my face to peer up at her, eyes squinting. She's sitting on the bed cross-legged, a shit-eating grin on her face. "You *really* need to stop referring to guys as nice. We hate that shit."

"Good thing I've never called *you* nice." Jameson pokes me in the arm with a teasing forefinger.

I scowl when she pulls away. "I've noticed."

"Are you pouting?"

"No."

"'Cause it sounds like you're pouting."

"Pfft. What do I care if you don't think I'm *nice?* Like I give a shit."

Jameson goes radio silent, peering down at me with those big, blue eyes.

Eventually, she says, "Liar."

I refuse to look at her. Study the ceiling that could use a fresh coat of paint. The fan covered in dust that could use a good scrub. The cracked drywall in the corner.

Everywhere but at her.

She nudges my bicep. "Why aren't you looking at me?"

Because you make me feel things I don't want to feel. Feelings I don't know how to manage, don't know how to deal with.

Get rid of.

Keep.

"Look Oz, just because you had a dream about me—that doesn't mean anything."

That gets my attention. "You don't believe dreams *mean* something?"

"Do *you?*"

"*Yes.*" I push myself up on my elbows and rise to a sitting position. "The whole thing is fucked. Up."

She scrunches up her nose distastefully like I've insulted her. "Why? Because *I* was in your dream instead of some blonde wrestling groupie? Someone with huge boobs who requires zero effort? Gee, sorry to disappoint you."

She's still not getting it. "No James, it's because I dreamed you were my *girl*friend and you were *cheating* on me." The words get stuck in my throat, bound as tightly as the mounting jumble of knots in my stomach.

Goddamn *knots.*

I'm gonna puke.

"You consider it a nightmare that I was your girlfriend?" Her voice comes out slowly. Small.

Hurt and confused, latching onto the least important detail.

Typical female.

I twist my torso to face her. "*No*. That's not what I'm saying. The dream was fucked up because—shit. I don't even know what the hell I'm saying any more." She's quiet so I fill the silence with more jabbering. "It's the same, reoccurring dream: I come home from out of town and I walk in on you boning my roommate. Hard. We argue and fight, then you cry and I kick you out. The first time it happened, I was shaken awake on the bus by a teammate; he heard me crying like a goddamn baby. How fucked up is that?"

"You were crying? Because I was your fake girlfriend who fake cheated?" Her head gives a tiny, confused shake. "Why would that upset you?"

"Because it didn't *feel* fake." I'm whining.

"I don't understand. You don't even *like* me like that—why would you dream about me?"

Spoken like it's something I can control.

"Don't you see? This is what I've been trying to tell you." My eyes float back to the ceiling as a puff of air expels from my chest. "Maybe I do."

Those three little words ripple in the air, tension thickening the atmosphere.

"But surely...not like *that*," she drawls, sounding cautious and doubtful, uncertainty etched across her pretty, perfect brows. I glance at her sharply.

"Why are you saying it like that?"

"I don't know."

"How can you not know?" I ask, genuinely curious. "Would it be the worst thing in the world if I did like you? I'm a great catch you know."

"You want the truth? Here it is: it bothers me sometimes that *all* you do is talk about sex. It's a turnoff for me. Like, let it go already, we get it, you're a walking hard-on."

"Is that your only impression of me?"

"Are you being serious?" she deadpans. "You spend half our

time together making *sex* jokes, and yet you expect me to take you seriously right now." Jameson throws her hands in the air, mumbling to the ceiling, "What *is* it with *guys?*"

Okay, but… "Seriously, you think that's all I want from you? Sex?"

Her chuckle is sarcastic and lacking enthusiasm. "What else is there? Do you honestly just want to be my *friend?*"

"No, I don't just want to be your friend." Not any more; now I want to be her friend *and* I want to bang her. Repeatedly. "Do you just want to be friends?"

"I did at first. I mean, you're vulgar and kind of a pig. I'm not sure where to start with a guy like you. You're like a set of Legos with a million tiny pieces and terrible instructions, and I'm not sure where to stick what. And then I end up stepping on the pointy edges in the middle of the night, which hurts like a bitch."

What the fuck is she talking about?

"What I'm saying is…I think you're really fun and great, but parts of you could hurt me."

I scratch my chin. "I'm not sure how to feel about being compared to a set of Legos."

"That's why I haven't slept with you." She bites down hard on her lower lip. "But you're growing on me and I hate it." Her head shakes back and forth, eyes squeezed shut. "*Hate* it."

"So my pointy edges are…?"

"Other girls."

I draw each word out slowly, carefully. "Sometimes sex is just *sex*, James, and that's all it is for me. A physical act to relieve stress."

Jesus, even to my own ears I sound like a huge ass; I basically just compared sex to working out at the gym. I curse my mother for not teaching me better manners.

And yet, it doesn't faze her. "That may be true, Sebastian, but I'm not into sharing or constantly wondering if my boyfr—the guy I'm sleeping with has his youknowwhat in someone else's youknowwhat. It's a deal breaker, and you said you weren't into being tied down, so…"

"Maybe I changed my mind."

"Have you told your fan club?" Her gorgeous pout makes my heart skip a beat and my pulse race, no fucking lie. It means she cares.

"Jameson Clark, I never would have pegged you as the *jealous* type." Even to me, my next question comes out sounding incredulous. "You're not jealous of the other girls, are you?"

Cause that would be great. I've had jealous, angry hate sex in the past, and believe me when I say, it's the *best.*

"Yes, I guess I am." Jameson gives a careless shrug, shocking me with her honesty. "I just know that all the times you've said you want to *fuck* me"—she winces—"it pushed me away—no, that's not the right word. It didn't push me away, but it does make me feel…" She struggles with her next choice of words. "Common? Like maybe how all the others feel. The girl in the hallway with the *red* hair."

I glower. "You are nothing like those other girls."

Jameson rolls her eyes, and blurts out, "*Duh.* I know that."

This unexpected statement surprises us both, and the way she says it makes us laugh. I fall onto the bed, roll onto my side, and prop myself up on an elbow, studying her.

I study her *hard.*

"You are *nothing* like those girls. Nothing."

I want her to *get it*; I need her to understand. Using the only tool I have to communicate, I show her with my body. Stretching my large frame across the bed, I scoot across the bed, dragging her down so she's positioned flat on her back. Balancing my elbows on either side of her face, I look down into her face.

She is truly beautiful.

I've always thought she was cute, but with her hair fanned out on my navy quilt, staring up at me all wide eyed and trusting, she's a total knockout.

I want to wrap the gleaming locks of her hair around my fist and tug, so I twirl some into a curl with my finger.

"I'm sorry Jim. I don't know how to do this."

"Do what?"

"Ask you out. Date you. I would never treat you—" I stop, not knowing how to finish my thought. "Jameson."

"Sebastian." Her lips twist into a patient smile.

"Nothing about you is easy…"

Her soft laughter fills the room. "Thank god for that."

"I can't believe I'm fucking saying this, but for someone who started off as just a study partner, you're all I can think about lately." Her glossy hair slips from my fingers, greedy hands raking through the hair spread across my bed. "Night and day. Being on the road and not seeing you is killing me. That's never happened before. Not talking to you was killing me. Dreaming about you—"

"Was killing you?"

I still, narrowing my eyes at her. "You didn't look like such a smartass the day we first met."

James cocks an eyebrow. "Oh yeah? What did I look like?"

"Smart and sexy." Confident and complicated.

Jameson snickers. "You did *not* think I looked sexy. You thought I was a dork, don't lie."

I respond by raising my eyebrows and lowering my voice. "I'm going to date you, and one of these days, *Jameson,* I'm going to pluck all the buttons off your cardigan, one at a time, and screw you senseless while you wear nothing but your pearl necklace."

"There are no buttons on this cardigan," she whispers.

I lean in closer, lips resting above her ear. "I know."

"That's not fair," she complains, shifting restlessly beneath me.

"What's not fair?" The tips of our noses brush while I finger the neckline of her soft, pink sweater. It's delicate and pretty and so very *Jameson.*

"The way you make *me* feel."

"How do I make you feel? *Tell* me," I plead.

I'm okay with begging.

I have to know what she's thinking, hoping it might help make sense of the tangled shit I've got going on in my own damn head.

"You make me think about not studying," she whispers, arching into me, nose nuzzling a trail up my neck to the valley below my ear.

Whoa!

I move my hands, bracing them on either side of her thighs, and tilt my head to give her better access to my neck. "Is that good or bad?"

"Both." She sniffs it. "*Mmmm.* You smell good, though half the time I want to strangle you with my bare hands."

"What about the other half?"

Jameson feigns a sigh in my ear so blissful and sweet it sends a shock straight down to my cock. I resist the impulse to climb all the way on top and pin her down.

"The other half, I want you to do all those dirty things you're always threatening to do to *me*. Like right now, I want you out of that shirt. I want to touch you, feel your bare flesh against the tips of my fingers."

"Oh yeah?" I croak.

"*Yeah.*" She's still running the tip of her nose up the side of my neck, up and down, up and down, breathing me in. "Allison says I should let you screw me into a coma." Her tongue flicks my earlobe and she blows lightly. "What do you think about that?"

"Holy shit, yes." I breathe, dick officially hard inside my mesh athletic pants—painfully so. The thin fabric strains and pulls against my erection. "I knew I liked Allison."

"But what I think I should do now is…"

"Yes?"

"Leave."

"Leave? Why? We're just getting started."

Jameson pulls back, cupping my face gently in the palm of her hand. "If we don't stop, we won't stop, and I don't want whatever this relationship is to be based on sex. That makes sense right? Oz, tell me it makes sense."

"It makes sense," I echo unhappily, crossing my arms to pout.

She's right, of course; this relationship shouldn't be based on sex. Or orgasms. Or blowjobs. Or round, perky tits. It should be based on getting to know her personality and her likes and dislikes. Her hopes and dreams and—

Holy shit, what the hell am I even saying?

Her lips are moving and she's speaking, but the stiff dick in my pants is straining angrily against my boxers, cutting off the blood to my brain and making it impossible to concentrate.

"So you agree?" Jameson says, licking her lips. Her glossy, juicy, pouty lips...

I jerk out a nod. "Whatever you just said, I agree. Okay. I'll do it." I expel a shaky puff of air and gulp back my raging disappointment. "Wait. What did I just agree to?"

"If you're going to date me, I insist on rule number ten: No sex until the fifth date." She bites down on her lower lip, carefully extracting herself from under me and scooting toward the headboard, where she props herself up and begins the process of buckling her heels. "Or maybe the third or fourth, depending on how it goes."

No sex until date number five! Is she fucking insane?

"Oz? Do we have a deal?"

My eyes catalog every single one of the delectable curves I won't see naked for at least five dates. *Three if it goes well.* Three, three, focus on three. Focus on her crotch, her flat stomach, her boobs, her chagrined mouth—

"Oz?"

I like her. I can do this. We'll just crank out the dates, one after the other, rapid fire.

I nod again, lips arching into a wicked grin. "Yes, yes. Excel-

lent."

She beams at me and I feel a million feet tall walking her to her car. I plant a chaste kiss on the top of her head to leave her wanting more.

I stand, watching her glowing taillights travel down the empty street, stop at the light, and disappear from sight once she turns left.

"Brace yourself Jim; I'm going to date the *shit* out of you."

#DOUCHEBAG

"On a scale of 1 to 10,
what are my odds
of you doing anal?
I need to know if I should
stop talking to you or not."

Jameson

"God. This ugly-ass thing is actually really cute on you," Oz says, reaching to adjust the blue batting helmet resting on my head. Giving it a little tap, he leans in and—

"You did *not* just kiss the tip of my nose."

"It's an adorably perky little nose." He steps back, letting his eyes scan the rest of my body. "Almost as perky as your boobs."

I whack him in the gut harder than I intend to. My hand stings like a mothertrucker when I pull back, prickly like needles are stabbing from within, and I slap it over my mouth to quiet my dismay. "Oh my god, I'm so sorry! I didn't mean to hit you that hard. I mean—I meant to *tap* you, not smack you."

"If that was your apology, it sucked."

"My hand hurts," I whimper, cradling it like a baby.

"Want me to kiss it and make it better?"

I do. I do want him to kiss it and make it better, so I step toward him, palm extended. "Be gentle."

"Here, let me see it." He drops his helmet to the pavement, moving toward me with a purposeful stride, taking my hand in his. "Poor baby."

Oz makes a grand show of examining my hand, my fingers, then soothes his palm up my goose bump-covered arm, back down again. When he lowers his head and drags his nose along the delicate skin of my inner wrist, my eyelids flutter closed.

When his lips find my pulse, I moan.

"Poor." Kiss. "Poor." Kiss. "Baby." One more kiss and he lifts his head. Winks. "Be more careful next time. When I have you, I want you in one piece."

"It was my special brand of flirting." No doubt my expression is wobbly. "I hope I didn't hurt you."

A slow smile creeps across his face and he dips, reaching for my arm. Drags me closer by the wrist he's just branded with his lips. Drags my flattened palm over his stomach and over his hard abdomen.

"Feel these abs?"

"*Yes.*"

"Rock. Solid." He moves that palm over the flat plane of his six-pack, the muscles constricting under my feather-light touch. His arm slides around my waist as he moves my hand up over his firm pecs. Up over his right shoulder. Forces me to step even closer. "You can't hurt me, James."

You can't hurt me.

Flirtatious words with a bewildering wallop of fiction.

Those four words cause me to look up into his dark, expressive eyes. His mouth has a smile tugging on it but...those sullen eyes? Those eyes are saying something else completely: you *can* hurt me.

All this time I was worried about myself and my own heart, never once stopping to consider that *I* could hurt *him*. How selfish.

Shamefaced, my head drops for a split second, considering his bald-faced lie. He's lying. This behemoth, mountain of a guy, gazing down at me with jokes and smiles and laughter, is *lying.*

"You really do like me," I say breathily, the words full of wonder.

"You like *me*," he breathes back.

"But you *like* me, like me," I challenge like a ten-year-old on the playground. "Do you have a crush on...my cardigans, Sebastian?"

I get an eye roll for that one. "Get over yourself, Clark."

Oz tilts his head to study me, one hand rising between our two bodies to cup my chin. Leans in. Lands his mouth squarely on mine and presses gently as his other large palm squeezes my butt cheek. "Pick up the bat, slacker."

"But it's heavy," I complain when he hands me the wooden

Louisville Slugger. "My arms are like noodles."

"Stop stalling, Clark. Get to it." He gives my ass another squeeze then a light tap before nudging me toward a yellow line drawn on the pavement where I should take my mark.

I giggle like a schoolgirl and take the wooden baseball bat from his outstretched hand.

"Check your helmet," he pesters. "Make sure it's on straight. I don't need you getting a concussion."

I straighten the helmet, my long hair swept to one side. "Better. Okay, I'm ready, Coach."

Oz nods and crosses his arms, satisfied I've properly cross-checked my equipment, then begins rapidly doling out instructions.

Spread your legs. Bend at the knee. Elbows out. Eyes on the ball.

Swing at everything.

"Got it?"

"Got it."

The white ball flies out of the machine, whizzing past me at warp-like speed. It hits the canvas backdrop with a hollow thump, drops to the ground, and rolls a few feet before stopping at the chain-link fence.

Too late, I swing.

"Damn. Don't got it," I joke.

Oz laughs, walking a few feet to the green mechanical box hanging on the fence, and opens the lid. Turns a few dials, snaps the lid closed. "That might have been a little too fast for a beginner. I adjusted the speed."

"I hope it's slower than the rate at which girls fall into bed with Zeke Daniels," I drawl, taking the proper stance while anticipating the next pitch. "Because if that's the case, I'm screwed."

"You're funny."

"Why thank you." I lift the bat, bend my elbows, and stick my butt out, glancing at the nude wedges strapped to my feet. At the hot pink toenails playing peekaboo. At my fitted jeans and aqua blue silk top.

The delicate turquoise necklace sways between my breasts when I glance over at Oz. "You could have warned me you were bringing me here so I wouldn't wear heels; it would've been the *polite* thing for a gentleman to do."

He leans against the chain-link fence. "I've always preferred the element of surprise."

"But I wouldn't have worn this."

One thick eyebrow crooks over eyes fastened on my denim-clad rump. "*Exactly.*"

The gorgeous ass grins at me and I roll my eyes. "Let's get this show on the road and put an end to my misery."

Ball after ball shoots out of the machine; I swing and swing and swing and miss every ball flying past me with a *whoosh* at alarmingly rapid speeds.

Frustrated by my incredible suckage, I stomp a foot. "Dammit, Sebastian! Are you going to help me or not?"

The bastard grins. "Only if you insist."

Eye roll. "I insist."

Pushing himself away from the fence, he saunters over, slower than molasses, approaching from behind. Rests both hands on my hips. Slides them slowly up my ribcage, down my arms, and grips the base of the bat over my hands.

His hard muscular body imprints on my backside; I bite down on my bottom lip when that splendid chest encounters my shoulder blades, his pelvis creating an erotic friction against my derriere. I loll my head slowly to the side as his nose brushes the hair alongside my neck, nudging it aside.

Those lips speak, inadvertently igniting infinite sparks inside my body, his suggestive words a sexy, sensory caress.

"Grip it like this, not too firm, not to soft." He repositions my hands. "Open those beautiful legs for me a little wider, James. Yeah, that's it." His knee taps the inside of my leg, spreading them wider on the asphalt. "Straddle the plate." Those fingertips momentarily leave the bat to dig into my hips and cradle me in closer.

I can feel his cock straining against my ass crack and fight back a moan. "There *is* no plate." It's a batting cage, not a ball-park.

"Close your eyes and visualize it then. Imagine yourself straddling it."

My eyes flutter closed, a ballpark the furthest thing from filthy mind. Graphic images fuel my imagination, my dirty, dirty imagination: Sebastian on his back, covered in sex sweat. His bare chest, lean hips, and a light dusting of hair trailing from his belly button straight down to the delicious V...*dipping, dipping down* and disappearing into a tangle of white sheets. Rising above him on a big bed, my hair spills in a cascade over my naked—

"Are you seeing it?" His voice cuts into my fantasy.

"*Yes. I'm seeing it...*" The throbbing between my legs is no figment of my imagination. The wet underwear. The want. The, "*Mmm.*"

Oz releases his grip on the bat so he can drag those massive paws along the front of my denim jeans. I almost can't stand the tension of his middle and forefinger dragging up and down that sensitive vale of my bikini line, rubbing. *Coaxing.* So close to my crotch the telltale sign of an orgasm threatens to have me moaning out embarrassingly loudly.

The resistance from his fingers on the denim is like flint and fire.

Intoxicating.

He strokes my lower abdomen.

Groans into my shoulder.

Drags that rock-hard dick across my ass.

We both groan when his fingers drag themselves up my rib-cage and reposition themselves around the barrel of the bat.

"Coming here was *such* a fucking terrible idea," he growls.

"No crap." *Don't drop the bat James, don't drop the bat.* "This is the worst place ever."

I clutch it tight.

"Rule number eleven: any and all future dates will now have a no-contact clause implemented."

"That sounds like a rule within a rule." I pant, mentally attempting to steady my palpitating heart. "Maybe we should head back. Clearly you can't be trusted to behave."

"Me? You're the one gyrating your tight little ass into my—"

"Am I?" I'm trying to focus on his words, I really, really am…and I really am gyrating my ass into his junk… but I swear, I can't help myself. My body suddenly has a mind of its own.

"You are," he maintains. "You're gyrating like a stripper."

He says it like it's a bad thing. "Sorry?"

"Say sorry *without* moaning." Oz chortles in my ear with a sigh. "We should probably leave before I come in my pants like a thirteen-year-old and we embarrass ourselves."

A family of seven is picking out helmets and bats in the gated batting cage to our immediate left.

"Good idea."

Neither of us make a move.

"Jim, let go of the bat."

"*You* let go of the bat."

His hips swivel, giving my rear a little bump, a little grind. "One of us should let go of the bat."

"All right." Biting down on my lower lip, I nod. Oz's warm body heat is making my knees weak, turning my otherwise level-headed brain to mush. "Okay. We should definitely go."

So we do.

We return the bats and helmets then climb back into his black pickup truck. Drive the few short miles back to my house. Sit in his vehicle in the street, under the bright overhead security lamp.

It's gotten dark outside and the streetlights flicker on one by one along the empty avenue, casting shadows and slashes of light inside the cab of Oz's truck. Across his dark eyes, lips, and chest.

He looks foreboding. Mysterious.

Sexy.

I swallow, glancing out the window before unbuckling the seatbelt that's been holding me secure.

"Wait there," Oz instructs, swiftly undoing his own seatbelt and hastening to open the door. He jumps out, jogs to my side, and wrenches open the passenger side door.

I bite back a grin at his good manners; he's *a lot* rusty, but the potential is there.

"Thank you."

Nonchalantly, his hand slides into mine as we stroll, unhurried, up the sidewalk to the door.

I turn to face him, hand still in his, leaning casually against the front porch. I suck in one unsteady breath after the other in an attempt to stabilize my rapidly beating heart.

"Is this weird?" I whisper under the dim light.

"Is *what* weird?" Oz whispers back. "Why are we whispering?"

"This. Us. I feel like we should be doing something else. Studying or something." I try to laugh, but the laugh gets caught in my throat. "Get back into our element."

"You want to go to the library, we'll go to the library," Oz says pragmatically, the need to please me evident in his harried persistence. "I can wait here while you grab your backpack, then we'll swing by my place and I'll get—"

"That's *not* what I meant." I chuckle. "This dating thing—does it feel weird to you?" Oh god, what am I saying? *Stop talking Jameson, you're going to sabotage everything!* "I'm sorry, don't listen to my babble. I'm just super nervous."

Oz pauses a few seconds, watching me under the hazy porch light with one burnt-out bulb. Steps closer then reaches between us to grasp my other hand. Drags it to his powerful chest. Flattens my palm and places it over his heart.

His wildly racing heart.

So wild I can feel it beneath my fingers, its rhythm like a thin string drawing me toward him with every beat. Connecting us, heart to heart.

"Do you feel that, Jameson?" he implores breathlessly. "Can you *feel* it beating?"

I can.

"That's for *you*. No one else makes me feel this way; no one has ever made me feel this way. No woman. No coach. No opponent makes my heart race the way—"

"Stop talking."

Suddenly I'm up on my tiptoes, silencing him with the crush of my mouth. *Crush*—what a cliché, and yet I'm shoving him against the house, kissing the dickens out of him with my hand twisted unexpectedly in the collar of his shirt, pulling him closer, kissing the words off his lips, downing them like a thirst-quenching drink to my soul. Kissing him like he's a deployed soldier I won't see for months. Years.

Hints of delectable tongue.

Bodies flush.

Sounds I didn't know people made while kissing.

We kiss and kiss until a light goes on inside the living room, the soft glow from the flimsy curtains catching my eye and giving me pause. Allison pulls back the curtain to glance outside, visibly startled to see us making out on the porch.

Quickly closes the curtains, but rips them back open seconds later to get another look. Begins fist pumping in the air, leaping and jumping around the room in a silent victory dance until my making out with Oz turns to giggle fits and he pulls away, confused.

Allison's eyes get guiltily wide and she lunges toward the curtains, whipping them closed, but we can hear her hysterical laughter.

"She's a goddam delight." Oz laughs, planting another firm kiss on my lips.

I perk up. "You think so?"

"No. She's a boner killer."

Oh god.

One date down.

Four to go.

#DOUCHEBAG

"Wanting to be honest up front—
I actually swiped right
for your hot, blonde friend
in the picture on the left.
Can you show her my profile and
find out if she's interested?"

Jameson

If you would have told me a few weeks ago I'd be watching a wrestling match on a *Wednesday* night in a packed campus stadium, I would never have believed you.

Not in a million years.

But I'm here, Allison beside me for support, because no way was I coming alone. Not when the two tickets handed to me last night were front row floor seats.

Freaking front row. On the floor.

"We get these to give our families but I want you to have them," Oz had said as he slid them into the pocket of my backpack, landing a sloppy kiss to the center of my surprised mouth; I still cannot get past his unencumbered displays of PDA.

"You still plan on coming, right?"

I gave a shaky nod, fingertips touching the spot on my mouth where his lips had just been. "Yes. Allison's coming with me."

"Good. I don't want you to be alone on our second date." His pencil had tapped the edge of the hard, wooden table.

"How is this considered a date if you're not even going to be there?"

"What do you mean, not going to be there? You're going to be watching me in action. And then afterward..." He'd hesitated. "Maybe we could celebrate the big W with dinner."

I'd scrunched up my forehead, confused. "Big W?"

My mind had gone immediately into the gutter: Big O.

Orgasm.

Big D.

Dick.

Oh god, it was official: I had sex on the brain twenty-four-seven, and there was only one person to blame.

"Big W stands for win." He'd laughed. "What were you

thinking it stood for?"

"Definitely not that?"

"What then?"

"Big big things."

"Oh my god," Oz howled. "I can't believe what a pervert you are."

"I'm not a pervert just because it made me think of sex!"

"Busted!" He'd laughed again, harder, head thrown back against the leather desk chair in the study room. "I never said that's what you were thinking about."

"James. James, are you paying attention? You're in that guy's seat."

Huh?

"You have to scooch over a seat James. Earth to James. James?"

"Oh crap, sorry!" I hustle to move over, shooting an apologetic smile at the man waiting patiently for his stadium seat. Grabbing my jacket and the giant Iowa foam finger Allison bought me, I scooch.

"I cannot believe these seats!" Allison squeals beside me, chatting me out of a daydream. "They are amaze-balls, James." She digs for her phone, taps open SnapChat, and takes a selfie with the wrestling mats in the background. Her finger flies through the filters. "Sweet, there's an Iowa wrestling geofilter!"

I smile at her enthusiasm and try on the foam finger, giving it a few waves before setting it back on the ground in front of me.

The butterflies in my stomach multiply by the hundreds when the lights in the stadium suddenly flicker and go black. Our Iowa mascot appears on the jumbotron and a single spotlight appears in the center of the huge, hardwood court that's been converted into a wrestling stadium.

The light shines on the center mat as the broadcaster's baritone voice booms. The marching band begins the fight song and the cheers from the packed house are so deafeningly loud I resist the urge to cover my ears.

"This is crazy!" I shout to Allison, truly astonished. The number of people filling the seats is incredible; the stands are lost in a sea of black and yellow. Banners, signs, and flags fly. Across the gleaming hardwood, a hand-painted poster announces, ZEKE DANIELS! I WANT TO MAKE BABIES WITH YOUUU, one boldly sparkles, OZZY 4 THE PIN in gold glitter, and another next to it begs, OZ OZBORN, PIN US WITH YOUR BIG D***! WE DO 3SUMS!

I cringe at *that* one.

One by one, the wrestlers from the visiting team are announced and their stats pronounced as they run from the locker room and take the floor. Jog around the perimeter. Drop to the ground and do pushups.

Strip off their warm-up suits.

And holy sweet *Jesus*…

"Dear. God. You can see—*everything*," Allison shouts over the band when they begin a bleat of chants to fire up the crowd while our cheerleaders twirl their metallic yellow pompons and—wait.

"Since when does wrestling have cheerleaders? Is that a thing?" I yell to my roommate.

"Oh, it's a thing all right." She laughs loudly. "You really don't get into sports much, do you?"

I shake my head.

The overzealous crowd around us goes wild when strobe lights flash, the faces of our team appearing on the giant screens of the scoreboards and jumbotron high above our heads. First some kid named Rex Gunderson jogs out. Another named Jonathan Powell. Monaghan. Lewis. Fairchild. Pittwell. Bower. Rodriguez. Ebert. Schultz.

That giant douchebag Zeke Daniels.

Sebastian Osborne strolls out last—every masculine, muscular inch of him. Reaching the edge of the mat, he bounces in place on the balls of his feet, covered from head to toe in a black track-suit with his last name screen-printed in bold yellow across the back.

I stare, transfixed as he unzips the jacket and slides it down past his shoulders. The straps of his tight singlet are not yet pulled over his defined pecs; rather, they hang down at his sides. He's *naked* from the waist up, tattoo sleeve expanding as he warms up with the team. Skin already damp with perspiration, he's the epitome of rock hard, unyielding, sexy—

"Sweet. Baby. *Jesus!*" Allison shouts with an elbow to my ribcage so hard it hurts. Her arms go out, widespread, beseeching. "Why have I never paid more attention to the wrestling team? Why, god, why! This is...this is..."

"Amaze-balls?" I tease.

"No. It's *better*. It's majestic. It's the eighth wonder of the freaking world is what this shit is." She shoots me a look. "Would it be weird if I took pictures for my spank bank?"

"Girls *have* those?" I refuse to say the words 'spank' and 'bank' together in a sentence.

"*This* girl does. I mean, Jesus, James. Look at all the poly-covered c-o-c-k in this room." She covers her mouth. "Shit, sorry. I just... It's just that you can literally see *every*thing. I mean, that guy from Wisconsin looks like he stuffed an entire eggplant emoji down his—"

"I'm well aware." But thanks for mentioning it.

Allison stares pointedly across the room at the female fans in the student section. With their lewd signs and skimpy outfits, their objectives are evident to anyone with a set of functioning optical senses.

My roomie states the obvious with a hair flip. "You don't honestly think they're here to actually *watch* wrestling, do you? Bitches, please."

"Remind me again why I brought you?"

"Because after this meet is over, you're gonna have to elbow your way through that crowd of *hoes* to properly congratulate bae on his v-i-c-t-o-r-y and I'm going to help you do it."

Hoes?

I sputter on the pink water bottle poised at my lips. "There were *so* many things wrong with that run-on sentence."

"Shhh, shhh, they're starting." Allison hops up and down on the balls of her feet. "Oh em gee, I'm going to have a million pictures on my Snap story. Everyone is going to be so jelly."

I roll my eyes, but my face lights up with a smile. "Whatever you do, do *not* tag me in those. I'm not kidding this time Allison— those pictures you posted on Instagram last week weren't funny."

She snaps a selfie and shoots me a sidelong glance. "But you were wearing a *puffy* coat."

"So?"

"It was forty-five degrees!"

"Some people get cold, Allison."

"Stop being so huffy, hardly anyone saw it."

Deep breath, James.

"Allison," I reason with her calmly. "Two hundred and sixty-seven people double-tapped to heart it."

She disregards my annoyance with a flippant, "Are you going to watch your wrestler or start an argument?"

Dammit, she has a point. Resentfully, I direct my attention back to the action, to the collegiate athletes in front of us. Two young men grapple on the center mat while their coaches hover near the ground, getting low and shouting out directions. Referees lie flat on the mats, arms spread wide to catch every move, whistles at the ready for any point or penalty.

It's loud. Chaotic.

Exhilarating.

My heart pounds as one Iowa wrestler after another fights for victory in the center ring. The lightweights Gunderson and Pitwell. Bower. Middleweights. Some *insanely* good-looking Hispanic named Diego Rodriguez.

Zeke Daniels.

The crowd goes bat-shit *crazy* when Oz begins the warm-up set for his match, the cheers deafeningly loud while he goes about the simple stretching of his hamstrings. Arms. Bending at the waist and touching his toes.

My hungry eyes fly to his fantastic…round …squatter's…*ass*. That ass. Those thick, powerful thighs.

Without even thinking, I lick my lips, the blush creeping up my chest, neck, and cheeks as Oz goes through the groom check. I press my hands to my face to cool it and resist fanning myself with the program we were handed on the way in.

"You should see yourself right now." Allison laughs. "Seriously. You look like you want to rip your sweater off."

I want to point out that my cardigan is cotton, not a sweater, but the words get caught in my throat because I do—I do want to rip it off. I'm burning up, and it's not from the temperature of the auditorium.

Anxiously, I watch the match begin, hear the ref's whistle blow from a false start. They begin again. Hand fight. Grapple. A few hips are thrown before Oz gets his opponent in a headlock—then in seconds they're both on the ground.

It looks like they're fish flopping around, and—

"Does it bother you that everyone can see his balls through that singlet?" Allison asks.

"Oh my god, Allison, you can't just say shit like that!"

"What! Why? I'm just saying what you're thinking. Be honest. I mean…that junk is right. There."

"Right, but I don't need to hear about it." Because now all I'm going to be doing is looking at it.

"Face it, James: every girl in here is checking out his cock-a-doodle-do."

A nervous, inappropriate laugh bubbles up within my throat and I'm helpless to stop it. "Stop it Allison!"

My roommate bumps me with her hip. "You're so cute when

you get all hot and bothered. That's it, isn't it? You want him to make sex with you and this gets you all turned on."

Make *sex* with me?

I give one jerky nod because if I'm being honest, yes—I totally want him to *make sex* with me.

"Shit. I should totally text Parker and see where he's at. I'm getting horny."

"Um…"

"Calm down." She shoots me a look, typing furiously on her cell. "Not from staring at your boyfriend, from the room full of *peen*." A shrug, as if that explains everything. "I'm a hormonal teenager stuck inside a twenty-one-year-old body, James."

Evidently, so am I.

Sebastian

I'm drenched with sweat.

Hot.

Keyed up, I walk, arms braced behind my head, circling the mat at a slow pace to cool off. Slow my heart rate.

Every match is a high akin to riding a shockwave of adrenaline and testosterone, my body conditioned, primed to perfection, and powered on high, slow to decompress.

So I walk.

Out of the locker room, hair still damp from a quick shower, I pace the long corridor of the athletics building. Return to the gym and avoid the custodians rolling up the equipment, despite the crowd.

I walk, measuring every step. Sidestep school spirit and concession debris—poster board signs, foam fingers, streamers, popcorn.

Measure every cleansing breath, until—

James.

She's being led through the throng of fans by blonde-haired Fuck Buddy—sorry, *Allison*—who's strong-arming my...who's strong-arming *James* by the forearm. 'Led' is too loose a term; she's being hauled toward me, and grudgingly.

I slow my gait and grin. Chug from the water bottle clenched in my grip.

Watch as Allison gives her one final nudge. Jameson stumbles forward, head hanging low, pulling at the yellow cardigan layered over her black Iowa tee shirt. Snug boot-cut jeans. A low, sleek ponytail draped over her left shoulder secured by a thin yellow ribbon. A ribbon tied with a prim little bow.

A fucking *bow*.

I hone in on that bow, dissect it in the most erotic way possible.

Something about it suddenly makes me fucking *stupid.* Gets me *hot* in a way no tight, low-cut top or skimpy panties could. I imagine untying that bow and watching it drift to the floor; I imagine dragging it across her bare breasts.

A startling surge of adrenaline comes back full force and before either of us know it, I'm pushing through the crowd, closing the distance between us. My arms wrap around her narrow waist. I effortlessly sweep her off the ground. Twirl her around. Press my mouth over her startled lips. They're warm and pouty and juicy—exactly how I like them.

I suck on her lower lip and tug with a growl.

My hands *crave* her, itching to roam her body. Run under her conservative sweater. Untie that carefully tied ribbon.

Instead, I lower Jameson until her feet are planted firmly on the ground.

"Woo, oh boy!" Jameson fans herself with the program in her hand. "Rule number twelve: no manhandling in public. You have no self-control." She breathes.

"Good luck with that one," I quip, going in for another kiss, because there's just something about Jameson Clark I can't keep off my damn mind. I cannot stop thinking about her. Cannot keep my hands from touching her.

Literally.

And Christ—I don't want to.

"Ready for dinner?"

She attempts a nod and I grin.

I'm riding this roller coaster all the way to the fucking end.

Jameson: *I don't know if I told you, but thank you for the tickets to the match. And thank you for dinner.*

Oz: *You're welcome. Knowing you were in the crowd tonight gave my adrenaline the biggest rush; I can't believe how fast I pinned McPherson.*

Jameson: *Who's McPherson?*

Oz: *The kid from Wisconsin. I was on fire tonight, and it's because you were there watching me.*

Jameson: *You really were incredible.*

Oz: *You know what else is incredible? Your lips. I could have stood on your porch tonight and made out with you forever.*

Jameson: *That was really sweet...and hormonal.*

Oz: *Hormonal? Nah, that's not it at all. It's you. If you said 'Oz, get in your car and come climb through my bedroom window', I would do it without hesitating.*

Jameson: *My bedroom is on the second story...*

Oz: *Exactly.*

Jameson: *LOL what else would you do?*

Oz: *The better question is, what wouldn't I do?*

"The furniture store didn't have the one-night stand I was looking for. Maybe you could help me with that."

Sebastian

Oz: *Hey sexy.*

Jameson: *Sexy? You talking to me?! *points to self**

Oz: *Who else would I be talking to?*

Jameson: *Hmmm, good question…*

Oz: *What are you up to?*

Jameson: *Just getting ready for girls night. My roommates want to Netflix and chill.*

Oz: *You're definitely staying home tonight?*

Jameson: *Yeah. Hayley wants to watch Ten Things I Hate About You. She's hating on men right now—some guy won't text her back. Why, you asking for a reason? ;)*

Damn. I was hoping maybe…

I palm the phone in my hand and stare down at it, oddly disappointed that she's staying home with her friends. It's been days since I've seen her; work and school and wrestling have driven a wedge into my social calendar, not to mention whatever obligations she's had, and—

I miss her.

I miss her like fucking crazy.

Jameson: *Now that we know I'm having girls night, what does Oz Osborne have planned for tonight after his big WIN against Princeton?*

Oz: *Looks like I'm staying in, too. Roommates are gone and I* *have the place to myself tonight. Maybe I'll watch the MMA fight on HBO. Maybe I'll study. idk*

Jameson: *Must be nice having the house to yourself. What does that feel like?! The only time I'm ever alone is during the day when my roomies are at class.*

Oz: *Freakishly quiet. Zeke is usually pre-gaming on a Friday night before getting completely plowed; he went home to see his cousin. Or maybe it's his...who knows. I'm not sure where he's been lately, but he'll be back tomorrow for a party.*

Jameson: *lol. I'm not so sure about him. Yeesh.*

Oz: *Yeah, he's kind of a dick.*

Jameson: *Kind of? ;)*

Oz: *Hey James?*

Oz: *Are you sure you can't*

Jameson: *Am I sure I can't...what? Did your phone die again?*

Fuck it. I'm just going to put it out there.

Oz: *Are you sure you can't ditch your friends? LOL*

Shit. It sounds really insensitive after I hit send. I should have added a goddamn wink face or something.

Jameson: *I'm looking at Hayley and she's shoving Ben & Jerry's into her face with a shovel at an alarming pace. I'd say for the time being, I'm stuck here.*

Oz: *When can I see you again?*

Jameson: *Honestly? Not soon enough.*

Jameson: *I can't believe I just sent that. Groan.*

God, this freaking girl.

Oz: *I really fucking miss you.*

Jameson: *I miss you too. Is that weird? It's only been a few days since I've seen you.*

Oz: *Doesn't matter. Not seeing you is making me slightly unstable. I should probs go run a few miles to burn off some of this nervous energy.*

Jameson: *Oddly, I find that very sweet—I find YOU very sweet. And charming.*

Oz: *You are...the sexiest fucking thing I've ever seen.*

Jameson: *Stop it! You're making me blush and giggle, and now my roommates are all staring at me.*

Oz: *I fucking love that about you.*

Jameson: *What? What do you love about me? (trying to be modest and blushing like crazy over here)*

Oz: *Everything. I fucking love everything.*

Jameson: *You can't say things like that in a text message!*

I laugh out loud and tap out a quick *Why not?*

Jameson: *Because! Don't you know anything about girls? That's something I want to hear in person. That's like...panty dropper material right there.*

My eyebrows shoot straight into my hairline and I stare at the words on my screen, stunned that they came from her. *Panty dropper, panty dropper, panty dropper.*

Jameson: *My point is—that was really sweet and unexpected.*

Oz: *Did it make you wet hearing I love everything about you?*

Jameson: *I'm not sexting you right now! I'm in a crowded room!*

Oz: *Come on—give me something! I'm cold and alone and it's Friday night.*

Jameson: *Yes. It got me wet. And "excited".*

Oz: *EXCITED, excited?*

Jameson: *Yes (Yes! Yes!)*

Oz: *I'm beginning to think you're naughtier than you look.*

Jameson: *Remember what I said to you the first time we met?*

Oz: *Something about being curious to sleep with me because of my incredible body?*

Jameson: *LOL, no! (but also yes) Never judge a girl by her cardigan.*

I'm in my bedroom, stretched out across my bed, the latest episode of *The Walking Dead* playing in the background on the TV, when I hear the faint knock. Tipping my head to make sure my ears aren't playing tricks on me—I'm not expecting anyone—I hear it again: several soft raps to the front door.

A pause.

Another knock.

Curious, I minimize the open window on my laptop, set it aside, and pad barefoot to the door, taking my sweet time. Stop in the kitchen and grab a bottle of water from the fridge. Turn the TV off in the living room, but not before flipping through a few channels.

When I finally pull open the front door, my eyes widen at the sight of James standing on my stoop, dressed head to toe like a preppy do-gooder. Like a librarian. Navy dress coat buttoned from the bottom to the top and tied at the waist. Pearls peeking out from the collar of her jacket. Navy blue, black, and green plaid skirt. The same black patent leather ballet slippers that still haunt my dreams.

"What took you so long to answer the dang door? I knocked five times!" Her obvious irritation is punctuated by the chattering of her teeth.

"I..." I stare dumbly down at her. "You're *here*."

"I am." She nods with a shiver, wrapping her arms around herself in a hug. "Can I come in? I'm f-freezing and this jacket isn't keeping me warm."

It's not her usual puffy winter coat.

"Shit!" I scramble aside so she can enter and give her a wide berth so she can step into the house. "Come in. Wow. What are you doing here? Not that I'm not happy to see you, but I thought Hayley needed you..."

"The guy finally texted her back so it was a false alarm." A coy smile. "Besides, I realized she didn't need me as much as *I* needed *you*."

Are my ears deceiving me, or does her voice sound sexier than usual? Almost like she's here to...

I shake the feathers out of my brain and swallow when she breezes past me into the living room. Glancing around, Jameson takes stock of the small space four of us call home. Her eyes hit the huge, sixty-inch television. The two couches, shades of diarrhea-brown. Bare beige walls. The Xbox Live and the unorganized stack of games that go with it.

Zeke's and Dylan's beeramid.

"Love what you've done with the place."

Jameson turns gradually toward me, making a show of untying the belt of her jacket, unbuttoning the toggles, pulling it open and shrugging it off. Her shoulders and slim figure are dressed in a baby blue cardigan with shiny navy buttons. It's buttoned to her neck, but it's thin, and holy shit—I don't think she's wearing anything under it. The pearl necklace circles her neck like a collar.

Nipples. Hard.

Stiff.

My eyes hover over her boobs.

Shit, is she wearing a bra? Why the hell wouldn't she be? Why is she wearing a plaid skirt? Surely she was just at home hanging with her roommates in yoga pants? Causal shit girls wear?

I gape like an adolescent schoolboy at her incredible rack, at the hard nipples poking through the soft fabric of her sweater, almost one hundred percent positive she's *naked* beneath it.

I shake my head again in denial—there is no way.

Jameson would *never* go braless in public.

Would she?

Stop looking at her tits, dude. Get a fucking grip.

Jameson makes a little humming sound as she drapes her coat over the arm of our recliner, a demure smile parting her lips. Coolly rests her hip against the back of the chair, legs crossing at the ankles. Folds her hands over her lap.

"So. Now what?"

My eyes fly back to her chest. "Uh."

I can think of eight hundred things to answer that and they all include nudity, nakedness, and bare flesh.

She gives another pleasant little hum. "I'm thinking we should go to your bedroom?" She's the epitome of innocence and class, minus the bra. "You know, for privacy, in case your roommates come home."

If Jameson wants to go to my room, on purpose, wearing nothing but that plaid skirt and cardigan, she'll get no objections from me.

I've had girls at my place before, a steady stream of one-night stands and hookups. Virtual strangers in my bed for the night, good for nothing but a quick screw and a swat on the ass, then straight out the door the way they came. Not *one* of them has lasted through the night; not *one* of them has made it to morning. Regardless, I'm not about to pass up the opportunity to find out what's under that sweater.

I'm not a *complete* fucking moron.

I grab Jameson's hand, lacing our fingers. Guide her down the long hall, switching lights off in the process. Cringe when I open the door to my room. "Shit, sorry it's such a mess. I didn't make the bed. Didn't think I'd be having company."

I release her hand and rush the room, hastily yanking the covers up on my bed. Throw the pillows back into place near the headboard. Toss a dirty tee shirt into the open closet.

"Hold up a minute."

"Sebastian, it's okay. Really." Jameson eases herself onto the bed, crossing her legs, and kicks her ballet flats to the floor. Pushes them out of the way, dangling her feet off the edge, her pretty bright pink toenails polished and shiny.

My eyes follow the movement of her fingers as they toy with the hem of her plaid skirt. Her plaid. Fucking. Skirt. She parts the fold, giving me a rare glimpse of creamy upper thigh, the elusive crevasse between her legs, the shadow of underwear.

Blood rushes to the brain inside my pants, my hands shooting to my hair. I pace to the far side of my bedroom as the sight of her skirt alone does shit to my cock that—*fucking A.*

It twitches.

If she's doing all this sexy shit on purpose—trying to make me horny and out of my mind—it's working.

The electricity from our chemistry has my hair standing on end. I find my voice, testing it out. "Are you doing that on purpose? Because you're testing my patience."

Her fingers find the bottom button of her cardigan and tug then flip the bottom hem of her skirt, affording me another peek. "I'm sure I don't know what you mean."

Those glossy lips tip into an angelic smile. Teeth bite down on that tempting bottom lip.

"Fine. All right." I grip the nearby desk chair, white knuckling it when she leans back on the bed and uncrosses her legs. Sits there with her knees spread apart, toying, *toying* with that bottom button of her top.

Toying with *me*.

"Although..." Jameson sighs. "It did occur to me earlier that—" She pauses, tips her head, and studies me, blue eyes alive and sizzling. "These feelings aren't going away, are they? In fact," she demurs. "They're getting worse."

I'm confused. What feelings is she talking about? Our friendship? Our dating?

"So I'm here to do something about it. Five dates is a long time, and we already have something most couples don't. We're friends." The bottom button gets pushed through its hole, her expression impassive even as it's released. Then another...and another, until I can see the flat plane of bare stomach and cute innie belly button. "And don't you think we both deserve it after being so patient?"

It.

It?

The death grip on my chair gets harder. Is she—

Holy fuck, is she about to *strip?*

"Jesus Jameson." Eager (to say the least), my leg involuntarily starts to twitch. "Are you seducing me?"

A low *mmm*. "I like you, Sebastian," comes her husky whisper. "I like your brains and your body, and I'm tired of saying *no*. Tired of rules. Tired of waiting for date number five."

"I want to—wait." Am I hearing her correctly? "*What?*"

A smirk. "You heard me."

HOW TO DATE A DOUCHEBAG

"Yeah, I *heard* you. I'm just not sure I *heard* you."

Her nimble fingertips travel down her flat stomach, teasing the waistband of her plaid skirt. Finger the delicate gold buckle fastening it. Pull the leather strap through the loop with a gentle tug.

"Listen close: I'm telling you *yes*."

Spellbound, I watch when she stands. The wool skirt parts, revealing only a pair of lavender lace panties. The panties I've fantasized about over and over again the past few days. The panties that have literally haunted my dreams. Pale purple, they hug her slender hips but conceal nothing. Absolutely. *Nothing.*

Naught but a scrap of lace constructed solely to plague my testosterone levels. They're indecent. Racy.

Magnificent.

A sexually repressed librarian fantasy come true.

I release the desk chair and forcibly raise my eyes to her face, advancing on her. "Shit, seriously?"

"Yesss," she whines through clenched teeth when my grasping hands close in on her tiny waist then drift south along her backside. Down her spine. Down her flawless skin. Down to that taut ass. My large palms slide into her lace panties, cup her butt cheeks, and...

Squeeze.

"How far do you wanna go?" She moans when I give her ass a smack, rubbing the sting away in slow circles.

"*All the way*." I bury my head at the base of her throat, groaning, grinding my erection against her stomach. "Tell me what you what James; tell me and I'll do it."

"I want to spend the night. This isn't a booty call." She rattles off demands. "This isn't a one-night stand. I want respect. You do *not* get to kick me out afterward, or in the morning. I want breakfast and I want you in the kitchen cooking it for me."

The pads of my palms continue stroking her brilliant backside, pulling her in flush. "How do waffles sound?"

273

"Waffles sound *delicious*." She gasps and my dick weeps in celebration. "But I want your shirt off."

"Yes, ma'am."

Reaching for the hem of my navy blue wrestling tee shirt, I pull it up and over my torso and toss it to the hardwood floor. It lands in a heap near her shoes.

"What else do you want gone?"

"Everything." Jameson leans forward, licks the smooth skin of my collarbone, and blows, humming her approval. "But we'll start with your track pants."

She lays her hands on me tenderly, feather-light fingers leaving a pleasure trail as they trace the corded muscles of my biceps. Forearms. Down my rock-hard abs, her fingertip drawing a leisurely circle around my belly button until it reaches the elastic band riding low on my hips.

Together we untie the corded knot at my waistband. Slide my pants down until I'm kicking, tripping over myself to get them off. Standing in just my tented gray boxer briefs.

Jameson gives me a small shove toward the foot of the bed, instructing me to, "Sit."

Like an excited, obedient puppy, I comply, practically panting.

Bracing herself over me, Jameson leans in, her silky brown hair skimming my bare chest. Her mouth brushes the corner of my lips. "*My* turn."

She goes for the middle button on her cardigan.

"Be gentle with me, James. I haven't had sex with anyone since before Utah. I've done so much jerking off my junk is chafed—legit chafed."

How's that for brutally honest?

Jameson leans in, kissing the side of my mouth and crooning in my ear. "You want me to make sweet, sweet love to you, baby? Not give it to you hard?"

Holy shit, give me the dirty talk.

"Yeah—that first one sounds about right. Then I want you to cuddle me until it's time for breakfast."

"Thinking 'bout that sex, but also 'bout them waffles," comes her coo.

We both laugh; shit she's funny. And smart. And beautiful. And the sound of my name on her lips feels better than any victory.

Sexier than any moan.

"If your left leg was lunch
and your right leg was dinner,
I'd want to snack between meals."

Jameson

I'm taking what I want.

   I'm taking my time.

   I'm taking off my skirt.

Standing in front of the bed now, the discarded plaid skirt pooled in a puddle at my feet, I step out of it and set to work on my sweater.

There's no shame in my game: if a guy can get laid whenever the hell he wants, with whoever the hell he wants, so can I.

I *want* what I want, and I'm done telling Sebastian *no*.

Done waiting.

I want the tension gone and I want to get…

Laid.

I want him—every last part of him: the foul mouth, the stupidly hectic schedule, the needy groupies, the obnoxious roommates. The good, bad, and ugly. He's gained my trust and I'm ready to take the next step.

I trust him.

I trust Sebastian Osborne.

On my mind constantly, I cannot stop thinking about him. Day and night. Night and day. Consuming me like a fever.

Like a drug.

36

#DOUCHEBAG

"I just finished a round of golf.
Want to be my 19th hole?"

Sebastian

My eyes go to her fingers. The creamy skin of her stomach. Her soft lower abs. The thighs I just had my hands on.

"Take a guess: what am I wearing under this sweater?" Jameson whispers in my direction, plucking another navy button free. A mere three buttons hold the sweater closed.

"Nothing?" I wish out loud.

Jameson drags a hand up her ribcage, looping her forefinger around the necklace circling her neck. She gives her head a shake. "Wrong."

My breath catches. "What then?"

"This. I'm wearing *this* under my sweater."

"The necklace?" I croak.

"Mmm hmmm."

"No bra?"

I fucking knew it.

Stepping forward, she closes the gap between us in one, two, three dainty steps, then bends and clasps my hands in hers, placing them on either side of her waist. My thumbs hit the tantalizing span of belly. Raising her arms, Jameson takes a sweeping handful of hair and holds it back, both hands behind her head.

Her blue sweater gaps open, revealing smooth skin. Stomach. The tantalizing underside of her bare breasts.

"Go ahead," she urges with that sexy whisper of hers. "Take it off."

Like I have to be told twice.

My trembling palms glide up her stomach. My nimble fingers pluck one button free. Then another.

I part the sweater, hands sweeping across her ribcage, the tips of my thumbs brushing over her stiff, dusky nipples. My eyes are fastened on them, palms stroking them tenderly, caressing.

Her tits are perfect, full and round, filling the palm of my hand. I want to suck and fuck them both. Taste them until her panties are soaking wet.

Jameson inches forward, whimpering, her arms coming down, grasping the back of my head. Her fingers plow through my thick hair when I lean forward and drag my tongue over her nipple, flick the tip, draw the entire thing in my mouth.

Suck it. Lick it. Suck it some more.

Her labored moan fills the room, a moan so loud and arduous I thank fuck my roommates are gone for the night.

I suckle her fantastic tits. Run my tongue along her collarbone. Lick the side of her neck. Our lips connect, tongues so wet and needy with want we're desperately seeking ecstasy. Deliriously frantically *fucking* with our mouths.

She mounts my lap. Straddles my thighs. Lines herself up and covers my giant erection with her hot, wet, pussy.

Hovers there.

Shamelessly, Jameson grinds down on my dick, giving a lap dance worthy of a goddamn *stripper*, working her pelvis until my eyes are rolling back into my skull, breasts shoved in my face.

"Shit, fuck, shit." I'm close to coming from the erotic gyrations. Jameson's ass cheeks fill my hands, and, unable to handle the sensations building inside my junk, I bear down, bracing myself before rising to my full height.

Turn. Dump her into the center of the bed.

I watch her perky boobs bounce from the fall on the mattress. Watch her nipples glisten, still wet from my tongue. Watch as she shrugs out of the pale blue cardigan, spread out before me in nothing but her scanty lace panties and prim necklace.

She squirms impatiently.

Inviting me to devour her.

"When I'm done with you, I'm going to *fuck you* in those pearls," I growl, shucking my boxers and climbing toward her across the bed.

Jameson spreads her thighs—spreads them wide—luring me in.

So tempting my mouth begins to water—I'm insatiably hungry and only Jameson can satisfy me.

I linger over her, balanced above where she wants it most. Lean in and drag my flattened tongue up the inside of her shaved bikini line. Pull back the scrap of fabric covering her smooth pussy and lick.

Once. Twice.

Husky, surprised, moany gasps fill the air when I flick her clit with the tip of my tongue, up and down.

"*Oh shit, oh shit*," she cries, pulling at my hair. "Don't you d-dare...stop. *Ohhh...*"

I don't intend to.

Hooking my fingers in the sheer waistband of her panties, I tug them down. Down her hips. Down her thighs. Down her legs. Jameson spreads herself wider, wriggling her hips on the bed, impatient and naked but for the gleaming, shiny strand of pearls around her pretty neck.

My fingers part her and I suck, tongue going deep like our lives depend on it.

37

#DOUCHEBAG

"You remind me of a pinky toe:
small, cute…
and I'll probably bang you on my
kitchen table in the
middle of the night."

Jameson

"Lay on your back."

The command comes out more demanding than I intended, but has the desired effect. Sebastian scurries to his back, naked as the day he was born, and I marvel at the sight of him. He's hard angles and calloused hands and firm everything.

But gentle.

I marvel at the fact that my cardigans turn him on.

My pearls turn him on.

So much so that when I reach behind my neck and unfasten the gleaming strand, Sebastian's dark eyes glaze over with fascination. Lust.

"Why are you taking those off?" he rumbles, weight shifting on the mattress beneath us when he puts his thick arms behind his head to study me. "Please keep them on. I like 'em."

My eyebrows rise as if to say, *You* know *why I'm taking these off.*

"You like these?" I pinch the gold clasp between two fingers and let the ivory rope dangle over his solid, heaving pecs. They hover until I lower them, dragging the warm pearls over provocatively erect nipples.

Sebastian licks his lips, dragging his teeth slowly over his tantalizing lower lip. "Did I say like? I meant love."

The pearls slide lower across his naked body, down the slick skin of his sternum. Down the ridged plane of his chiseled, rock-hard abdomen. Down his pelvis. I let them dip into the valley between his legs, over his thick pale thighs.

Slowly, I tease. Dragging the pearls up. Then down.

Up. Down.

The moan he lets out is guttural. Raw. So filled with hunger that when his hips twitch, his arms frenziedly reach for me, hands as shaky as his legs. "Come here, baby, come here."

"Yes." One word and I'm grasping the glossy necklace. I lower myself to the mattress, core pulsing and throbbing.

He's hot; I'm hotter.

I need it. He needs it.

We both want it.

Beg for it.

"Yes. Please, get a c-condom on." My post-orgasm voice shudders and tremors as hard as my ovaries. I clutch the pearls tighter in my hand. "I want you so bad."

"I'll wrap up after you put the pearls back on for me," he gruffly demands, eyes blazing when I have them securely around my neck and I'm flat on my back, hair fanned out on his pillow. "You're so sexy."

Sebastian begins the slow creep up my body, stiff dick and pre-come dragging along the inside of my leg when he hangs off the side of the bed to grab a condom from his bedside table. My nerve cells strum on high, buzzing. Vibrating. Thighs itching to be filled.

He peels back the foil package, slides the condom carefully out of its wrapper. We watch breathlessly as he guides it down the length of his shaft, arms and muscles straining from the anticipation.

Lust-filled air and sexual tension overtake us.

We watch *breathlessly* when he kneels between my legs. My thighs.

I spread my legs and lift my ass off the bed, head thrown back when he finally pushes in slowly. Pushes *home*. Slides that big dick in, deliberate in his continuous rhythm, in each and every thrust.

His moan is gruff. Masculine. Intoxicating.

"Oh. Fuck. Yeah. *Yeah* sweetheart...you feel so good James...so good, baby," he chants, planting a sloppy kiss on my lips. I open for him, sucking on his tongue while those lean hips rail into me, wet and messy and wild.

Sweetheart. Baby.

Our eyes meet. Lock.

Watching my partner's face while he *screws* me isn't something I normally do; I've always found it too intimate. Unsettling. Maybe it's because I wasn't in love with any of my previous partners, so gazing into their eyes while they bang me into the bedposts? Not my thing.

But when Sebastian lifts his intense, broody eyes to mine, I'm a goner. Mesmerized.

His rotating pelvis become unhurried, dark eyes fixated on mine. Slowly but steadily the mood changes; his feverish fucking suddenly becomes…

Kisses to my temple. Aching, desperate moans in my mouth.

"You're beautiful…so gorgeous," he murmurs hoarsely as his massive palms reach under my ass, lifting. Rocking deep, so deep I *gasp*. And gasp again and again. Stars shine behind my eyes and my vision blurs. I thrash my head, hair spilling on the pillow as this glorious—

"Jameson, Jameson. I…*I*…" Whatever words he's trying to say get lodged in his throat, emotion overwhelming his expression. His throaty grunts are music to my lady bits and I—

"Wanna be on top," I plead against his neck. "Pull out, Oz…p-pull out…"

I can have another orgasm if I'm on top. Maybe two.

The words spill out of my mouth as my legs go wide—wide as they'll go, pulling and tugging him by the hips a few more frantic seconds so he'll grind deeper. Push harder. Deeper and deeper he pumps those athletic hips, working me over, his stamina a thing of beauty.

It's a miracle he hasn't come yet.

Sebastian stops and I give a little whimper when he pulls out, moan like I'm *dying* from the loss of penetration. Eight limbs tremble when he rolls over and lies flat on his back, reaching for me, slick cock standing at attention.

I lay on top of him, relishing the skin-on-skin contact before straddling his waist, dragging my tongue across his for an open-mouthed kiss. It mimics our sex. Our lovemaking.

My knees hit the mattress when I climb on top, Sebastian's hard cock brushing against my ass cheeks in the most delicious way. Channeling my inner stripper, I swivel my hips, watch his half-hooded eyes slam shut from the pleasure when the slippery tip teases my back door before I lower myself.

I undulate my hips so excruciatingly slowly I want.

To.

Die.

Sebastian's fingertips grip my thighs, easing up my body. Cup my breasts. He runs his flat palms in slow circles around my hard nipples. And if it were possible for him to be any deeper inside me, Sebastian flexes, tightening his torso. Rises into a sitting position. Wraps his powerful tattooed arms around my waist and buries his nose in the crook of my neck, impaling me farther.

"Jameson," he croons, stroking my back, thrusting up into me. "Jameson, *Jameson.*"

Loving me.

It's heaven.

It's *hell.*

It's bliss.

"God, I love the sounds you make," he moans. Groans and thrusts. Strokes my damp hair as his dick strokes my g-spot. His deep-throated grunts are in sync with my breathless gasps. "You feel *so good...so good...* shit...*uh...uh*...shit...I'm close...James, *baby,* I'm gonna come."

"Oh god, *yes! Yes!* Me too," I damn near sob. "Hard, push...yes, ohgod*ohgod*, yes, hard... *Oh!* Right there, *right there.* Oh!"

It's loud and beautiful and sweaty.

It's real.

"I can't do it any more, Sebastian. Leave me alone and get me food."

"Come on, Jameson. One more time before we go out. Please?"

"You're insatiable—stop begging. I've created a monster."

"Once more and I'll leave you alone. Promise."

"What a load of crap. You've said that *twice* already."

"But I didn't mean it those other two times."

"Sebastian, I need a shower. And I need food—I'm hungry!"

"I can think of a few things to satisfy your appetite."

"Ew."

"You weren't saying 'ew' when you were blowing me during Game of Thrones."

"First of all, could we not call it 'blowing you'? It makes me feel cheap. Secondly, you promised me a hamburger from Malone's."

"Ugh, fine."

"Hey pal, you're just lucky I'm still here. We've been in bed for what feels like a hundred godforsaken hours."

"Is it sick that I'm beginning to find it sexy when you roll your eyes at me like that?"

"Um, yeah, it's a *little* weird."

"I can't help wanting to blow a load every time I see you."

"Is it weird I find that horrible, somewhat degrading sentence mildly erotic?"

"Will it get me laid if I say it's not weird?"

"Probably."

"Then no. It's not weird."

38

#DOUCHEBAG

"I just swiped right with someone knowing I would get in an argument with her. She had "that look" about her. So that's my pathetic Friday night so far."

Sebastian

Watching Jameson across the crowded room, a few things immediately cross my mind:

1. I hit that—four times in the past twenty-four hours.
2. Four times.
3. Best sex of my life—and trust me, I've had plenty of it.
4. She's just as horny and depraved as I am in bed, thank. Fucking. God.
5. I am harboring some serious feelings for her.

A smug grin crosses my face, like I've stumbled across an untapped gold mine not a soul before me has discovered. Because no one—*and I mean no one*—would look at Jameson and suspect what I already know: she's hiding a banging body under those conservative clothes. Fucking fantastic boobs. Round, toned ass. Flat stomach.

Tight pussy.

Slipping into that shit? Toe-curling *ecstasy*.

Men pass her over; they see preppy cardigan sweaters and dainty shoes. They see *boring*. Staid. Buttoned up. A prude with a very smart mouth. They assume she's sexually repressed, too much work for not enough output.

Like I did.

Which is fine—more Jameson Clark for me.

Every inch of her is all mine.

Holding court near the kitchen, the little vixen glances up from her conversation and I watch as she drags her exotic blue gaze up and down my physique, undressing me with her eyes, mouth curling into a knowing smirk above her red beer cup.

I return the favor, sizing her up: the light pink, tight-fitted sweater with the V-neck showing only a conservative amount of cleavage. Cropped skinny capris. The high, strappy wedge sandals she debated a full ten minutes on before deciding it wasn't too cold to wear them outside.

In her pearl necklace's place? A delicate gold chain with the word *karma*.

Her roommate, Allison, leans into her just then, speaking into her ear, causing James to laugh cheerfully. She throws her head back, exposing a column of neck I know smells like sweet coconut and tastes like dessert when it's sucked on.

"Why do you keep looking over at Parker and his slam piece?" asks my teammate Pat Pitwell good-naturedly. For all his rough edges, he's a really nice guy. Decent. He's at school to wrestle, get a degree, and get out. He doesn't sleep around, and he doesn't make trouble.

So I'm honest with him. "I'm dating the girl in pink."

"No shit?" Pitwell's black bushy eyebrows shoot straight to the cornrows braided in his hair. "Seriously?"

"Seriously."

"Goody two-shoes?"

I let the comment slide. "Yeah. I think she's my girlfriend."

"A girlfriend? Good for you, man." He chugs from his red solo cup. "Pink sweater got a name?"

Pink sweater—*that* makes me smile. "James."

"Seriously?" he asks again. "For real? Her name is James?"

"Yeah, seriously."

"That's a dude's name."

"I know." We both study her from across the room. "But it suits her."

"Home girl got class," Pitwell observes over the top of his beer.

"She sure does."

"Still wondering how she ended up with a brother like you, are you?"

"Every day."

"Well good for you, man." He looks her over. "She sure is a pretty little thing."

A nod. "Sure is."

"She can't keep her eyes off you, brah. You should go over there, lay claim to that shit."

His hand clamping down on my shoulder propels me forward. I cross the room with long, purposeful strides, making it to Jameson's side in fifteen footsteps flat. Approach her from behind. Wrap my arms around her waist, lacing my fingers just under her breasts, lips pressing a kiss to the curve of her neck while giving Parker and Allison a nod. "What was that look you were giving me from across the room?" I ask into the shell of her ear.

She snuggles, sagging into me, but rolls her eyes. "Pfft, what look?"

"You know the look."

Jameson taps a finger to her chin. "You'll have to be more specific. Was it my 'I'm thirsty and need another drink' look, or my 'I'm undressing Sebastian with my eyes' look?"

"Yes." Ignoring Parker and Allison, I can't keep my hands off her and I drag them down her ribcage, settling them at the empty belt loops of her jeans. Tug and pull closer.

She makes no attempt to pull away, but rather, seems to melt into me.

Getting her into bed later will be a piece of cake.

"Fine, then yes. Guilty," she teases. "It's your fault for dragging me here—I just assumed I'd be spending tonight in pajamas watching a movie."

"So what you're saying is, you want to go back to bed?" I purr low in her ear so only she can hear me—not that anyone would be able hear us anyway, not with the music blasting through the surround sound, high-def speakers. The room practically vibrates.

Her laugh curls my toes. "Oh god, no—my crotch can't handle any more Sebastian Osborne."

"Wanna make a bet?"

This earns me another laugh; soft and sexy, her glossy hair beckons. I lift a hand to run my palm down the locks, fingers intimately straining through each satiny strand like sand through an hourglass.

Fuck, even her hair makes me hard.

I tug at the waistband of her jeans impatiently. "Come on, let's get out of here and go back to my place before my roommates get home."

I'm a young, randy, walking erection; she can hardly fault me for that. Jameson's lips part to refute—or *agree*—but her response is cut off by her damn roommate, whose timing is for shit.

"This party is fun!" Allison banters shrilly, oblivious to the negotiations taking place, and frustrated, I grumble my displeasure into Jameson's hair.

"Make her go away."

"Thanks for the tickets to your meet the last week Oz. I had a great time, didn't I James?" She nudges Jameson with her elbow—hard—prompting her. "They were amazing seats. Weren't they amazing seats James?"

Great. She's drunk.

Speaking of drunk, obnoxious friends—over Allison's shoulder, I see a few guys from the wrestling team approaching, curiosity driving the nosy bastards forward. They've wasted no time encroaching on my territory.

Awesome.

"Heads up ladies, assholes approaching." I step closer to Jameson and tighten my hold around her waist in solidarity.

Protectively.

A united front.

Leading the pack is Zeke Daniels, perpetual dickface, pushing through the crowd like a gladiator heading to battle. Determined and proud—and bearing a grudge.

His hard, steely crosshairs are on Jameson, then dart to Allison, dismissing her. Those untrusting gray eyes begin their perusal of Jameson, beginning at her feet, swiftly moving up her denim clad legs. Pausing at the apex of her thighs. Linger too long on her breasts. Face. Hair.

Zeke's jaded perusal misses not a single scrap of fabric or inch of exposed skin on Jameson's body.

My guard goes up when frozen regard hits her pristine pink sweater...the elegant necklace...the glossy lips. They narrow, irritated. Nostrils flare.

Shit, he really doesn't want me dating this girl. I don't know why or what his problem is, but I have a feeling at some point, I'm going to find out.

The hard way.

"Park. Ozzy. You gonna introduce us to your playthings?" Zeke's sullen gray eyes hit the arm I have resting under Jameson's tits and he plants a sneer on his face.

Dude is just so fucking *miserable*.

"Guys, this is Jameson," I give her tiny waist a squeeze. "You know her roommate, Allison."

Allison tips her hand in a perky, friendly wave. "Hey guys. Congratulations on your wins this week."

We didn't just beat Stanford—we decimated them, individually and as a team.

"Hi." One of my teammates steps forward, arm extended in a greeting like he's meeting the homecoming queen, his expression is eager. "I'm Gunder—I mean, I'm *Rex*. Rex Gunderson. Hi."

Enthusiastic doesn't do Gunderson justice.

Wrestling in the lightweight class, Rex might be a winner on the mat, but he's obviously out of practice with ladies; I can practically visualize the growing chub inside his pants and hear the internal dialogue: *Hi, I'm Rex. You're pretty. Can I take you back to my dorm and date you? I've never touched boobs. Can we date? And by date, I mean hump.*

"Rex, it's nice to meet you." Jameson's hand goes out for a handshake and Gunderson works it like a water pump. Once, twice. Three times.

Four.

Five.

I glower. "Okay dude, that's e-fucking-nuff."

Beside him, Zeke makes his move.

"Jameson, Jameson, now where have I seen you before?" he asks, casually rubbing the stubble along the square jawline he hasn't bothered to shave in days. Beefy fingers snap in her direction. "Right! Sexy Librarian. I *almost* didn't recognize you without all the books. You must be a fantastic lay to have our boy Ozzy here following you around like a dog in heat—without being paid, too."

My arms fall from Jameson's waist, prepared to—

"I know all about you betting him to kiss me, so don't bother bringing it up." Chin tipped up, Jameson takes the wind out of his sails with blatant animosity.

Allison snorts and becomes the next target of Zeke's rapid-fire loathing. "Allison, Allison, *Allison*. You're another story entirely. Want to know what we call you behind your back?"

Oh shit, he's gonna say it.

In front of everyone.

"Zeke, dude, don't." I put my arm out to stop him, fingers braced against his rock solid chest in protest.

He laughs, shoving me back. "Around our place we call you Fuck Buddy."

Fuck.

"Wow. Just...w-wow." Allison's lip quivers but she holds her ground. "Y-you...you are *rude*. I should slap you," Allison chastises him, small spray-tanned fists clenched at her sides. "I want to slap you. James, can I slap him?"

Drunk Allison is a tigress.

"I know I'm rude." Zeke shrugs, raking those weird gray eyes down her body, stepping into her personal space, leaning in close. "I just. Don't. Care."

Allison takes a step back, glancing from me, to Zeke, and back. "I cannot believe this dickhead is Parker's roommate."

I can't believe it either and become desperate to extinguish these flames. "Can someone find Parker? Gunderson. Go. And hurry the fuck up."

"You are a piece of shit," Allison shouts above the music. "Who do you think you are?"

Everyone watches the sparring match between Zeke and Allison, enthralled by the live entertainment. Someone even turns down the sound system to a dull roar.

Allison continues challenging Zeke, undaunted. "What's your problem with us? Huh? Answer me!"

Zeke's hot head is decidedly cool. "When you *deserve* my respect, I will give it to you." His gaze sweeps over Jameson. "She is a gold-digging *bet* he shouldn't have won, and you're just a Tinder swipe."

Arms crossed, Jameson's laugh surprises us all. "You still haven't paid him for the bet *I* helped him win, by the way," she innocently chimes in, expression schooled. "You owe him five hundred bucks."

Emotionless silver irises slide in my direction. "See what I mean? She's only after your money."

"*What* money?" Jameson laughs. "You're a deadbeat. Unlike you, Oz is actually a nice guy who works his *ass* off for your team, and look how you're treating the people he cares about."

"People he *cares* about?" Zeke grits out through clenched teeth. "You are a waste of his time."

"Whoa, son, show some respect." Pat cuts in before I knock Zeke to the ground, arm braced across Zeke's chest, forcing him to stand down. "Brother, I think you timed out. Walk away before Osborne and his girls knock yo pretty white boy teeth out yo skull." The big black wrestler bumps Zeke with his meaty arm.

"Sorry ladies. His mama never taught him no manners."

Allison continues to stare Zeke down, pure loathing aimed in his direction as she salutes him with a solid middle finger salute. "Bye, bye Daniels. Nice meeting you."

A retort is on the tip of his sharp tongue, but he hesitates—long enough for Pitwell to shove him toward the kitchen and away from the confrontation, women, and all people in general. Daniels turns, shuffling across the carpet into the other room—but not before shooting a glare over his shoulder.

At Allison.

At Jameson.

"He's got a real chip on his shoulder," Jameson says, nestling into the crook of my arm. "I wonder what his problem is. For real."

"Abandonment issues, obviously," her roommate theorizes as Parker finally drags his sorry ass over. Allison hiccups, recounting the entire exchange, narrowing her eyes toward the door Zeke disappeared through. "I want to scratch his dead lifeless eyes out."

"He can be a decent guy once you get to know him," Parker throws in diplomatically, having missed all the action.

"*No*—he is a major *douche*bag," Allison counters. She throws her hands up. "And you! Did you hear what he called me? Maybe I should be pissed at you, too! What is wrong with you? How dare you disrespect me like that?"

"I haven't done anything!" Parker argues, red faced.

"He called me *Fuck* Buddy!"

"I was in the backyard playing beer pong, babe." Parker goes on the defense. "And I've never called you fuck buddy in my life!"

"That's true, Allison. He hasn't." But then again, he's also never defended her when we say it.

"Let's just leave. This party is a train wreck." Jameson steps out of my hold and into Allison's for a hug. "What do you want to do?"

"My head hurts. I want to go home," Allison murmurs, elbowing Parker in the ribcage. "Parker, take me home. And this time, you're *spending* the night."

I shoot good luck Parker's way and give him a fist bump, glad Jameson and I weren't the center of all the drama, glad I'm not on the receiving end of what's sure to be one hell of an ass ripping.

A few quick nods, a few more hugs.

"We're out. I'm getting James the fuck outta here." I give Allison a pointed look, glancing down at James. "Don't wait up."

"My walk of shame is about to
become positive reinforcement;
I stopped for coffee
and walked out looking like
someone on their way to work."

Jameson

I can't get Zeke Daniels off my mind. His indifference. His rude behavior. His callous demeanor.

Something about the way he was watching Sebastian and me from across the room caught and held my attention; long before his careening gaze turned to a scowl, it was filled with something completely unexpected.

Pain.

I'm no psychologist—and I've been wrong before—but there is no denying it: Sebastian Osborne has something Zeke Daniels wants, and he's as petulant as a child who can't express his feelings, dealing with it the only way he knows how—through frustration and anger.

And mini bitch fits.

But *why?*

Why did he find it necessary to degrade Allison? Why did he find it necessary to demean my budding relationship with Oz? I assumed they were friends, but now I'm not so sure.

No one would treat a friend like that.

Not if they cared.

I consider this fact while Oz uses the toilet, emerging from the bathroom moments later to collect me where I'm perched on the end of the sofa in the living room.

He leads me by the hand down the short hall to his bedroom, lacing our fingers together when we cross the threshold. Flipping on the light, he presses me gently against the back of the closed door. Large hands cup my face, thumbs brush the underside of my chin in slow strokes. Dark, penetrating eyes scan my face as we wordlessly study each other.

The rough pad of his forefinger traces the line of my skin in a slow trail, over my cheekbone and along the curve of my eyebrow.

His thumb tracks down the bridge of my nose until he reaches the cupid's bow of my lip. Rests it there.

Rubs his thumb back and forth across my soft, parted lips, his gentle touch leaving a mark on my skin like a brand.

As he intends.

Sebastian slides those magnificent hands across each side of my neck, raking them through my hair, and leans in, nostrils flaring. Settles his mouth on mine.

Kisses me. Softly. Tenderly.

It deepens.

Wide, open-mouth kisses, heavy on the tongue.

Pinned to the door, my back arches when he moves those magic hands lower. Over my shoulders and down my arms, painstakingly slowly. Grasps my hips. They snake around to my rear, grabbing a handful. His knees bend, and before I can react, he's effortlessly hauling me up and off the ground like I weigh nothing, our mouths still fused together.

With Sebastian, I'm dainty and petite and deliciously vulnerable.

Suspended in the air, my legs instinctually wrap around his waist. He leans into me, all our yummy, private bits smashed together in perfect symmetry, lined up like a sexy, heavily panting puzzle.

We fit.

"I've been wanting to kiss you all night." I gasp when his lips hit the corner of my mouth.

"Yum. You taste like beer and honey." He hums in my ear. "And me. You taste like me."

"I like that you taste yourself on me." I purr at him in between kisses. "It's sexy."

"Jesus James, I can't get enough of you. You're—"

A booming crash stops whatever he's about to say; Sebastian goes lethally still, listening.

A door slams shut, the thud accompanied by muffled voices

and raucous female laughter. Giggling. More than two people are obviously stumbling down the hallway and falling into furniture. Another door slams, voices resonating from the next room. The telltale noises of mattress springs creaking. The sounds of a girl being tickled.

Moaning. Tittering.

Oh jeez.

"Great, dickwad is back with groupies," he complains stridently against my lips. "We need a house rule about that."

"Shhh, quiet," I whisper. "They'll hear us."

"I will not *shhh*." His velvety voice raises defiantly. "That dickhead can kiss my lily white ass, especially after that shit he pulled at the party." Calloused fingertips dip into the neckline of my pink angora sweater, exploring the swell of my breasts. "You've been waiting to kiss me all night and I've been waiting to get you alone."

"But we've been together since last night." I nip his earlobe playfully. "I only went home to shower and change."

"Doesn't matter." Deft hands sweep back my hair while his seductive lips find purchase on my neck, nipping gently, tendons in his biceps flexing with *every* movement as he balances my weight. "So soft and pretty…your sweater is driving me to fucking distraction."

His voice is low and gruff and hot—*so hot*. I moan when his mouth does a leisurely lap up the column of my neck in a single stroke, rolling that naughty tongue across my skin like he's lapping up honey.

And I've never, *never* been one for licking—ever. But I like *this* licking. Love his mouth and his lips and his tongue. They're provocative in a way that gets me so deliriously hot and bothered and ten shades of turned on.

Wet.

My hips swivel, rocking toward the throbbing length between his muscular thighs, my eyes wandering toward the bed against the far wall. I must be gazing at it longingly because he asks, "You wanna get naked?"

"Yes." I feel more alive than I have in years, more sexually awake than I have in my entire freaking life.

I feel sexual. Sexy. Desirable.

Safe, protected with his strong arms wrapped around me.

Adored.

I feel powerful and respected, and there's no doubt I'm calling the shots here.

Sebastian walks us to the bed, lays me on the edge, and gets down on one knee. Unbuckles my platform wedges, one thin leather strap at a time, before sliding them off my feet and setting them off to the side. Massages my heels before kissing my pink toenails.

Our hands reach for the zipper of my jeans at the same time.

Snap.

Zip.

I lift my hips and shimmy them off with ease. Oz kisses my knees, running his rough hands up my thighs until every last nerve in my body tingles. Quivers.

Jolts alive.

My shaking legs involuntarily spread as I reach for the hem of my sweater, pulling it up and over my head. It hits the ground at the same time Sebastian's fingers meet the bare skin on my abdomen. He scoots up, bending forward to press his warm lips near the space below my breasts, his big hands caging my ribs.

I stare down at him, at the top of his head, astonished when his tattooed arms wrap around my waist in an embrace and he lays his forehead against my stomach, holding me.

Just...*holding* me.

It's strange.

And beautiful.

My fingers rake through his short hair then skim over the firm planes of his deltoids; they're rock-hard and potent, one of my favorite parts of a man, especially from behind. Flattening my palms, they graze his shoulder blades and thick neck, kneading and massaging his dense, muscular body.

Relaxed, Sebastian hums.

Content.

After a time, butterfly kisses pepper my stomach, that gorgeous mouth moving across my skin toward my décolletage.

"Jameson," he mumbles against my scorching flesh, his fingers tracing the outer cup of my lacy, demi-cup bra. The sheer lace is nude and almost see-through, and I watch transfixed when Sebastian nuzzles my left breast with his nose. Sucks gently on one hard nipple through the fabric. Fondles the right breast in his oversized palm, mesmerized.

My head tips back and I gasp, pawing at the mattress beneath me when he licks and teases my nipples, dampening my bra. Sucks. Flicks the tip with his tongue.

He watches me the entire time, dark eyes burning with desire.

For me.

Our eyes collide, ablaze and aroused. Half hooded and hazy.

Drunk on lust.

My lips part. Tongue runs along my bottom lip as my head rolls, hair falling in waves, stunned that Sebastian already knows how to work my body.

Knows the tells that make me orgasm.

My boobs being one of them.

"Naked," I whimper. "Get naked."

"I wanna fuck these tits," he growls, releasing one and rising to stand. Hands hasten to his zipper and I watch as he tugs, frantically propelling the metal teeth…open. Full access. Relief when his jeans finally get shoved down over his erection.

Next, he whips off his tee, tossing it aside, and I revel in his body. It's gorgeous, a work of art. Muscular doesn't begin to describe it. Strapping. Strong. Powerful. All broad shoulders and hard pecs. Smooth in all the right places, with a pleasure trail dipping down into his boxer briefs—a path I follow with my index finger.

"God I'm hard as a fucking rock."

He throbs beneath his light gray boxers, the outline of his cock straining to bust through the cotton. I reach for the waistband, caressing just inside the elastic with my fingertips, back and forth (a total tease, I know) before running my flat palms along the smooth span of his waist, behind to his firm ass, inside his boxers. Squeeze that *ridiculously* shapely ass.

Push his underwear down the leanest hips I've ever had the privilege to touch, guide them over his erection until my palms cup his glutes and squeeze.

He's eyelevel. *It* is right in front of my face and *it* is huge.

Mouth watering, I eagerly lower my head and lick it like a lollypop, teasing beneath the tip with quick flicks of my tongue before wrapping my lips completely around it, sucking. Just. The. Tip.

"Fuck James, fuck. Shit." He pants a little frenziedly, hips thrusting toward me. "Suck it."

I suck just the end, tongue swiping at the clear pre-come and gloating with every grunt and groan coming from his strapping chest. Sebastian's fists clench and unclench at his sides, a sure sign he's trying to retain his composure.

"Fuck, stop. I need you to stop, but shit...*oh shit*... that feels f-fucking good." His tattooed arms go behind his neck and his head dips, eyelids fluttering like butterfly wings. He peels them open, watching my teeth friskily nip with glassy eyes. "Take it all, take it all," he begs, voice raising a few octaves. "*Please* Jameson, please just fucking *suck* it."

I do. Hands grasping his fine ass, I let them wander south at the same time I draw his thick, hard dick farther into my mouth. Hands continue onward, seeking, effortlessly discovering the secret spot under his balls I've only read about online, and I press down, rub it with circular motions while I suck.

"Oh...my...fucking...g-god," he rasps, his loud groan sounding like a tortured mixture of pleasure and pain. "Jameson...mmph...*uh*...uh...fuck..."

Sebastian's brawny muscles contract, biceps flexing behind his neck, hips driving forward. "Shit, shit, I'm gonna come, I'm gonna come," he repeats. "And then I'm gonna...f-*fuck*...fuck you."

40

#DOUCHEBAG

"Having a penis is like having a
really stupid, drunk best friend.
You see it doing all this dumb shit,
but you're not the one in charge.
And sometimes you take
pictures of him."

Sebastian

Jameson's warm sexy body is burrowed in the crook of my frame, head tucked under my chin, ass nestled against my groin. Like two pieces of a complex puzzle we've finally managed to solve, we fit together.

Perfectly.

I don't think we slept this way throughout the night. When we finally finished fucking, she told me I was a "hot box" and settled on the far side of the bed facing the window, sighing contently, happy with her own space.

Like a dude.

Jameson Clark is *not* a cuddler, but when I awoke to yet another raging boner, there was no resistance to my hauling her naked body to my side of the bed. No complaining. Only blissful sighs when I enveloped my strong arms around her, drawing her close, immediately folding her into my body.

Tenderly, I nuzzle her neck. Sniff her hair and brush back the loose strands so I can kiss the long column of skin below her ear. Palm settling on her breast, I tease her areola until her nipple puckers beneath my wanton fingertips, waking up.

Wanting to play.

Mission accomplished.

"Mmm…" She yawns, stretching beneath me, elongating her torso and making it easier for my hands to roam, drag them up and down her feminine curves. Marvel at her smooth skin.

"That feels good." She luxuriates beneath my touch. Kissing the spot between her shoulder blades, I move upward, sucking gently on her neck, careful not a leave a mark on her flawless skin. I nestle the tip of my erection into her ass crack.

I'm affected by every one of her muttered coos.

"*You* feel good." I lightly caress her hip while rotating mine

307

and land a kiss on her shoulder. She has a smattering of freckles, and I rest my lips there.

Moaning, her arm comes up to cradle the back of my head while I palm her breast, raking her fingers along my scalp—damn, aren't we the picture of domestic fucking bliss?

"Sebastian." Jameson gasps softly, pelvis beginning to rock, ever so slowly.

Yes, baby, *just* like *that*.

"You're never wearing clothes to bed again," my brusque voice informs her.

"I'm not?"

My head gives a definitive shake. "Now that I've seen you naked? *Hell* fucking *no.*"

The words settle on the air; we're quiet then, basking in each other. When Jameson rolls onto her back, she smiles up at me, satisfaction on her relaxed brows. "Does this mean you're keeping me around for a while?"

My chest swells with pride. I feel like I've done something *right* with us, something long lasting.

Something permanent, and goddammit, I suck at this emotional bullshit, but baser instincts prevail and have me wrapping my arms around Jameson's waist. Embracing her. Planting open-mouthed kisses on her neck. Resting my hands on her lower abdomen, the most womanly part of her body.

The source of her feminine power.

"Do you want to be around for a while?" I ask the crook of her neck.

"You know I wouldn't be here if I didn't." Her soft lips kiss the side of my forearm, and, as if she senses the change in me—the pensive silence—she tilts her neck toward my face.

"Sebastian? I thought you were going to..." Jameson prompts, bright blue eyes coyly reading my expression, and she shifts position, reaching between our bodies. Enfolds my thick morning wood in her hands, squeezing. "Have your way with me this morning."

Up and down…up and down, my cock pulses in her hand with every even stroke until my thighs are shaking—the need for her is *that* urgent. That real.

"Is that what you want? Me to have my way with you this morning?" The question comes out in a hiss when her hands round the tip of my dick, thumbs brushing the head.

"*Yes.*"

It takes me a few seconds to grab a condom, tear it open, and slide it on, position myself above her. Jameson's eyes cloud, hazy with lust and desire when I slip in. She's warm, dripping wet, and willing. So willing.

Soft.

Sexy.

Hair pooled around her like some kind of goddamn angel, she watches me quietly, braced above her.

We go methodically, painfully slowly, the only sound in the room our labored breathing and the headboard bang, bang, banging the wall with each and every languid thrust. The thumping sound gets me harder.

Toes rooted and digging into the mattress, I glide in and out of her slick heat like it was made just for my cock.

Jameson's palm strokes my cheek and I bend my head, covering her lips with mine, breathe her in and out, then in again, like she's the air I need to survive.

Because she is.

Somehow…

Shit, this girl means everything to me.

"Mmm, *mmm*." She moans sweetly into my mouth when her body begins to climax, the muscles in her tight pussy contracting and squeezing the shit out of me in the best possible way.

I come moments later, the shockwaves quivering my lower body.

"Baby." I speak the promise into her hair, lovingly stroking the damp locks away from her temple as I cradle her in my arms. "Jameson."

She is mine.

#DOUCHEBAG

"At birth I was given the choice
between a good memory
and a big dick.
I cannot for the life of me
remember which one I chose…"

Sebastian

Zeke is waiting for me in the kitchen when I return from taking Jameson home, seated at the kitchen table wearing nothing but boxer shorts and a scowl.

I walk past him, pull open the fridge, and take out the cream cheese. A bagel. A butter knife from the drawer.

Zeke crosses his brawny arms and shifts in his seat. "I heard you *fucking* last night. All night."

I pop the bagel in the toaster and turn to face him, adopting his posture by crossing my own arms. "So? What the hell is your problem, dude? You brought home who-knows-how-many chicks last night after that scene at the party, and you're pissed you had to listen to Jameson and me?" The toaster ticks, and I give it a shake and a smack to keep it working. "Get over it."

"If you're pity fucking her out of some twisted obligation. I can find ten girls to bang you *right* now."

Pity fuck? What the—

I flex my fingers to avoid clenching them into fists and stare down at my toasting bagel. "Could you stop calling it *fucking?*"

Christ, now I'm starting to sound like a girl. Scowling at the thought, I pull the toaster cord out of the outlet then dig inside the toaster with my knife to retrieve the only carbs I'll eat today.

"You don't like to call it fucking any more? You want something a little more flowery?" He says it with a sardonic laugh. "Don't tell me—you call it making love."

"Actually, yeah." I smear tons of cream cheese on my bagel and stuff a hunk in my mouth. Talk and chew. "That's exactly what I'd call it, and I don't need to be discussing it with you. My shit, what I do is none of your business."

"It used to be my business."

"Well it's not any more, and someday, Zeke, I hope you find

someone special who makes you change your mind."

If possible, his expression darkens. "Wow. This bitch has done a number on you—really messed you up, hasn't she? Don't you dare fucking let her inside your head man."

"Is that what this is about?" I ignore the fact that he just called Jameson a bitch because I know it will only lead to a physical altercation. "The team?"

"If you lose a single match, I'll—"

"You'll what? You're in no position to threaten me."

Zeke stares at me, the cold pallor of his gray eyes disarming. "I'm warning you now, Osborne. Don't let this girl affect your place on the team."

This girl? Okay, now he's just being dramatic, so in true Jameson fashion, I give my eyes a solid roll. "She won't."

"She better not, because you barely fucking know her."

Because he's wrong.

I do know her.

I know Jameson Clark better than I know him. I know that she only watches reality television and loves *The Bachelor* so much she's in a fantasy league. I know she has two sisters and an eleven-year-old Schnauzer named Leopold. I know she wants stability and a good job, but she wants to be a mom even more. When she was twelve, she died her hair a putrid shade of green. When she was fifteen, she kissed some dude name Kevin behind the baseball dugouts and he tried to touch her boobs.

Jameson knows why I want to be in human resources. She knows I don't want to wrestle professionally, but will do it if the money is good, if any coaches want me before I get a "real job". She's texted with my sister, knows that when I was fourteen, I cried watching *Marley & Me*, and that I love dogs. And traveling. She knows family comes before friends, and how hard my parents work to pay for my education.

She's one of the few people who know I have a night job.

I trust her.

I—

"Are you even listening to me jackoff?" Zeke's voice cuts in. "You check that shit at the damn door, hear me?"

This time, I do clench my hand into a fist. "You are seriously overstepping yourself my friend."

"Because you're *not* fucking *listening*."

Setting the butter knife in the sink, I spin back on my heels to face him. "That *girl*, as you keep calling her, is my friend. My *girl*friend. And if I ever catch you—or anyone—disrespecting her, I won't hesitate to choose her over you." I lean against the counter and speak slowly. "In fact, I'd chose Jameson over the entire team if I had to. So don't test me."

"Ozzy, just listen to me—"

"No, you listen to me: this conversation is over and we are never having it again."

Surprisingly, he lets it go, and because I'm not a pansy, I let him sit and stew in an awkward silence as I unemotionally finish my cold goddamn bagel before walking back to my room and slamming the door shut. I pace from the closet to the bed, hands behind my head, and take short, even breaths.

They're right; Zeke is a complete douchebag.

I pull out my phone and text the only person who calms me.

Oz: *Hey pretty girl. Fancy yourself a study date?*

Jameson: *On a Sunday?*

Oz: *I really just need to be somewhere quiet.*

Jameson: *<3 Yeah, okay. I could probably hit the books if that's what you want. My lit paper isn't going to write itself.*

Oz: *I have practice today at 11:30, but I should be done around two. After that, I am all yours.*

Jameson: *All mine?! I definitely like that sound of that. But*

314

you have to promise to behave yourself. None of that hanky panky stuff...

Oz: *Hanky panky? My grandma says shit like that.*

Jameson: *Then I guess your grandma and I have something in common.*

Oz: *Right. But now all I can think about is my Gran.*

Jameson: *Consider that your punishment for years of misbehaving.*

#DOUCHEBAG

"Some creeper at the bar tried
hitting on me last night,
so I excused myself
and told him I had to go
change my tampon.
Works every single time..."

Jameson

"Where are you going dressed like that?"

I glance down at my cuffed jeans, my Iowa sweatshirt, my brown half boots, then back up at Hayley, who's stopped me in the doorway.

Shoot. I almost made it out.

"Why are you carrying books? It's Sunday."

"I'm going to the library?"

She wrinkles her nose. "On Sunday? Weren't you just there?"

Yes, but…

"I mean…Oz has a test tomorrow and I have a paper due, so he thought we could study." She looks horrified, so I explain. "The library is where we met, so I guess in a way, that makes it our special place."

Hayley cuts me off with a loud, giddy laugh. "Okay, okay. I get it now; *study* is the new word for *screwing*, isn't it? And don't you dare lie to me."

"Screwing! Who's screwing who what now?" Another voice enters the conversation as Sydney breezes through the living room, pulling her blonde hair back into a high pony and securing it with a rubber band. "Girl, you know my ears perked right up when I heard that word."

I fidget uncomfortably, rocking back on the low heels of my boots. I haven't exactly been…*forthcoming* about my budding relationship with Sebastian, and I've been dreading this conversation, purposefully withholding information. Afraid of what she'll say, how she'll judge me. Worried she'll be pissed.

Or worse, *hurt.*

The very last place I want to have this conversation is the doorway while I'm on my way to meet him.

I don't handle things like this well, disappointing people I care about—in this case, my roommate, who admittedly gets infatuated with good-looking guys frequently, especially ones that play sports, are well-built, well-connected, and sought after by the entire female populous.

Sebastian ticks all those boxes.

And I know she thinks she has a crush on him.

Daunting conversations like the one I'm about to have are one of the reasons I haven't thrown myself into the college dating scene.

Guys like Sebastian come with drama, drama, drama.

But he's been worth it, so worth it. So please, just shoot me now and put me out of my passive-aggressive existence because I do not want to hurt my friend.

But I'm also not willing to give up what it took me so long to find.

Hayley, unfortunately, beats me to it. "You know, James and Oz have been hooking up."

That is not what I was expecting, and so startled am I that I almost drop the books in my arms out of complete shock. My face flushes from complete embarrassment; never in my life has anyone strung my name and the words 'hooking up' together in a sentence.

"I...w-we...we..." Oh god, I'm stuttering. "We're not hooking up," I finally manage, face a blazing inferno.

Sydney's face, well—that's another story. First her eyebrows shoot up, entertained. But then...the words sink in. *Oz. James. Hooking up.*

Her vivid blue eyes scan Hayley's smug expression, digest my quick denial and flaming red cheeks. I swear she can see the stress rash developing across my chest through my shirt.

"Of course you're not hooking up with him." Sydney blows out a puff of air and flips her hair in Hayley's direction. "James doesn't do hookups; *everyone* knows that."

I don't even have the fortitude to be insulted by her tone.

Our other roommate demurs angelically, "You're right, I

shouldn't have used the term hookup. They're *dating*, aren't you James?"

"I…"

But Hayley doesn't stop, hands flailing about her as she speaks. "He brought her to that fraternity party you missed last weekend when you went home. You should have seen him, totally glued to her side the entire night. Fetched things for her like a puppy dog. So cute."

"Uh…" It's all I can say, so bad at this someone should take away my girl card because Lord knows my backbone has disappeared.

"Then he hauled her off early. Well, because of that fight with that big wrestler—you went back to his place, didn't you? 'Cause I know you didn't come home." She snickers and I feel sick, like I'm gonna vom all over Hayley's trendy platform wedges.

Sydney's face scrunches up, whether from distaste or disappointment, it's impossible to tell. "James, for real?"

"I mean…" I shrug my shoulders. "Yeah?"

My feet shift beneath me, the books in my arms becoming dead weight.

Sydney glares at Hayley then turns her wounded stare on me. "Why didn't you tell me, James? Why would you let me go out with him if you liked him?"

Right. I did do that…

"Why wouldn't you have said something? I feel like such a jerk."

Because I was scared and embarrassed and a fool. Because I wasted time when I could have been spending it with Sebastian instead of avoiding him.

"I'm sorry."

Sydney throws her hands up, exasperated. "James, you're the one who said he was un-dateable. You're the one who said all he did was sleep around. You're the one who said—"

"I know what I said, Sydney! I was wrong."

SARANEY

Sydney—sensitive, understanding Sydney—shows me the reason why she's beautiful both inside and out. "God, I feel like such an idiot—I had no idea you liked him."

And now I feel like an idiot because she's the one apologizing when I'm the one who—

"If he's what makes you happy... Just don't let him break your heart. Don't let him do to you what you told me he would do."

And now I'm cringing because the words come back to me verbatim: *The guy screws everyone...I saw him getting a hand-job at a party in the hallway...It's probably a good idea to stay away from a guy like that, no matter how good looking he is...No doubt he's run out of room on his bedpost for notches...*

Blushing, I look down at the floor, embarrassed to have judged Sebastian before I knew him, and embarrassed to have kept my budding relationship from one of my best friends.

I'm the A-hole here.

"I won't let him hurt me." Then, to myself, I add, *And I won't hurt him.*

Sid eyes my outfit. "Casual study date then?"

"Sort of." I bite down on my lower lip and readjust my books. "I think something might be bothering him, so..."

"Any chance you're going out with us tonight? I have a new pair of jeans I want you to see."

I smirk. "Want to borrow a cardigan to go with them?"

"Heck no."

43

#DOUCHEBAG

"I know exactly where things
went wrong with her.
Besides me never texting her back,
I never used Ben & Jerry's
as a seduction technique."

Sebastian

Jameson is a sight for sore eyes, and I drink her in from head to toe when she slips silently through the door of our study room on the third floor of the library, the study room at the end of a long row of law school periodicals, research, and publications.

It's quiet, relaxed, and isolated.

Emphasis on *isolated.*

I rise to greet her, skirting around the long conference table, and gently take the books from her hands. Place them on the table. Place my hands at her waist and lean in for a kiss. Place my hands on her ass and give her butt cheeks a squeeze.

"Well that's a fine hello." She laughs, swatting at my hands to create some distance. "You said we were going to study, Mr. Grabby Hands."

"Yeah but your ass has gravitational pull—I'm drawn to it like a magnet. Can't keep my hands off."

She swats at me again. "I swear to god, Oz, if you keep manhandling me like this, we're never going to get anything done."

Reluctantly I back away and give her berth. "You're right; I didn't bring you here to accost you. The imprint of your ass on my hand will have to tide me over for the next hour."

"You're a raging hormone." Jameson sits, rearranging her study materials. She aligns her pens and pencils, pushing each one into place with the tip of her finger, lining them up as if they have a permanent place on the table. Calculator on the right. Computer in the center of her workspace.

She takes a small stack of notebooks out of her bag, shuffling them. Spreads them out next to the pens like a fan.

Watching her meticulously fuss over her school supplies turns me on.

Glumly, I hang my head. "I know. It's gotten worse since you let me in your pants. Bad move on your part."

I join her at the table and soon, we're both focused on our studies. Every so often I'm distracted by the sound of Jameson's sighs, her little hums of concentration. The tapping of her pen against the tabletop.

"Stop watching me," she mumbles without looking up.

"I'm not," I argue.

But I am.

"You've been watching me for the past twenty-five minutes. I timed it." Her pen scribbles in a black composition notebook and after finishing writing whatever it is she's writing, she looks up. Sets down the pen. Crosses her hands in front of her. "Something's bothering you."

Well shit. I wasn't expecting her to notice. "It is?"

Jameson cocks her head to the side and studies me. "Isn't it? It's just a guess, but you seem somehow, I don't know…off."

I scoff. "Can't I just want to be with you? Why does something have to be wrong?"

The room is quiet as the seconds tick by. She's thinking and I'm blankly staring and no one is talking.

Slowly, she gives her head a little shake. "You're right; nothing has to be wrong. I read you wrong. Let's just forget I said anything."

Her smile is sympathetic and lopsided.

And so sweet.

Jameson is the least judgmental person I know.

I trust her. I trust her, and she is the only person I've ever told anything to besides my sister, but she's not here right now and James is. So, I expel a deep breath and explain.

"No, you're right, something has been bothering me," I say, shifting in my seat, fighting the urge to fidget. "Since that party, Zeke has been riding my ass and it's wearing on my nerves. Not sure what to do about it." When Jameson doesn't say anything, I continue. "I live with the guy, right? So I know how he is, what an asshole he can be—but I also see a side of him no one else does, yeah? And I know he isn't always such a prick, especially when he's friends with someone." My fingers rake through my hair. "I don't understand what his problem is lately."

"Has he said anything?" Jameson asks carefully, watching me closely.

I give a curt nod. "This morning."

"*Ahhhh*." She drags out a breath, already seeming to know what I'm about to say.

"He's…" What's the word I'm looking for? "Angry."

"He is," comes Jameson's whisper. "Do you know why?"

This time I'm shaking my head. "No. I suspect I know the reason, but I'm not a shrink so…" I shrug. "It's just a guess."

"Have you tried talking to him about it?"

"This morning when he threatened me, I told him to piss off. That's about all the talking we did."

Her eyebrows shoot straight to her hairline. "He threatened you? *Why?*"

I fiddle with the keys on my laptop, aimlessly tapping at a few. "I'd tell you, but I don't want you in the middle of it."

Now her brow furrows with concern. "So you're saying it had something to do with me?"

"Want the truth? Yes and no."

"Why do I not like the sound of that?"

"Because the truth is that yeah, he doesn't want me dating you. I don't necessarily think he's jealous, I think he thinks…shit, I don't know. It's like he thinks I'm ditching him for good, almost like I'm abandoning him—it's the weirdest thing."

"Do I have cause to worry? He's not going to be hiding in the bushes when I get home to knock me off, is he?" She gives a nervous little laugh, and now I feel like the biggest horse's ass for mentioning it in the first place.

"He wouldn't hurt you. He's angry at himself, not at you. He just doesn't realize it yet."

"Okay," she says slowly. "But now it's starting to affect *you*, and that's what worries me."

"Why should it worry you?"

"Because, I..." She clears her throat. "Because I *care* about you Sebastian."

My girl adds an eye roll.

A huge grin spreads on my face and I lean toward her to change the subject. "You care about me, huh? That's it?"

Eye roll. "Don't be an ass. Of course I *care*."

Care. I wonder if that's a code word for a stronger feeling she's not ready to admit yet...the same way I haven't admitted it to her, or said it out loud.

It's too soon to know for sure.

Isn't it?

Once again, a palpable silence settles over the room, the weight of words lingering above us.

"Jameson, let me..." My voice trails off, the next words out of my mouth breaking the tension. "Sex you on the table."

"Oh my god!" She laughs, tossing a pen at me. It hits my chest and ricochets to the carpeted floor. "We are not having sex in a public place!"

I gesture around the room. "Come on, this is hardly public. There are four walls and a solid door, if you don't count the window. Besides, don't say you haven't thought about doing it with me every time we've been in here."

"Um, I can honestly say I have *not* thought about it, but *clearly* you have."

I stare at her like she's crazy. "Um, *clearly*. Hate to break it to ya, but screwing is pretty much the only thing I think about when I'm with you."

"Well put it out of your mind; we're not having sex in the library."

"What's it gonna take to convince you?"

"Nothing. *Nothing* is going to convince me to let you sex me on the table. It's not going to happen."

"Want to make a bet?"

Another eye roll makes three. "No Sebastian, because you still owe me for the *last* bet we made."

"How 'bout I pay you in orgasms? Two hundred and fifty of them."

"Hmmm." She taps her chin with a pink fingernail, considering my offer. "Fine. I'll think about it."

My smirk is smug. "The last time you said *I'll think about it*, you ended up sticking your tongue down my throat in the middle of the library."

"Shut up!" She pitches another pen. "Can we please get to work?"

"Oh god...*right there*...can't you do it any harder?"

"Baby, I'm trying...if I do it any harder, I'm going to break this shitty table. It's plywood."

"My ass...m-my ass in on the laptop keys and it's digging into my hip...oh god...don't stop doing that... feels so good..."

"Shit...shit...did you hear that cracking noise? I told you we were going to...break this...fuck...ing table..."

"It's worth it, s-so ssss...so worth it..."

"Don't stop don't stop I'm coming, I'm coming..."

"So much for not having sex in public, Little Miss Priss."

"Come on, baby." Jameson affects a staged, decidedly male voice. "This is hardly public. There are four walls and a solid door, if you don't count the window."

"Very funny, smartass."

"We don't have time to bask in the afterglow. You should probably pull your pants up."

"Bask in the afterglow—I like the sound of that."

"Awww, you really are a closet romantic after all."

"Yeah, I guess I am."

#DOUCHEBAG

"Sometimes she wakes me up in the middle of the night with a blow job. Once, afterward, she fed me a sandwich. Obviously I need to lock that shit down."

Sebastian

"**W**hat the hell do you think you and your crap are doing on my stoop?"

The wind blows, kicking up snow and sending frigid cold air whipping past me and into the hotel room. The gust has Jameson's long loose hair swirling around her shoulders.

I'm standing in front of the same hotel room door, letting my red duffle drop to the frozen, snowy ground. A bright lime green snowboard leans against the doorjamb, along with a black boot bag and my clothes. "My old pal Chad said your roommate bailed on you," I tease with a casual shrug of my shoulders.

"Chad you say? Hmmm...I heard he graduated and got a job at a tech company. You'll have to come up with a better line that that; I can't let just *anyone* pass through this door—my boyfriend would *kill* me, and he'll be here any minute."

"Your boyfriend sounds awesome—and really good looking."

Jameson crosses her arms and shrugs, noncommittal. "Meh, he's all right. I wouldn't push him out of bed."

I lean down to kiss her smiling lips, heft my bag, and shoulder into the hotel room. "Wow. Place looks just how we left it."

"Yu*p*." Jameson pops her P with a loud smack. "Same bed, same dresser, same tiny bathroom."

"Ah yes, the tiny bathroom of sin, scene of all masturbatory emissions." My laugh fills the outdated hotel room as I walk to the dresser to set my things down.

"Could you please not remind me?" Jameson's question hits my back.

I glance over my shoulder. "You stood and watched babe. It couldn't have been *that* awful."

"That's only because I was caught off guard."

"Righttttt...but then you listened at the door as I finished."

"I find it very rude of you to bring that up," she points out indignantly.

"Rule number twenty..."

Jameson holds up a finger and gives it a flirty little wiggle. "Nuh uh—we're up to twenty-three."

"Oh pardon *me*, ma'am. Rule number twenty-three: while we're on vacation this weekend, we have to try to do everything the way we did it last time we were here."

She's skeptical. "You want to go to the lobby and watch me give my number to complete strangers?"

"Sure! It will be romantic."

"That trip was *not* romantic. It was exhausting."

"You didn't think it was romantic when I tackled you in the snow on the way back to the bus?"

"Not really, no."

"Bullshit. You *moaned* when I fell on top of you."

"No, you were squishing me and I was trying to push you off. There's a huge difference. Plus, I had snow down my pants."

"Hmmm." I think for a second, trying to think of all the nice things we did in Snowbasin when we were here last, but only a few things stick out in my mind. "You slept with me in the same bed because you couldn't resist me. Admit it, that pillow wall was a desperate ploy for my attention."

My gorgeous girlfriend bites down on her smile. "Fine, I'll admit it—I *might* have wanted to snuggle up to you in bed, but you have to admit you had a huge crush on me."

I look at her like she's crazy. "Pfft, of course I had a huge crush on you—probably from the moment we met. You're fucking adorable."

My delivery might be saying *What's the big deal*, but Jameson's expression rivals the time I gave her a dozen long-stem red roses. "Sometimes you say the sweetest things!"

"Only sometimes?" I move closer, teasing as she pulls the bed linens down and fluffs the pillows.

SARANEY

Jameson yawns, tired from traveling. "Fine. Most of the time."

And she's right; rarely am I an asshole to her. I've reserved the sensitive and softer side no one else has the privilege of seeing for Jameson. As lame as it fucking sounds, she's the light in my life.

And if anyone heard me saying shit like that, I'd get my ass beat.

Not that I'd care.

Slowly, James unsnaps the fly of her jeans, pushing the dark denim down her hips. "I'm exhausted."

"My family won't be here for, oh"—I check my phone for the time—"another twenty-four hours. How shall we *ever* pass the time?"

"Speaking of your parents, I can't believe you never told them we were going to arrive early. And I can't believe they're giving up their Thanksgiving holiday to come all this way to be with us."

I snort. "*Please.* My mom thought this would be more fun than cramming all those people into our tiny house. Plus, now she doesn't have to cook. She hates cooking and always fucks up the turkey."

"I know, but—"

"Trust me, they're pumped."

A frown mars her forehead. "I know, but are you *sure* you're okay giving up your spring break to be here *now?*"

"You're going to be with me in March, so what do I care if I go anywhere." I shrug. That's what we decided when we booked this trip: we'd spend the Thanksgiving holiday in Utah with my family, then stay home and work through spring break to save up money for an apartment. We plan on living together the rest of our senior year—as soon as we have enough money for a deposit. "Relax. You have nothing to be nervous about."

I watch as she nibbles the nail of her thumb nervously. "I'm anxious about meeting your parents."

"Babe, they're going to love you. And you've already texted with Kayla a bunch of times—she thinks you're the shit."

"Right, but moms are different."

Her concern has me dipping down to kiss her mouth. "Stop worrying. We're going to have a blast. And aren't you glad we have enough snow this early in the season to do some boarding, lift tickets compliments of Zeke Daniels and his five hundred bucks?"

That perks her up.

"Heck yes. So glad he finally paid you." Jameson unzips her purple suitcase to retrieve her snow pants and jacket, hanging them inside the small closet. "I'm ready to take on the mountain."

I dig mine out and they join hers. "Can you at least pretend to wait for me as I creep down the hill behind you?"

"We'll see. Try to keep up and we won't have a problem, will we old man?" With a cocky, confident flick of her hand, James gives her hair a toss.

"It's fine; I love watching you—especially your ass from behind."

"Same." She walks into the bathroom to plunk her toiletries on the counter. "I'm exhausted from the drive. Let's watch a movie and go to bed."

"Good idea. We should take advantage of tonight before my family gets here in the morning, because once they do, you'll be rooming with Kayla and I'll be camping out on my parent's floor."

"You're always trying to take *advantage*." The laugh comes from around her toothbrush.

I join her in the bathroom, stepping close so my hands can roam up her sides, burying my nose in the crook of her neck as she brushes her teeth. "I don't have to try very hard, do I?"

"Oh please, I can totally resist you. Remember that day you decided not to wear pants in a desperate attempt to get me to seduce you?" She removes the toothbrush and taps her chin as she recollects. "It was a useless attempt to reverse psychology me, but I lasted the entire day without jumping your bones. I practically

333

had super powers."

"What*ever*. That didn't count because you took off *your* pants as a counter attack, which didn't work. Ended up screwing anyway."

She sighs, toothpaste dripping form the corner of her mouth. "At least we gave it the old college try."

"We sure did."

My heart is pounding a million miles a minute, pounding like it's never pounded before. Not even when I was introduced to the scout for the Olympic wrestling team last semester. Not when I told him *no*, I wasn't going to be advancing my wrestling career and joining the team.

I was done. Mind was made up.

I plan to intern for a law firm in my hometown next summer with the hopes of getting a job in their human resources department. Then I'm going to buy a house with Jameson and we're going to live together, get married, and make cardigan-wearing babies.

I crack open the black velvet ring box, drop to one knee, and present it to her, lid open. Jameson's blue eyes widen, hands flying to her mouth in astonished surprise. "Sebastian." She breathes. "It's beautiful."

It doesn't escape my notice that she hasn't reached for the ring.

"Jameson Victoria Clark. Will you marry me?"

"I don't know what to say…"

"Say yes." I laugh, as if there isn't anything to discuss and this is a done deal. "Have I shocked the shit out of you? Why aren't you saying yes?"

"I can't," she whispers, her breath leaving her body in short puffs. The air turns frigid cold and steam rises from our mouths. "I can't marry you."

Can't marry me? What the ever-loving fuck.

"Can't?" I snap the ring box closed. "Or won't."

Her head gives a tiny, almost imperceptible shake. "Can't. Won't."

"Why?" I demand. "Why won't you marry me?"

"You don't even know me Sebastian."

I fumble to my feet, reaching for her. "Baby, please. What do you mean I don't know you? You're my best friend."

"And you're mine…"

"Then why aren't you saying yes?" I repeat, voice cracking. "I tell you everything; you know things even my parents and sister don't know. Things I've never told the guys, or my coaches." I suck in a breath. "James, I…I…"

The three little words I've never said to her get lodged in my throat, choking me, making me hesitate.

Jameson pulls away, her eyebrows going up. She glowers. "See? Right there. That's the reason I can't marry you."

"Big deal. It's only been seven months. Lots of people don't say the L word after only a few months."

"Stop talking, Sebastian, you're making it worse. The fact that you can't even tell me you lo—" Her sob cuts off whatever she's about to say.

"Baby, I'm an idiot…what do you expect?"

"I expect more than a man that makes excuses about why he can't tell me how he feels." Her anger turns to a cry, a steady stream of tears pooling down her flushed cheeks.

"Don't cry, *please* don't cry."

Don't cry. Don't cry.

"This dream is turning into a fucking nightmare," I moan.

"That's because you're dreaming."

"*No*," I argue. "*This is a goddamn nightmare*, Jameson—"

"Sebastian. *Sebastian* wake up, you're having a dream."

With a start, I gasp, jolting myself awake.

"Shhhh, you were crying." Jameson's delicate palm runs down the course of my spine in a gentle stroke, landing at my waist and wrapping around my middle. I feel the pillows of her pouty lips plant a kiss to the planes of my shoulder blades, her hot breath caressing my bare skin as she spoons me from behind.

"I was?"

"You were," she whispers with another kiss on my shoulder.

"Fuck, sorry. Did I wake you up?"

She nods. "You did, but it's okay."

Shit. "What was I saying?"

"You don't remember?"

I lay in the dark, staring at the wall before rolling to my back. Moonlight floods the hotel room, casting a warm glow on Jameson's beautiful, worried face.

"Yeah, I remember."

"Do you want to talk about it?" Her voice is a gentle caress from the shadows.

"I asked you to marry me, and you said no."

"Why did I say no?" Jameson is biting down on her lip to hide her smile. I can see her white teeth glowing against the light filtering into the room.

"Because I haven't told you I love you yet." My voice is small and aloof, because even though it was a dream, I feel like an asshole.

"Oh?"

And I haven't, not yet. We've been together officially for more than half a year and all I've ever done is show her with my body how much I care. That part I'm stellar at. *That* part is easy. The sex. The affection. Holding hands. Whispered words across the library table. The way every now and again, she lets me fuck her in a study room.

Not once have I told Jameson how my *heart* feels about her, how I love her intelligence and sarcasm. How I love her quick wit, and the fact that she doesn't put up with any of my shit. Or Zeke's nonstop bullshit.

How I love *her*.

No wonder she keeps rejecting me in my own damn dreams.

I'm a dick.

"James?"

"Se*bas*tian?" This time when she smiles, she doesn't bother hiding it.

I roll over to face her, repositioned so we're snuggled against each other in the center of the bed, her arms across my stomach. My fingers find and sweep away the stray hairs across her temple, and I stroke her forehead.

"I do, you know. Love you. More than probably anything."

There. I said it.

And wouldn't you know, her breath actually hitches—just like you see in the movies when the girl is so startled and pleased she loses her breath for a second.

"I know you love me." Wistful and filled with wonder. "I love you, too."

Somehow, it's not enough. "For real though, babe. The only person I love more than you is myself."

A loud laugh fills the otherwise darkened room. "Oh my god, tell me you did not just say that."

Am I missing something here? "What's so damn funny? I'm being serious."

"The only person you love more than me is *you*?"

"Yeah, so?"

"You're ridiculous."

"But you love me?"

"So much."

A floodgate opens, and now that I've said the words, they're easier to say than I could have ever imagined.

"I love you." My arms stretch toward her, dragging her flush against me then pulling her over my body. Hands grasping her face, I do my best to look in her eyes. "I love *you*."

Our lips meet and she sighs.

"I love you, Jameson. I'm *in* love with you."

"Desperately?" She breathes with a smile.

"*So* desperately." I open my mouth for another kiss with tongue. "So fucking much."

I don't stop dreaming about us.

Won't stop.

And when the time comes and I ask her to marry me and have cardigan-wearing babies?

She's going to say yes.

The End

AN EXCLUSIVE EXCERPT from BOOK 2

The following is an unedited, rough excerpt of, tentatively titled *How to Date a Douchebag:* The Failing Hours.

This is Zeke Daniels story.

A very small part of him.

The guy you love to hate.
Be gentle with him.

#DOUCHEBAG

"Ezekiel Daniel—
my parents must have known
from the beginning
that I was going to be a sinner
when they named me after
two books of the Bible.
Lord knows I'm no saint."

"Why does anyone stand him? The guy literally has no redeeming qualities."

Ezekiel

"**A**re you listening to me Mr. Daniels?"

I jerk my head toward the sound of my coach's voice, already aggravated to the point of distraction because he's determined to waste my time. His office is small, but so is he, and the cinderblock walls faded to a dull blue cast an eerie pallor over his skin.

The veins in Coaches neck strain as he fights to gain control of the impromptu meeting he's called me into. Except I'm not in the mood to listen.

With nothing to add, I keep my damn mouth shut, instead giving a terse nod.

"I said, are you listening to me, son?"

I want to remind him that I'm not his son; not even close. My own father doesn't even call me son.

Not that I'd want him to.

Jaw locked, teeth clenched. "Yes, Sir."

"Now, I don't know where that chip on your shoulder comes from, and I'm not going to pretend to give a shit about what goes on when you leave here—but I'll be damned if I stand by and watch one of my boys self-destruct in my gym." His weathered skin stretches along with the grimly set line of his mouth.

He continues. "You think you're the first prick to come through this program thinking his shit don't stink? You're not. But you're the first prick to come with an attitude I can't seem to quit. You're also one sarcastic wisecrack away from getting a fist slammed through your pretty face. Even your own teammates don't like you. I can't have discord on my team."

My jaw ticks when I clench it, but having nothing in defense, I clamp my jaw shut.

He rankles on.

"What's it going to take to get through to you, Mr. Daniels?"

Nothing.

You've not nothing that will fucking get through to me, old man.

He tips back in his old, wooden desk chair and studies me, fingers clasped into a steeple. Balancing on the legs, Coach taps his chin with the tips.

It's on the verge of my tongue to tell him that to start, he can stop calling me *Mister* Daniels. Second, he can cut to the chase and tell me the real reason he pulled me into his office after practice.

After a long stretch of silence, he leans forward, the springs on his chair releasing a loud, scrapping metallic sound, his arms coming to rest on the desktop. His hands glide over a sheaf of paper and he plucks one off the top.

"Tell you what we're going to do." He pushes the paper toward me across the desk. "The director of Big Brothers Mentorship Program owes me a favor. You have any experience with kids, Daniels?"

I shake my head. "No."

"Do you even know what Big Brothers is?"

"No, but I'm sure you're going to enlighten me," I can't stop myself from retorting. Crossing my arms, I adopt a defensive pose most people find intimidating.

Not Coach.

"Allow me to educate you, Mr. Daniels. It's a program designed to match a youngster with an older volunteer—usually they prefer college-aged students—that act as a mentor. Hang out with the kid. Show him he's not alone. Be that someone dependable that isn't going to bail him. Typically, they're good kids, from single parent households—but not always. Sometimes the kids are left alone a lot, deadbeat dad. Sometimes their parents just don't give a shit and they're left to fend for themselves. Know what it's like growing up like that, son?"

Yes. "No."

343

The sadist drones on, shuffling the stack on his desk. "There's an interviewing process I think you'd fail with flying colors. But that's why we're cutting through the red tape and pulling some strings. You know why? Because you have potential to be successful and you're pissing it away by being a little asshole."

His chair creeks in the cellblock of an office. "Maybe what you need is to give a shit about someone other than yourself for a change. Maybe what you need is to meet a kid whose life is shittier than yours. The pity party is over."

"I don't have time to volunteer, Coach," I grit out.

Coach grins up at me from his desk, the overhead lights reflecting off his thick glasses. "Too goddamn bad then, ain't it? You either take the volunteer hours, or you're off the team. I don't need a smoking gun on my hands. Trust me, we'll find a way to carry on without you."

He waits for my answer, and when I don't immediately respond, he presses. "Think you can handle that? Say, *Yes, Coach.*"

I nod tersely. "Yes, Coach."

"Good." Satisfied, he grabs a yellow number two pencil and tosses it at me. "Fill that sheet out and take it with you. You meet your Little Brother tomorrow at their downtown office. Address is on the form."

Reluctantly, I snatch the paper off the desk but don't look at it.

"Don't be late. Don't fuck this up. Tomorrow afternoon you're going to see how the other half lives, got it son? Now get the fuck out of my office.""

I glower down at him.

His raspy chuckle hits my back when I turn toward the door. "And Mr. Daniels?"

I stop in my tracks but refuse to face him.

"I know it will be hard, but try not to be total prick to the kid."

Coach is a total asshole.

Not that I give a shit, because I'm an asshole, too. But there isn't much I care about these days, so why would he think I'd care about some strange fucking kid being involuntary forced on me?

My friends call me merciless. Heartless.

They claim cold blood runs through my veins—and who knows, it probably does.

But I like it that way; I like creating distance. No one needs me, and I need them even less. Happiness is a myth. Who needs it? This anger brewing inside me is more real than any happiness I've forgotten how to feel.

Walking into the grocery store, I grab a cart from the corral, pushing it with purpose up and down each aisle, tossing shit in without slowing my stride.

Steeled oats. Agave nectar. Walnuts.

I saunter to the nutrition and organics, hands automatically reaching for the Protein Powder, gripping the black plastic container in one hand, and lob it in among the deli meat, bread, and bottles of water.

Turning the aisle and pushing the cart on the right side of the aisle, I skid to a halt, almost plowing into a little girl on her tiptoes, reaching for a box of ice cream cones. Her black, curly hair pulled tightly into two pigtails, she strains with her string bean arms toward a shelf she'll never reach.

Even on the balls of her feet.

"Shit kid, I almost hit you," I growl. "Pay more attention."

"Can you get that down for me?" Her little index finger wiggles toward a red box of sugar cones. I note that her tiny digits are painted glittery blue, bits of dirt encrusted under her nail beds.

"You shouldn't talk to strangers." I scowl down at her, plucking the box off the shelf and gruffly shove it toward her grasping hands. "Jesus Christ, where's your Mom?"

"She's at home."

"Who the hell are you with?"

The little squirt tilts her head, narrowing her unblinking beady eyes at me. "You're saying bad words."

I'm not in the mood for this, so I narrow mine back. "I'm an adult. I can say whatever the hell I want."

Her little mouth puckers and I can feel her silently judging me.

"Summer? *Oh my god*, Summer!" A flurry of gray and white flies by when a woman tears from around the corner, gasping for breath and latching onto the kid's puny arm. "Oh my god, you cannot just walk off like that! You scared me half to death. Didn't you hear me calling you?"

The kid holds her ground. "I was getting ice cream cones."

"Summer." The woman gets down on her knees, pulling the little girl into an embrace. Takes a shaky breath. "Summer, when I couldn't find you I thought I was going to have a heart attack."

"I was right here," the kid squeaks out into the bare skin of the woman's shoulder, combating to breathe through the struggle cuddle. "This boy was getting my cones."

This *boy*?

I put my hands up. "Whoa kid, do *not* drag me down into the gutter with you."

It's then that the woman senses my presence and looks up. Up. Up, into my impassive eyes. No, I'm startled to realize—she's not a woman—she's a *young* woman. About my age, her eyes widen with a flash of panic and fear at the same time her lips part.

She recovers quickly, hugging the girl tighter. "Where you waiting with her?"

A snort escapes my nose and I ignore her question. "Lady, you make a shitty nanny. She could have been kidnapped."

"I know." The girls mouth clamps shut, chin trembling. Taking a few deep breaths to compose herself, she swallows nervously before, "T-thanks for helping her."

"I'm no good Samaritan," I snort, not wanting her thanks. "All I did was prevent her from crushing herself by tipping over the display rack."

"Thank you nonetheless." Another quick squeeze around the little kid's shoulders, and the young woman stands. I take her measure, sizing her up. Petite, I gauge her height at around five foot five. Hazel eyes. Blonde hair so pale it looks *white*, falling down over her shoulder in a thick, wholesome braid. My gaze immediately falls to the neckline of her gray Iowa tee shirt, and I appraise her non-existent chest.

Bummer. Must suck.

She hunches her shoulders self-consciously and clears her throat. "Come on, Summer. We should go. We have more stuff to grab."

"Yeah, you should go, because you're totally in my way." I give my cart a jostle, jerking it forward so they move and I can skirt around in what little room they're *not* taking up. Before I round the next aisle, I stab an accusing finger their way. "For the record, *Nanny*, that kid shouldn't be out in public; it should be in bed."

Acknowledgements

A h, my favorite part… The acknowledgements.
        The "letting people know who made this journey a little more amazing along the way" part.

Thank you Internet for providing the inspiration for the dating quotes at the beginning of each chapter. They're all based on *real* conversations, pick-up lines, come-ons, and texts between actual people. Yup. This is how singles talk to each other these days….and we wonder why chivalry is dead!

Shocking, I know.

To my brother, Jeff, who suggested I dedicate this entire book to him. He's bossy and rude, and was the perfect person to call when I needed to make Sebastian just a tad douchier. The guy goes and helps solve one plot dilemma, and suddenly he takes credit for the *entire* story.

Typical douchebag.

To my Beta family: Tami Estes, Nikki Kroll, author ME Carter, Laurie Darter, author Emma Doherty, and author Kristann Monaghan—I know some of you were nervous to give me honest feedback, but without you, I couldn't have struck the right balance between "douchey" and "likeable."

All in all, I think we did okay.

Shirl Rickman. I <3 You.

Christine Kuttnauer, my right hand and PA: the fact that you're starting to hug me says it all. You keep me organized, scheduled, and always tell it to me straight. If we worked in an office, you would be my work wife. Don't tell Laurie I said that.

To my fan group *Ney's Little Liars*; thank you for loving me enough to join and stick around, except for Melinda, whom I added

without permission: "FFS Sara, did you add me to your group?"
Yes. Yes I did.

BS'ers. Our safe place.

Alina (Hoot Nanny) for taking such good care of my baby
while I work.

To Doug for giving me the space to be myself and letting me
be creative. Because let's face it, I'm a tad... weird.

My parents: Lori, Jim, Jean and Harold for being so proud.

Jenna P, Kirstin K, Abby S, Jenny C...for still thinking I'm
cool even though I'm way older than you. My new friends Renee
and Jody, who will probably never see this because I have to *force*
them to read when they'd rather be Jazzercising. Or eating ice
cream.

Swag hags:

Tami with the etsy shop MockingbirdApparel, thanks so much for
designing and printing the "Date the D" tee shirts that I wear and
sell at my signings. They are a real crowd pleaser, and the decals
aren't half bad either.

Kristen & Andy with the Book Boyfriend Candles for creating the custom "Douchebags Smell Good" candles. The best.
Swag. Ever. It's true: "One whiff and you're in love..."
Design & Editing:

To Sarah Hanson with Okay Creations for designing an eye-
catching cover. It's fantastic in every way. And Sarah? I might be
irritating to deal with via email, but I'll grow on you, *trust* me.

To Caitlyn with C. Marie Editing, your attention to detail
made a huge difference. I never thought I'd get through all those
red edits.

To Julie with JT Formatting, the last person to touch the book
before it gets published. Thank you for turning my manuscript into
art. I marvel at your work.

And to you.
Thank you.

For more information about Sara Ney and her books, visit:

Facebook
www.facebook.com/saraneyauthor

Twitter
twitter.com/saraney

Goodreads
www.goodreads.com/author/show/9884194.Sara_H_Ney

Website
kissingincars.weebly.com

Instagram
www.instagram.com/saraneyauthor/?hl=en

**Don't forget to join the official
Ney's Little Liars group on Facebook!**
www.facebook.com/groups/1065756456778840/

Other Titles by Sara

The Kiss and Make Up Series

Kissing in Cars
He Kissed Me First
A Kiss Like This

#ThreeLittleLies Series

Things Liars Say
Things Liars Hide
Things Liars Fake

With M.E. Carter

FriendTrip
FriendTrip: WeddedBliss (a FriendTrip novella)